BLACK GLASS

ALSO BY KAREN JOY FOWLER

We Are All Completely Beside Ourselves

What I Didn't See and Other Stories

Wit's End

The Jane Austen Book Club

Sister Noon

The Sweetheart Season

Sarah Canary

Artificial Things

KAREN JOY FOWLER

BLACK GLASS

short fictions

A MARIAN WOOD BOOK

Published by G. P. Putnam's Sons

an imprint of Penguin Random House

New York

A MARIAN WOOD BOOK
Published by G. P. Putnam's Sons
Publishers Since 1838
An imprint of Penguin Random House LLC
375 Hudson Street
New York, New York 10014

Originally published by Henry Holt and Company Inc.

Library of Congress Cataloging-in-Publication Data

Fowler, Karen Joy.
[Short stories. Selections]
Black glass : short fictions / by Karen Joy Fowler.
p. cm.
"A Marian Wood Book."
ISBN 978-0-399-17579-4
I. Title.
PS3556.O844A6 2015 2015007425
813'.54—dc23

Printed in the United States of America
1 3 5 7 9 10 8 6 4 2

Book design by Chris Welch

FOR SHANNON

FOR RYAN

MY HOMEGROWN INSPIRATION

AND ALSO TO THE STARRY URSULA LE GUIN,
FOR LIGHTING THE PATH

Contents

Preface

I was raised by professionals. My father was a behavioral psychologist and my mother was a highly educated nursery school teacher. Already, I know how you expect this story to end, with my confessing that, despite their education and qualifications, or better yet, *because* of all that, they made quite a hash of being parents.

Nothing could be further from the truth. They were pretty wonderful. The household ran on the scientifically supported principle of positive reinforcement. I was loved, admired, encouraged, disciplined gently, and listened to seriously. All this will be confirmed by my older brother, who had much the same experience and remembers it better. Those mistakes we have gone on to make are entirely our own.

Recently, I did an event with another writer who said, in answer to a question, that he had become resigned to his material. "We all had the childhoods we had," he said. "Nothing can be done about that." I might change that to "We all think we had the childhoods we think we had," if it weren't, in addition to being true, also nonsensical. We'll stick with his configuration, but asterisk it.

I'm far from the only writer to have had a happy childhood. But I think we writers who did share a nagging sense of it not being very writerly, all that early happiness. We suspect, as Maeve Binchy once said, that a happy childhood is an unsuitable beginning for a writer. (She said "Irish writer," but why quibble?) We wonder why, reared in relative contentment, we became writers in the first place. What *is* our material?

For many years I never asked myself those questions, as I could see no way in which the answer would be helpful to me. I like to think of myself as wide-ranging, no book much like the last. I like to think I follow whatever obsession has its current hold on me. I like to think my material changes. But when, as in this book, I'm confronted with a collection of my stories written over a number of years, certain themes become impossible to ignore.

My father is a clear obsession—I sometimes wonder if I write about anything else. We fell out when I was an adolescent and he died before our relationship could right itself. I am always trying to fix that.

As an adjunct, the scientific study, particularly when focused on human behavior, seems to come up often in my writing. Scientists appear frequently as extraterrestrials. I imagine that not only speaks for itself, but also demands an apology.

I have always suffered from the Rosencrantz and Guildenstern syndrome—an excessive concern with peripheral characters. This first manifested when my ninth-grade English class was taken to see *Prometheus Bound*. My idea of great storytelling at that time was *The Man from U.N.C.L.E.* There were no sexy Russians, no triumph of good over evil, no action, no ending of any kind in *Prometheus Bound.* There was, however, a strange tormented cow that caught my interest. I asked my teacher about her and was given some extra reading to do as a consequence. This is how I learned that most of the male gods were horrible rapists and most of the females, jealous harpies. (For the record, I have never minded being asked to do additional reading. It is a privilege.)

At its core, this focus on the peripheral is a struggle against literature's ubiquitous suggestion that some people are more important than others. This is a deeply outrageous, globally damaging thing to believe. But I haven't yet found a way to write that doesn't inevitably partake of it.

And finally there is also this recurring theme: Eden lost. This popular plot was standard in many of the stories I loved as a child—*A Little Princess, The Hobbit, The Wizard of Oz, The Once and Future King, Cinderella, Snow White, Black Beauty.* My own first stories, written when I was about five years old, never deviated from it. But at five, while I understood that happiness could be lost, I expected it would also return. A return home was not only possible; it was the way stories ended.

THIS IS THE THING about a happy childhood—it ends, and not in the way of those stories. "There is always one moment in childhood when the door opens and lets the future in" (Graham Greene).

For me, that door into the future was, of course, a book. One day, when I was maybe eight or nine years old, I was looking through the case in the hall and I pulled something off a shelf for no other reason than this: I had never seen a book that tried less hard to get someone to read it.

The spine was a plain black with a barely discernible title: *The Black Book of Polish Jewry*. There were photos inside, so I turned at once to those. What I saw made no sense to me: pictures of beings who mostly looked human, but not completely—their bones too prominent, their heads, their eyes, too big. My first thought was that I was looking at some alien life-form I had never been told existed. I called on my mother to explain.

Her explanation was the worst thing I had ever heard. It is no exaggeration to say that I lived in one world before my mother began to speak and a completely different one when she was done. Why didn't everybody stop it? I asked, and my mother had no good answer.

I was surprisingly angry with my parents about this.

As was quite common in the time and place of my childhood though quite rare today, I had enormous freedom, both in space and time. I wandered at will, unsupervised and unscheduled, having my own adventures, making my own plans. There was a lot of room in my childhood.

In their actions, in letting me roam as I had roamed, my parents had as much as said that the world was a safe place, that people could be trusted. I felt in some indirect and unclear way that they had lied to me, that my whole life had been a lie.

My school was about four blocks from my house. I usually walked there. One day, a woman I often stopped to chat with as she worked in her yard asked for my phone number. That night my mother told me that she'd invited me to lunch. By myself. I was nervous about this, because I was extremely fussy about food back then, not liking most of it. Being asked to eat something I didn't like was the greatest horror I was capable of imagining. Not to worry, my mother told me. It had all been covered in the phone call.

Sure enough, my hostess was ready with my favorites. We ate off china plates and she told me stories about her own childhood. Before the lunch was over, she'd promised me a kitten from her cat's next litter and she was as good as her word. It turned out that she wrote a gardening column for the local paper. A few days later, I was in print, being publicly celebrated for my sweetness and sunshine.

This was how strangers treated you: they brought out the good china and made your favorite foods; they entertained you with stories; they gave you kittens; and they wrote laudatory newspaper columns about you.

They didn't snatch you from your mother and father, then beat and starve and gas you.

More revelations followed. *Life* magazine did an article on abused children that included a pair of siblings raised in a basement. Once again, there were pictures. Once again, I was looking at an image of something dreadfully wrong written on someone's body. The children were stunted. They were bonsai children. And the people who had done this to them were their very own parents.

I'VE LIVED MY ADULT LIFE at the exact halfway point between joy and rage, gratitude and dismay. There is surely no need to say that, at sixty-five, I've had a great many disappointments and suffered some agonizing losses. No one gets through unscathed. Still, by any reasonable reckoning, life has treated me gently.

I like almost everyone I know, easy enough as the people I know are quite lovely. I would think well of us as a species, if I'd never read a history book. Or the newspaper. Or the comments sections of the Internet. Quite recently I learned of a new app, a way to quickly assure your family and friends that you've survived a shooting, a bombing, a drone strike, a military assault. The app is called I Am Alive. Developed for those in Lebanon, but useful in so many places around the globe. A great future is predicted for such an app.

This, I now believe, is the place my writing comes from; this is the central puzzle of my life. Is the world more beautiful than terrible? Is it more terrible than beautiful?

How can I praise such a world?

How can I be so ungrateful as to not?

Some days I answer these questions one way and some days the other, but I am always asking the questions. As I work my way through any given story, the answers often change as I go. What doesn't change is this—I am always aware that, beautiful as the world sometimes is, deeply as I sometimes feel that beauty, there is no denying or forgetting that I once lived somewhere so much better.

Karen Joy Fowler

January 21, 2015

BLACK GLASS

It was a Wednesday afternoon in the Senate Bar. Schilling, the proprietor, stood behind the curved counter, stroking the shot glasses with a towel. Every part of the bar was reflected in the mirrored wall behind him: the marble and black onyx floor, the oiled cherry-wood counter, the brass bar rail. A chandelier hung in the center of the ceiling. Rows of cut-glass decanters filled the shelves. Schilling ran his towel over their glass stoppers. In the corner, on the big screen, Cher danced and sang a song for the U.S. Navy. Schilling had the sound off.

There were three customers. Two sat together at a table near the door. They were businessmen. One of them smoked. Both of them drank.

Every time either of them picked up his glass and set it down again, he made a new wet ring on the table between them. They were careful to keep the spreadsheet out of the water.

The third customer, a college student, sat at the bar, drinking his way through an unexpected romance with a woman old enough to be his mother. He'd asked Schilling to bring him three drinks at once, three different drinks—a Bloody Mary, a Sex on the Beach, a Velvet Hammer. As a compromise, Schilling had brought him the Bloody Mary and put in an MTV tape, picture only, out of deference to the businessmen and as a matter of personal preference.

A fourth man came into the Senate Bar from the street. A shaft of sunlight sprang into the room when the door opened and vanished when it closed. "Give me a drink," the man said to Schilling.

Schilling glanced at the man briefly as he polished the wood bar with his sleeve. "Get out of here."

"Give me a drink."

The man was dirty and dressed in several tattered layers, which still left a bare hole the size of a tennis ball above one knee. He was smoking the stubby end of a cigarette. It was not his cigarette; there was lipstick on the filter. He had retrieved this cigarette from the sidewalk outside the bar. "You pay your tab first," said Schilling.

"I don't have any money," said the man. Cher closed her eyes and opened her mouth.

"Where's my Sex on the Beach?" asked the boy.

"You're disturbing my customers," Schilling told the man at the door. "You're stinking up my bar." He reached under the counter for a bottle of gin.

"He gave me my first drink," the man at the door said to the boy at the bar. "I used to be just like you." He took two steps into the room, leaving two gritty footprints on the black onyx. "Finish what you started," he told Schilling.

"Get out," Schilling said.

The boy rolled a quarter down his nose and let it drop, catching it loudly in his empty Bloody Mary glass. "Can I get another drink?" he asked. "Am I going to get another drink?"

A second shaft of sunlight appeared in the room, collided with the mirrored wall. Inside the sunlight, barely visible, Cher danced.

She turned her back. Schilling heard a woman scream, and then the Cher in the mirror broke into five pieces and fell behind the counter. The sunlight disappeared. "Madam," said Schilling, hardly breathing, in shock. A nightmare dressed in black stood at the door of his bar, a nightmare in the shape of an enormous postmenopausal woman. In one hand she held a hatchet. She reached into the bodice of her dress with the other and pulled out a large stone. She wore a bonnet with black ribbons.

"Glory be to God!" shouted the woman. "Peace on Earth! Goodwill to men!" She hit the big screen dead center with the rock. The screen cracked and smoked, made spitting noises, blackened. She took a step, swept the cigarette from the shabby man's mouth with one hand. "Don't poison the air with your filthy gases!" she said. Then she held her hatchet at the vertical. She charged into the bar, clearing the counter. Maraschino cherries and stuffed olives flew. "Madam!" said Schilling. He ducked.

"You purveyor and protector of obscenity!" the woman shouted. "Has your mother ever been in this place?" The boy at the bar slipped from his stool and ran for the rear door. In three steps the woman caught him. She picked him up by the neck of his sweater as if he were a kitten, throwing him to his knees. She knelt over him, singing. "Touch not, taste not, handle not. Drink will make the dark, dark blot." He struggled, and she let him go, calling after him, "Your mother did not raise you for this!" The back door slammed.

The businessmen had taken cover under their table. Schilling remained out of sight. The shabby man was gone. The woman began, methodically, with her hatchet to destroy the bar. She punctured the decorative keg behind the counter and then, apparently disappointed to find it empty, she brought her hatchet down on the counter, severing a spigot from one of the hoses. A fountain of soda exploded into the air. She broke the decanters. Pools of liquor flowed over the marble and onyx floor. The woman's bonnet slipped to the side of her head.

"That brandy costs seventy-five dollars," Schilling said.

"Broth of hell," she answered. "Costs your soul." She gashed the cherry wood, smashed the mirrored wall. She climbed onto a stool and brought the chandelier down with a single stroke. Schilling peered over the bar. She threw a rock at him, hitting a bottle of bright green crème de menthe behind him.

He ducked out of sight again. "You'll pay for this," Schilling told her. "You'll account for every penny."

"You are Satan's bedfellow," she said. "You maker of drunkards and widows. You donkey-faced rum-soaked Republican rummy." She lifted the hundred-and-fifty-pound cash register from the counter and held it over her head. She began to sing again. "A dreadful foe is in our land, drive him out, oh, drive him out. Oh, end the monster's awful reign, drive him out, oh, drive him out." She threw the register at what remained of the big screen. It barely missed the tabletop that hid the businessmen and crashed onto the marble and onyx floor.

She worked for twenty minutes and stopped when there was nothing left to break. The woman stood at the door, straightening her bonnet, tightening the ribbons. "Until the joints close," she said, "the streets will run red with blood." She opened the door. Schilling crouched lower behind the bar. The businessmen cowered beneath the table. Nobody saw her leave.

"The sun was in my eyes," Schilling explained to the police. "When she opened the door, the sunlight was so bright I lost sight of her."

"She came in screaming?" A man from the press was taking notes.

"Shrieking." The first businessman tried to read the reporter's notes, which were upside down from his point of view and cursory. He didn't enjoy talking to newsmen. When you dealt with the fourth estate, accuracy was your social responsibility. You could still be misquoted, of course. You wouldn't be the first.

"Kind of a screek," the second businessman offered.

"She's paying for everything," said Schilling. "Don't even ask me to be chivalrous."

"She was big," said the first businessman. "For a woman."

"She was enormous," said Schilling.

"She was as big as a football player," said the first businessman carefully.

"She was as big as a truck," said Schilling. He pointed with a shaky finger to the register. "She lifted it over her head like it was a feather duster or a pillow or something. You can write this down," he said. "You can quote me on this. We're talking about a very troubled, very big woman."

"I don't think it's such a good idea," the second businessman said.

"What's not a good idea?" asked the reporter.

"Women that size," said the second businessman.

"Just look what she did," said Schilling. Rage made his voice squeak. "Just look at my bar!"

PATRICK HARRIS HAD BEEN a DEA agent for eight years now. During those eight years, he had seen some action. He had been in Mexico and he had been in Panama and he had been in LA. He had been in one or two tight spots, but that didn't mean he couldn't help out with the dishes at home.

Harris knew he asked a lot of his wife. It couldn't be the easiest thing in the world, being married to a man who disappeared into Latin America for days at a time and might not even be able to get a message out that he was still alive. Harris could run a vacuum cleaner over a rug without feeling that he was doing his wife any favors. Harris could cook a meal from the very beginning, meaning the planning and the shopping and everything, without feeling that anyone needed to make a fuss about it.

He stood with the French bread and the Gruyère cheese and the imported Emmentaler Swiss in the nine-items-only-no-checks checkout line, wondering how he could use the tomatoes, which he hadn't planned to buy but were cheaper and redder than usual and had tempted him. The woman in front had twelve items. It didn't really irritate Harris. He was only sorry that it was so hard for some people to play by the rules.

While he waited for the three extra items to be tallied and worried in an ineffective, pleasant way over the tomatoes, he read through the headlines. Evidence of prehistoric alien cannibals had been found in Peruvian cave paintings, and a statue of Elvis had been found on Mars. A husband with bad breath had killed his wife merely by kissing her. A Miami bar had been destroyed by a sort of half woman/half gorilla. Harris saw the illustration before he read the story, an artist's rendering of Queen Kong in a black dress and bonnet. He looked at the picture again. He read the headline. One of his tomatoes spun from the counter to the floor. Harris stepped on it, squished it, and didn't even notice. He bought the paper.

He had never been in so much trouble in his life.

THE DOORS WERE HEAVY and padlocked. A hummingbird dipped through the entryway twice, held for a moment over an out-of-season fuchsia, and disappeared. The largest of the MPs tried to shoulder the doors open. He tried three times, but the wood did not give. One of the women smashed through a window instead. Harris was the fifth person inside.

The soldiers searched for fugitives. They spun into the hallways, kicked in the doors. Harris found the dining room on the other side of some broken glass. The table was set with china and the flatware was gold. An interrupted meal consisted of rack of lamb, braised carrots, curried peach halves served on lettuce leaves. The food had been sitting on the china plates for at least twenty-four hours.

He started into the library, but one of the MPs called to him from farther back in the house. The MP's voice sounded self-consciously nervous. I'm still scared, the tone said. Aren't I silly?

Harris followed the voice down a hallway and through an open door.

The MP had her rifle slung over her back. In her hands she held a large statue of St. George, spear frozen over the neck of the dragon. The dragon was considerably smaller than St. George's horse.

Behind the MP, three stairs rose to an altar with red candles and white flowers and chicken feathers. The stairs were carpeted, and a supplicant could kneel or lie supine if the supplicant weren't too tall. The room itself was not carpeted. A black circle had been painted on the stone floor, with a red triangle inside. The four cardinal points of the compass were marked.

Harris looked east. The east wall was a wall of toads. Toad-shaped stones covered every inch of seven shelves, and the larger ones sat on the floor. The toads were all different: different colors, different sizes. Harris guessed there were four hundred, five hundred toads. "Why toads?" Harris asked. He stepped inside.

The MP shook her head and put the statue back on the altar. "Shit," she said, meaning nothing by it, merely making conversation. "Is this shit for real?"

One of the smallest toads was carved of obsidian. Its eyes were a polished, glassy black; it was no bigger than Harris's thumbnail. It attracted him. Harris reached out. He hesitated briefly, then touched it. At that moment, somewhere in the room, an engine cycled on. Harris started at the sound, closed his hand convulsively over the toad. He looked at the MP, who gestured behind him.

The noise came from a freezer back by the door. It was a small freezer, not big enough to hold the body of an adult. A goat, maybe. A child. A head. Harris looked at the MP. "Groceries," he said.

"Stash," the MP suggested. This made opening the freezer Harris's job. Harris didn't think so. He would have stared the MP down if the MP had only looked at him. Harris watched to be sure the MP wasn't looking. He put the black toad in his pocket and went to open the freezer. He was simply not thinking about the toad. Otherwise he would never have taken it. Harris was DEA, and even when he was undercover he played by the rules. Taking the toad marked the beginning of a series of atypical transgressions. Harris was at a loss to explain them. It was not as though he wanted the toad.

The freezer worked laboriously. When Harris and his wife were first married, they'd had a noisy refrigerator like this. They would argue: arguments of adjustment, kitchen arguments as opposed to bedroom arguments, as vehement and passionate as they were trivial. And the refrigerator would be a third voice, grumbling in dissatisfaction or croaking in disbelief. Sometimes it would make them laugh. Harris tried to resurrect these comfortable, pro-appliance kinds of feelings. He closed his eyes and raised the lid. He opened his eyes. The only thing inside the freezer was a stack of pictures.

Harris pushed the lid up until it caught. Some were actual photographs. There was a Polaroid of the General's wife seated in a lawn chair under a beach umbrella, a fat woman who'd left the marks of her nails on more than one of the General's mistresses. There were some Cubans, including Castro, and some Americans, Kissinger and Helms, pictures cut from magazines, but real photographs of the President and the ex-President. There was a fuzzy picture of two men shaking hands on the steps of a public building. Harris recognized one of the men as the Archbishop. The edges of every picture had been dipped in red wax.

HE STILL HAD the toad in his pocket that night when he attended a party at the home of Señora Villejas. Many American officers were there. Señora Villejas greeted him at the door with a kiss and a whisper. *"El General llego a la embajada con calzoncillos rojos."* The General had turned up in the Vatican embassy wearing red underwear, she said. She spun away to see that the band had refreshment.

A toad in a hole, Harris thought. It was Christmas Eve. Harris arrived late, too late for the champagne but just in time for the mixed drinks. The band was ethnic and very chic. Harris could hear a concertina, a bobla, a woowoo, the triangle. They played a waltz.

"Have you heard the one about the bitch at the dog kennels?" one of the American captains asked him. The captain had a strawberry daiquiri; he stirred the strawberries with his straw.

"I have now," said Harris.

"Don't pull that shit with me," the captain said. He drank. "You some kind of feminist? You got a whole lot of women working undercover in the DEA?"

Harris ignored him. He spotted Ruiz by the windows and made his way toward him. Some couples had started to dance in the open space between Harris and Ruiz. Harris dodged through the dancers. A woman he had never seen before put a drink in his hand, alcoholic, but hot and spiced. "What am I drinking?" he asked Ruiz.

Ruiz shrugged. "You had a chance to call your wife?"

"This afternoon," said Harris. "I'm on my way home tomorrow. You?"

"South," said Ruiz. "What any of this shit has to do with anything I do not know."

"It's a statement," said Harris. "At least it's a statement."

"It's an invasion," said Ruiz.

Well, of course there was that. Harris was sorry Ruiz was choosing to see it that way. "He collected toads," Harris offered, by way of changing the subject. "Stone toads."

"He collected yachts," Ruiz said. "The *Macho I*, the *Macho II*, and the *Macho III*. Don't ever tell me he had a problem in this area. And don't tell me he lacked imagination."

Harris took a sip of his drink. It stung his mouth. "Why toads?" His eyes were watering. He took a larger sip, drained the glass halfway.

"Maybe they were hollow," Ruiz said.

"No."

"Maybe just one was hollow and the others were all to hide the hollow one."

A young woman refreshed Harris's drink. "*¿Que estoy bebiendo?*" Harris asked the woman, who left without answering.

"Have some of mine," Ruiz said. He was drinking a margarita.

He handed it to Harris. Harris turned the glass to a virginal part of the salt rim and sipped. He rotated the glass and sipped again. "Go ahead and finish it," said Ruiz. "I'll get another."

The music had begun to sound odd. A man stood in the middle of the dance floor. "I'll tell you who's coming here. I'll tell you who's coming here!" he shouted. He threw the contents of his drink into the rafters of the house. Others did the same. Harris laughed and drank his margarita instead. He started to say something to Ruiz, but Ruiz was gone. Ruiz had been gone for a long time.

The dancers began to stomp, and the high treble sound of the triangle reached too deeply into Harris's ears. It hurt. Harris could smell alcohol and herbs, drifting down from the roof. The drums and the stomping worked their way into his body. Something inside him was pounding to match them. Harris resisted finding out what. He pulled the little toad from his pocket. "Look what I have," he said to Ruiz, but Ruiz had gone; now Harris remembered, Ruiz had gone south to get a margarita. It was quite some time ago.

"In short, you were stoned out of your gourd," said Harris's superior.

"Now it gets a little blurred for a while," Harris told him. This was a lie, one of several lies. The story Harris was actually telling was far from complete. He had certainly not mentioned stealing the toad. And now he was not mentioning remembering a woman in an evening gown who smiled at him, holding out her hand. There were flowers in it. They bloomed. Everyone was dancing.

"My ears hurt," Harris told her. "Ants are crawling on me."

He tried to brush them away, but his hands wouldn't move. She knelt and was still above him so he must have been on the ground. The flowers turned into a painted egg. "This is your brain on drugs," Harris said, laughing. She held it out to him, knowing he couldn't reach for it, teasing him.

"What do you want?" Her shoulders were bare; she answered the question as she asked it by breathing deeply so that her breasts swelled at the neckline. "In your heart, what do you really want?"

Harris's soul detached from his body and floated away.

"I think I had a very narrow escape," Harris told his superior.

"It's a hazard of fieldwork. Sometimes you draw suspicion to yourself by refusing. We know that." The tabloid Harris had purchased was spread out on the desk between Harris and his superior. His superior was adding a mustache to one of the cannibal aliens in the Peruvian cave painting. He blacked in the teeth. It pained Harris, who was not the sort of person to deface pictures and certainly not prehistoric pictures. "I appreciate your coming in, but I don't think I'm even inclined to report this. I mean, in your case, it wasn't even advertent. You were inadvertently drugged."

"I was poisoned," said Harris.

"What does it have to do with gorilla women?"

"Guerrilla women?" Harris repeated. "Everything. I was poisoned by female agents of the Panama Defense Forces." He took a deep breath. "You got anything here I can drink?"

His superior gestured to the wet bar. Harris poured himself a shot of whiskey. He swallowed it all at once. "The toad is an important Mayan symbol of hallucinosis." Whiskey warmed his tongue and his throat. "In medieval European witchcraft, they used to decompose toads in menstrual blood for use in potions.

"'Toad, that under cold stone, / Days and nights has thirty-one / Swelter'd venom sleeping got, / Boil thou first i' the charmed pot!'" Harris said.

Harris's superior was staring at him. Harris's superior was not an educated man. "Shakespeare," Harris said, by way of apology for showing off. "I've been reading up on it. I mean I don't know these things off the top of my head. I'm not really a toad man." Harris's superior continued to stare. Harris poured another drink to steady himself. "In Haiti, the toad is a symbol of the zombie." Harris tossed his whiskey into his throat and avoided looking at his superior. "What do you know about Carry A. Nation?" Harris asked.

"Make it a written report," his superior said.

Item one: There are real zombies.

The woman could see where Harris was floating above his body. She began to sing to him, low, but he could hear her even over the drums. "Ti bon ange," she sang. The egg in her hand became a jar made of clay. She held it out so he would come down closer and look. She wanted him to look inside it and not at her, because her shape was not holding. She was not a beautiful woman at all; she was an ugly woman, old and ugly. Her skin folded on her neck like a toad's. Harris found this transformation a little insulting. He remembered how much he loved his wife. He had spoken with her only today. He couldn't wait to get back to his body and home to her. He refused to be seduced by an ugly old woman instead. "Ti bon ange," she sang, and her voice was low and croaked. "Come look in my jar."

Item two: the ti bon ange. Ti bon ange means the little good angel. Every person who has ever lived is made up of five components. These are the z'etoile, the n'ame, the corps cadavre, the gros bon ange, and the ti bon ange. We need concern ourselves here only with the last three.

The gros bon ange is the undifferentiated life force. It binds you to the rest of the living world.

The ti bon ange is your personal life force. The ti bon ange is your individual personality.

The corps cadavre is your body.

Harris could see the dark opening of the jar beneath him, a circular pool of black. The circle grew until he could have fit inside it. He didn't know if it was growing because the woman was raising it or if he was slipping toward it like sand sucked into the throat of an hourglass. Either way was perilous. Harris looked for someplace dark to hide. He slid into the bright blackness of the stone toad, resting in the hand of his inert corps cadavre.

The American captain came and knelt on the other side of Harris. "What have we here?"

"DEA." The beautiful woman was back. The American captain wouldn't have even spoken to the ugly old woman. She turned her jar into a wineglass and drank from it innocently.

Item three: creating a zombie. In order to create a zombie, you need to separate the ti bon ange from the gros bon ange. You need to take the ti bon ange out of the corps cadavre and leave the gros bon ange behind.

The bokor accomplishes this with bufotoxin, an extremely potent poison milked from the glands of the *Bufo marinus* toad, and tetrodotoxin, taken from the skin, liver, testicles, and ovaries of the Tetraodontiformes, a family of fish that includes the blowfish. Bufotoxin stimulates cardiac activity. Tetrodotoxin causes neuromuscular paralysis. In proper doses, taken together, they produce a living corpse.

It is critical that the dosage not be too high. Too much poison and you will kill the body, forcing the gros bon ange to abandon it as well.

"I know," the captain said.

The woman wanted the captain to go away so that she could sing to Harris again. "He's had too much to drink."

The captain flicked a finger at Harris's nose. Harris saw him do it. "Undercover is pussy work. I wish just once the DEA would send out an agent with some balls."

The woman was angry and it made her old, but the captain wasn't looking.

"Pompous self-righteous pricks," he said. "The most ineffective agency in the whole U.S. Government, and that's saying something."

The captain looked at her. She was beautiful and drank red wine. Her eyes were as bright as coins. "I wish . . ." said the captain. He moved closer to her. "Shall I tell you what I wish?" he said. Harris was relieved to see that the captain was not going away, not unless the woman became old before him, and this was something she was, apparently, reluctant to do. Perhaps she wanted to surprise the captain with it. It served the captain right, seducing some old crone. The party spun around Harris, dancing couples, drinking couples. The black opalescence of the toad cast a yellow filter over the scene, but Harris could still see, dimly, that inside every woman there, no matter how graceful, no matter how beautiful, there was an old crone, biding her time.

"WHAT ARE YOU WRITING?" Harris's wife asked him. She had come in behind him, too quietly. It made him jump. He leaned forward to block the screen.

"Nothing," he said. Harris loved his wife and knew that her dear, familiar body did not conceal the figure of a hostile old woman. Hadn't he always helped with the dishes? Hadn't he never minded? He was safe with her. Harris wished she wouldn't sneak up on him.

"What are you reading? Children's books?" she asked incredulously. She taught British, American, and women's literature at the junior college. She was, Harris thought, but lovingly, a bit of a snob. In fact, he had a stack of books on his desk—several Japanese pharmacologies, several volumes of Voudon rituals, and a couple of temperance histories. Only one was for children, but this was the one Harris's wife picked up. *The Girl's Life of Carry A. Nation,* it said on the spine. "Are you coming to bed?" Harris's wife asked.

"In a moment."

She went to bed without him, and she took the book with her.

. . .

FIVE-YEAR-OLD CARRY MOORE sat on the pillared porch and waited impatiently for her mother to come home. Her father had bought her mother a new carriage! Little Carry wanted to see it.

The year was 1851. Behind Carry was the single-story Kentucky log house in which the Moores lived. It sat at the end of a row of althea bushes and cedar trees. The slave cabins were to the right. To the left was the garden: roses, syringa, and sweet Mary. Mary was Carry's mother's name.

Carry's mother was not like other mothers. Shortly after Carry was born, Mary decided her own real name was Victoria. She was not just playing let's pretend. Mary thought she was really the Queen of England. She would only speak to Carry by appointment. Sometimes this made Carry very sad.

Carry saw one of the slaves, Bill, coming down the road. Bill was very big. He was riding a white horse and was dressed in a fine red hunting jacket. Didn't he look magnificent? He carried a hunting horn, which made loud noises when you wound it. *Honk! Honk!* The Queen was coming!

Carry could see the carriage behind him. It was the most beautiful carriage she had ever seen. It had curtains and shiny wheels and matched gray horses to pull it. Henry, another slave, was the coachman. He wore a tall silk hat.

The carriage stopped. Mary got out. She was dressed all in gold with a cut-glass tiara. She wanted to knight Farmer Murray with her umbrella. Farmer Murray was their neighbor. He was weeding his onions. Farmer Murray tried to take Mary's umbrella away.

"Oh, Ma," said Carry. She ran down the road to her mother. "Take me for a ride."

Carry's mother would not even look at her. "Betsey," said Mary. Betsey was one of the slaves. She was only thirteen years old, but she was a married woman with a baby of her own. "This child is filthy. Take her away and clean her up."

"Ma!" said little Carry. She wanted so badly to go for a ride.

"We don't want her in the house," said Mary. Queens sometimes say *we* when they mean *I*. Mary was using the royal *we*. "She is to sleep with you tonight, Betsey," said Mary.

Carry didn't mind sleeping with Betsey, but it meant she had to sleep with Josh, Betsey's husband, too. Josh was mean. "Please don't make me sleep with Josh," Carry asked, but her mother had already walked past her.

Sometimes Carry's mother was not very nice to her, but Carry had lots of friends. They were her slaves! They were Betsey; and Judy, who was very old; and Eliza, who was very pretty; and Henry, who was smart; and Tom, who was nice. Carry ate with them and slept with them. They loved Carry.

One night Henry told a scary story. It was dark in the slave cabin, and they all sat around the fire. The story was about a mean slavemaster who died but came back in chains to haunt his slaves. They all believed in ghosts, which made the story even scarier. The story made Carry shiver.

Suddenly there was a knock at the door. Carry jumped right out of her seat. It was only Mr. Brown, the overseer. That made Carry laugh. "We thought you were someone bad coming," Carry said. Mr. Brown laughed, too. He had just come to talk to Eliza. He took Eliza away to talk to her in his cabin. Judy and Betsey scolded Henry for telling a story that frightened Carry.

> Item four: On Christmas Eve, at a party at the house of Señora Villejas, I narrowly survived an attempt by the Panama Defense Forces to turn me into a zombie. The agent of the attack was either a beautiful young Panamanian woman or an old one. She appeared to me as both.
>
> Under ordinary circumstances, the body's nerve impulses are relayed from the spine under conditions of difference in the sodium and potassium concentrations inside and outside the axon membrane. The unique heterocyclic structure of the tetrodotoxin molecule is selective for the sodium channels. A change in the sodium levels, therefore, alters the effectiveness of the drug. My escape was entirely fortuitous. I had just drunk half a margarita. The recent ingestion of salt was, I believe, all that saved me.
>
> I hardly need point out the usefulness to the drug cartels of a DEA agent entirely under their control.

Harris's hands were sweaty on the keyboard. He licked a finger to taste the salt. There was a map on the wall beside him, marked with five colored pins. One pin went through the Vatican embassy in Panama. One was in the Senate Bar in Miami. The others continued northward in a more or less direct line. If extended, the line would pass through Washington, D.C.

> Item five: the loa. At death, the ti bon ange survives and returns to live in another body. Each of us has a direct spiritual lineage back through history. After many such renewals, the individual spirit metamorphoses into disembodied, undifferentiated energy. It joins the cosmic pool of life where the loa reside. When a loa is called back, it returns

from this pool as a purified, mythological version of itself. The individual ti bon ange has become archetype. The same mythological figures we know as saints of the Catholic Church also appear to the Voudon as loa.

On the evening of December 24, 1989, I convinced several DEA agents to join me in calling forth a loa. We did not call forth a specific spirit by name. We called to our own spiritual ancestors. We asked for a weapon in our struggle against the drug cartels.

"Send us a DEA agent with balls," Harris shouted. He was laughing, ecstatic to be in his body again. His hands tingled, his lips were numb, his thighs were warm. The war was over and he was not among the dead. It was Christmas Eve. Ruiz and Casteneda and Martin and several others, ties loosened, suit jackets askew, shoes off, danced the dance with Harris in Señora Villejas's garden. They threw the contents of their drinks into bushes pruned to the shapes of elephants and camels and giraffes. They crushed flowers with their hands, and Martin had unzipped his pants, rezipping them so that a white hothouse iris extended from his crotch. Of course, it hadn't really been the dance. It had only been something they made up.

I would prefer not to identify the men who joined me in this ceremony since the suggestion was entirely my own. I would like to repeat, in my defense, that I was at this time under the influence of bufotoxin, known for its hallucinogenic properties, as well as alcohol. I was not conducting myself soberly. We did not for a moment believe that we would be successful in calling up such a spirit. The entire enterprise was conducted as a drunken lark.

Clinically speaking, I suppose we were trying to protect ourselves from our fear of the Voudonist by making a joke of it. I had just survived an attack on my soul. That I did not believe in this attack, imagining it to be purely hallucinatory, does not change the fact that I was unnerved by it.

In the light of recent events, however, and with the benefit of hindsight, it seems possible to me that we have underestimated the effectiveness of the South American drug cartel Voudon. The Haitian zombie is typically described as dim and slow-witted. Among our top government officials are men who fit this description, men known also to have been in Latin and South America. The DEA should make a list of these men, meet with them on some pretext, and offer them heavily salted foods.

Ruiz was gaping at him. A z'etoile fell from the sky into the garden. It came in the form of a burning rock. It landed in one of the camel bushes and melted the garden.

The shapes of the flowers and trees remained, but now they were made of fire. The DEA agents burst into flames. Harris could see their shapes, too. They continued to dance, stamping their flaming feet into the liquid fire of the lawn, shaking their flickering hands.

A woman emerged from the camel bush, not a real woman but a woman of flame. She grew larger and larger until she was larger than he was, wrapped her fiery arms around him. The air was so hot he couldn't breathe it. Harris panicked. He fumbled for the toad in his pocket, remembering how he'd escaped into it once already, but she touched it with one finger, melting it into something small and phallic. She laughed and melted it again, shapeless this time, a puddle of black glass.

"Who are you?" Harris asked, and she told him. Then she scorched the bottoms of his feet until he fainted from the pain and had to be carried home.

The next morning, the toad was in his pocket and his feet were healed. Ruiz came to say good-bye. *"Feliz Navidad,"* said Ruiz. He brought a present of candied fruits. "Kiss your wife for me. You lucky bastard."

Harris thanked him for the gift. "Great party," said Harris carefully.

Ruiz shrugged. "You had a good time," he agreed. "You were a wild man."

They said little else. On his way to the airport, Harris directed his taxi past the home of Señora Villejas. The garden was green.

CARRY'S MOTHER WAS sometimes better when she had new places and people to see. Carry's father, George, had trouble with his real estate business. The Moores moved often, and they grew poorer. When Carry was ten years old, they moved to Cass County, Missouri. Carry missed Kentucky. She missed Bill and Eliza, who had been sold. She missed her beautiful Kentucky house.

But Cass County was an exciting place to live! Just across the border, in Kansas, people who liked having slaves were fighting with people who didn't. The people who liked slavery were called bushwhackers. The people who didn't were called jayhawkers. Kansas had an election to see if they would be a free state with no slaves. Bushwhackers from Missouri took the ballot boxes and said they would count the votes for Kansas.

They said that Kansas had voted to make it illegal to even say that you didn't like slavery. Anyone who said they didn't like slavery could be killed. So many died, people began to call the state "Bleeding Kansas."

This was a hard time for Carry. She went to bed for five years.

Psychologists now say maybe having a mother who thought she was Queen Victoria is what made Carry sick for such a long time. Psychologists are people who study how people feel and behave.

In 1857, her doctor said she had consumption of the bowels.

But George, her father, said her sickness was a punishment for not loving God. He came to see her sometimes in her bedroom. "Why won't you love God, Carry?" he would ask. He would have tears in his eyes. "You are going to die and break my heart," he would say.

Carry didn't want her father to be unhappy. She tried and tried to love God better. Carry thought she was a horrible sinner. Sometimes, when she was a little girl, she stole things for her slaves, little bits of ribbon, spoonfuls of sugar. Her own heart, Carry said, was the blackest, foulest place she ever saw.

One day when Carry was twelve, George took her to a revival meeting. "Who will come to Jesus?" the minister asked. Carry said that she would. Carry had a fever. George was afraid she was about to die, so even though it was winter, the minister and George took her right away to an icy creek. The water was cold! Carry waded into it, and the minister pushed her under.

When she came up, Carry said that she had learned to love God. She made her slaves come to her bedroom so she could preach to them. Carry told them that God sent you troubles because He loved you and wanted you to love Him. God loved Carry so much He made her ill. God loved the slaves so much He made them slaves. Now that Carry loved God, she began to get better, and in two more years she was able to get out of bed.

The slaves thought that since they loved God, maybe they didn't need to be slaves anymore. They told George they wanted to go to Lawrence, Kansas, where slavery was illegal. Lawrence, Kansas, was very close to Cass County, Missouri.

George told the slaves they were all moving to Texas instead. Texas was very far from Lawrence, Kansas.

Item six: I don't know where she got the body. A loa usually manifests itself through possession, but I remember no one at the party as large as this woman is reported to be. In addition, I have a memory of the loa materializing out of flame. I need not repeat that I was under the influence of bufotoxin at the time.

Item seven: The loa are frequently religious archetypes. Carry Nation, by her own account, spoke to angels when she was still a child and saw the Holy Ghost at her basement window. She performed two miracles in her life and applied for sainthood, although the application was turned down. Since the DEA agents and I performed only a quasi-Voudon ritual, there is a certain logic to the fact that we got only a quasi-saint in return. The loa I summoned was Carry Amelia Nation. She told me so herself.

Item eight: Ask the General why he left the Vatican embassy.

Harris already knew the answer to item eight. Harris had friends among the attorneys on Miami's "white powder bar." It was not that their interests were compatible. It was merely a fact that they saw each other often.

"So what was it?" the attorney told Harris he had asked the General. "Why did you come out? Was it the white room with no windows and no TV? Was it the alcohol deprivation?"

"It was a woman," the General said.

"You spoke to your mistress." The attorney knew this much. She had been in U.S. custody at the time. "She persuaded you?"

"No." The General shuddered violently. His skin turned the color of eggplant. "It was a horrible woman, a huge woman, a woman no man would sleep with." He was, the attorney told Harris, very possibly a homosexual. Hadn't he started dressing in yellow jumpsuits? Hadn't he said that the only people in Panama with balls were the queers and the women? "She sang to me," the General said.

"Heavy metal?" asked the attorney.

"Who Hath Sorrow, Who Hath Woe," said the General.

Harris did not include this in his report. It was an off-the-record conversation. And anyway, the DEA would trust it more if they found it themselves.

Harris pushed the key to print. Only the first part of his report fit on the DEA form. He stapled the other pages to it. He signed the report and poured himself a bedtime sherry.

THE MOORES DID NOT LIVE in Texas very long. Many of their slaves developed typhoid fever while walking there from Missouri. All their horses died. George tried to farm, but he did not know how. Mary told one of their neighbors that she was confiscating his lands and his title, so he threw all their plows into the river. Soon there was nothing to eat.

George called his slaves together. He told them he had decided to free them. The slaves were frightened to be free with no food. Some of them cried.

It was very hard for the Moores to leave their slaves. But Carry said her father had done the right thing. She believed that slavery was a great wrong. She admired John Brown, a man who had fought for the rights of slaves in Kansas and was hanged for it when Carry was thirteen years old. All her life, John Brown was a hero of Carry's. "When I grow up," Carry said, "I will be as brave as John Brown."

Between Texas and Missouri was the Civil War. The Queen's carriage had been sold. When the Moores went back to Missouri, they had to ride in their little wagon. One day the ground shook behind them. They pulled off the road. It was not an earthquake. It was the Confederate cavalry on their way to the Battle of Pea Ridge. After the cavalry came the foot soldiers. It took two days and two nights for all the soldiers to pass them.

On the third day, they heard cannons. The Moores began to

ride again, slowly, in the direction of the cannons. On the fourth day, the Confederate Army passed them again. This time they were going south. This time they were running. The Moores drove their little wagon straight through the smoking battlefield of Pea Ridge.

They spent that night in a farmhouse with a woman and five wounded Union soldiers. The soldiers were too badly hurt to be moved, so the woman had offered to nurse them. She told Carry she had five sons of her own. Her sons were soldiers for the South. Carry helped her clean and tend the boys. One of them was dying. Mary knighted them all.

"ARE YOU ENJOYING the book?" Harris asked, surprised that she was still awake. He took off his clothes and lay down beside her. She had more than her share of the comforter. He had to lie very close to be warm enough, putting an arm across her stomach, feeling her shift her body to fit him.

"Yes, I am," she said. "I think she's wonderful."

"Wonderful?" Harris removed his arm. "What do you mean, 'wonderful'?"

"I just mean, what a colorful, amazing life. What a story."

Harris put his arm back. "Yes," he agreed.

"And what a vivacious, powerful woman. After all she'd been through. What a resilient, remarkable woman."

Harris removed his arm. "She's insane," he suggested stiffly. "She's a religious zealot with a hatchet. She's a joke."

"She's a superhero," said Harris's wife. "Why doesn't she have her own movie? Look here." She flipped through *The Girl's*

Life to the collection of photographs in the middle. She skipped over Carry kneeling with her Bible in her jail cell to a more confrontational shot: Carry in battle dress, threatening the photographer with hatchetation. "She even had a costume. She designed it herself, like Batman. See? She made special dresses with pockets on the inside for her rocks and ammunition. She could bust up bars and she could sew like the wind. Can Rambo say as much?"

"I bet she threw like a girl," said Harris, trying for a light tone to mask the fact that he was genuinely upset.

His wife was not masking. "Her aim was supposed to have been extraordinary," she said in her schoolteacher tone, a tone that invariably suggested disappointment in him. "Women are cut off from the rich mythological tradition you men have. Women are so hungry for heroines. Name one."

"What?" said Harris.

"Name a historical heroine. Quickly."

"Joan of Arc," said Harris.

"Everyone can get that far. Now name another."

Harris couldn't think. She tapped her fingers on the page to let him know that time was passing. He had always admired Morgan Fairchild for her political activism, but he assumed this would be the wrong answer. If he hadn't been so irritated, he could probably have come up with another name.

"Harriet Tubman," his wife said. "Donaldina Cameron. Edith Cavell. Yvonne Hakime-Rimpel."

She really was a snob, but she was also a fair-minded woman. She was not, Harris thought, one of those feminists who simply changed history every time it didn't suit her. Harris got out of bed and went back to the study. His feet were cold on the bare wood floor. Blankets or no blankets, it would take a long time for his feet to warm up. He fished Carry Nation's autobiography out of his stack and brought it back.

"You haven't read about her daughter," he said. "There's nothing about Charlien in the pretty little version for children that you chose to read." He flipped through his own book until he found the section he wanted. He thrust it in front of his wife's face, then pulled it back to read it aloud. "'About this time, my precious child, born of a drunken father and a distracted mother, seemed to conceive a positive dislike for Christianity. I feared for her soul and I prayed to God to send her some bodily affliction which would make her love and serve Him.'"

Harris skimmed ahead in the book with his finger. "A week later, Charlien developed a raging fever," he told his wife. "She almost died. And when she recovered from that, part of her cheek rotted away. She had a hole in her face. You could see her teeth. But it was a lucky thing. Because then her jaws locked shut, and she wouldn't have been able to eat if there wasn't a hole in her cheek to stick a straw through." He made an effort to lower his voice. "Her jaws stayed locked for eight years."

There was a long silence, a silence, Harris thought, of reevaluation and regret for earlier, hasty judgments. "That is a very ugly story," his wife said. She took the autobiography away from him and began to turn the pages.

"Isn't it?" Harris wiggled his arm underneath her. There was a longer silence. Harris stared at the ceiling. It was a blown popcorn landscape, and sometimes Harris could imagine pictures in it, but he was too tired for this now. He looked instead at the large cobwebs in the corners. Tomorrow Harris would get the broom and knock them down. Then he would get out the vacuum to suck up the bits of ceiling that came down with the cobwebs, the little flakes of milky asbestos, the poisonous snow, the toxic powders. Nothing the vacuum couldn't handle. And then Harris would need a rag to remove from the furniture the dust the vacuum had flung up. And then the rag would need to be washed. And then . . . it was almost like counting sheep. Harris drifted.

"You can't possibly think those things happened because of Carry's prayers," his wife said.

Harris woke up in amazement. His arm had already gone numb from his wife's weight. He pulled it free. "So now she's Carry?" Harris asked. "Now we're on a first-name basis?"

"Look at the religious climate she grew up in. You don't believe God afflicted a little girl with such a horrible condition because her mother asked Him to?"

"What kind of mother would ask Him to?" said Harris. "That's the point, isn't it? What kind of a horrible mother is this?"

Harris's wife was still reading the autobiography. "Carry worked for years to earn the money for surgery," she told Harris.

"I've read the book," he said, but there was no stopping her.

"She ignored the doctors who said the case was hopeless. Every time a doctor said the case was hopeless, she went home and earned more money for another doctor." Harris's wife pointed out the relevant text.

"I've read the damn book."

"The condition was finally cured, because Carry never gave up."

"So she says," said Harris.

His wife regarded him coolly. "I don't think Carry would lie."

Harris turned his back on his wife and lay on his side. "It's very late," he said curtly. He turned off his light, punched angrily at his pillow. Unable to get comfortable, he flipped from side to side and considered getting himself another sherry. "What's to like about her? I really don't understand." Harris felt that his wife had suddenly, frighteningly, become a different person. They had always been so consensual. Not pathologically so—they had their own opinions and their own values, of course—but they had also generally liked the same movies, enjoyed the same books. Suddenly she was holding unreasonable opinions. Suddenly she was a stranger.

His wife did not answer, nor did she turn off her own light. "This is an interesting book, too," she said. He heard pages continuing to turn. "There are hymns in the back. Honey, if you dislike Carry Nation so much, why do you have all these books about her?"

Harris, who always told his wife everything, had not yet found just the right moment to tell her that, the last time he was in Panama, he had summoned a loa. Harris pretended to be asleep.

"You just don't like her because she had a hatchet," his wife said quietly. "Because she was a big, loud woman with a hatchet. You're threatened by her."

Harris sat bolt upright so that the comforter slid off him. Was that fair? Was that at all fair? Hadn't they had a completely egalitarian, respectful, supportive marriage? And didn't it make him sort of a joke in the DEA for his lack of machismo, and hadn't he never, ever complained to her about this?

"Good night," his wife said evenly, snapping her light off. She had her side of the comforter wound in her fists. It fell just a bit below her shoulders so he could see her neck and the start of her spine, blue in the moonlight, like stitching down her back. She breathed, and her spine stretched like a snake. She pulled the comforter up around her again. She had more than her share of the covers.

Beside the books on her nightstand was the little black toad. Harris had given it to her for Christmas. It stared at him.

And wasn't he, after all, the person who'd brought Carry back? Now he was glad he hadn't told her. Harris's feet were too cold, and he couldn't sleep at all.

"I'VE READ OVER your report," Harris's superior told him. "I took it up top. It's a little spotty."

Harris conceded as much. "The form was so small," he said.

"And not really designed for exactly this sort of problem." With tone of voice, phrasing, and body language, Harris's superior managed a blatant show of generosity and condescension. Harris's superior was feeling superior. It was not a pretty thing to see. It was not a pretty thing to see in the man who fought so hard to award the Texas Guard a $2,900,000 federal grant so they could station themselves along the Mexican border disguised as cactus plants and ambush drug traffickers.

Harris looked instead at the map on the wall behind him. It was a map much like the map in Harris's study; the pins were different colors, but the locations were identical. "This is the DEA's official position," his superior said. "The DEA does not believe in zombies. The DEA believes in drugs. One of our agents was inadvertently drugged on Christmas Eve and imagined a great many things. This agent now understands that the incidents in question were hallucinatory.

"If it is ever proved that this agent called forth a loa, then it is the DEA's position that he did so in his leisure time and that the summoning represents the act of an individual and not of an agency.

"The DEA has no knowledge of or connection with the gorilla woman. Her malicious and illegal destruction of private property is a matter for the local police. Do you understand?"

"Unofficially?" asked Harris.

"Unofficially they're reading your report in the men's room for light entertainment," said Harris's superior. "You'll see bits of it on the wall in the second stall." Harris already had. *Item six: I don't know where she got the body.* Scratched with a penknife or the fingernail-cleaning attachment on a clipper, just above the toilet paper dispenser.

His superior leaned forward to engage in actual eye contact with Harris. It took Harris by surprise; he drew back.

"Unofficially we were impressed with the report the General gave us. We were impressed enough to interview some of the Miami eyewitnesses. They're not the sort of wing nuts in sandals you might expect to find in the tabloids. Our agent spent two hours with a Mr. Schilling, who owns the Miami bar. He's a pretty savvy guy, and he says she performed feats of superhuman strength. How did she get into the Vatican embassy? No one ever sees her come or go. She took out a crack lab in Raleigh, North Carolina, a week ago. Did you hear about that?"

Harris had not. He was alarmed to hear she was already as

far north as Raleigh. He rechecked the map. There it was, a black pin through the heart of North Carolina. "Unofficially the DEA doesn't give a damn where she came from. Unofficially the DEA expects you to take care of her."

Harris nodded. He had always seen that the burden of responsibility was his. With or without the DEA, he had never intended to shirk it. He had already been spending his sleepless nights making plans. "With support?" Harris asked.

"At my discretion. And certainly not visibly."

It was more than Harris had hoped for. He moved to the map on the wall. "She seems to be moving directly north. Sooner or later, I figure she'll hit here." He drew a line north from Raleigh to Richmond, a small circle around Richmond. "Somewhere in here. So. We concentrate our forces in the larger bars.

"Now, the body is the real issue. Is it a real body? If so, it's doable. If not, we're in trouble. If not, we need expert help. But let's say that it is. She shows herself, we attack with the bufotoxin/tetrodotoxin package. This could be a bit tricky. She won't drink, of course. The potion can go right through the skin, and sometimes the bokor simply sprinkles it on the doorstep, but I'm guessing she's the sort who won't remove her shoes. We might try a Shirley Temple, load the tetrodotoxin into the cherry. Even if she won't drink the ginger ale, I'm willing to bet she'll eat the cherry. The dosage will be guesswork, and someone will have to take it to her. Of course, I'm volunteering."

"No hallucinogenics," Harris's superior said.

Harris's mind was filled with cherries. He had to blink to clear it. "I don't understand. We're just trying to persuade the loa to abandon the host body."

"You summoned a weapon. This weapon served us at the

Vatican embassy. It's a useful weapon. We don't want it destroyed."

"You don't understand," Harris said. "You're not going to control it. You can't talk to it. You can't reason with it. You can't hurt it. It doesn't feel pity or remorse or self-doubt. It makes no distinction between drugs and liquor and nicotine. And it will not stop. Ever."

"We want it on the team," Harris's superior said.

"You're tying my hands," said Harris. His heart had never beat faster except for maybe that time in Mexico when Rico had slipped and used his real name during a buy, and that time above the Bolivian mountains when two engines failed, and that time when his wife was supposed to be home by seven and didn't arrive until after ten because the class discussion had been so interesting they'd taken it to a bar to continue it and the bar phone had been out of order, and that time he was on bufotoxins.

"The problem is not here in the States with the consumers. The problem is down there with the suppliers."

"You're sending me on a suicide mission."

"We want your loa in Colombia," Harris's superior said.

HARRIS PACKED HIS CLOTHES for Richmond. He had no red underwear, but he had boxers with red valentines on them. They were a gift from his wife. He put them on, making a mental list of the other items he needed. Eggs dyed yellow, fresh eggs, so he would have to pick them up after he arrived. Salt. Red and white candles. The black toad, for luck. Feathers. Harris pulled his Swiss Army knife out of his pocket and reached for his pillow.

"Patrick?" Harris's wife called him from the kitchen. "Patrick, would you come here a moment?" Harris put the knife away.

His wife stood in front of the refrigerator. In one hand she had the picture of Carry and her hatchet, torn from *The Girl's Life*. The edges were dipped in red candle wax. "I found this under the Tater Tots," Harris's wife said. "What is it and how did it get in my freezer?"

Harris had no answer. He had to stall and think of one. He opened the refrigerator and got himself a beer. "My freezer?" he said pointedly, popping the flip-top. "Isn't it our freezer?"

"How did this get in our freezer?"

"I don't think I would ever have referred to the freezer as my freezer," Harris said sadly. He drank his beer, for timing rather than thirst, an extra moment to let his point sink in. Then he amplified. "I don't think you'll find me doing that. But with you it's always my kitchen. My Sunday paper. My bed."

"I'm sorry," said his wife. She held out the picture. Harris spoke again before she could.

"It signifies," he said. "It certainly signifies."

His wife had the tenacity of a hound. "What's with the picture?"

"I spilled wax on it. Accidentally." Harris had not survived in the Latin American drug theater without some ability to think on his feet. He took the photograph from her. "Naturally I wanted to remove the wax in such a way as to do as little damage to the picture as possible. This picture came out of a library book, after all. I thought I could remove the wax easier if the wax was hard. So I put it in the freezer."

"Why were you reading by candlelight?" his wife asked. "You

tore the picture out of a library book? That doesn't sound like you."

"The book was due back. It had to be returned." His wife was staring at him. "It was overdue," Harris said.

He missed the loa in Richmond. A few hours after his wife took the picture out of the freezer and before he'd hidden it under the bed, pinned beneath a glass of salt water to force the loa across an ocean, she struck. Harris's superior caught him on the car phone on the way to the airport. In addition to Richmond, there'd been a copycat incident in Chicago at a cocaine sale. The sale had been to the DEA. They had worked on it for months, and then some grandmother with a hatchet sent it all south. "I want her on the plane to Colombia yesterday," Harris's superior said.

Harris canceled his reservation and drove to Alexandria. She was coming so fast. For the first time, he asked himself why. Was she coming for him?

"STRAYING TONIGHT, straying tonight, leaving the pathway of honor and right. . . ." The song came from inside the Gateway Bar, punctuated with sounds of breaking glass, splintering wood, and an occasional scream. Harris had been beepered to the spot, but others had obviously arrived first. It was ten in the evening, but across the street two men washed a store window. One sat in his car behind a newspaper. Two more had levered up the manhole cover and knelt beside it, peering down industriously. One man watched Harris from a second-story window above the bar.

Harris set his case on the sidewalk and opened the latch. HAPPY HOUR! the bar marquee read, RAP SINGING! OPEN MIKE! HOGAN CONTEST! He took a bottle of whiskey from his case and poured himself something stiffening. Someone else would have to drive him home. If there was a ride home. Of course there would be a ride home.

He began to sprinkle a circle of salt outside the bar door. He drew a salt triangle inside it. There was a breath of silence; the awful singing resumed. "She's breaking the heart of her dear gray-haired mother, she'll break it, yes, break it, tonight."

A young woman in a wet T-shirt flew out of the bar, landing on his knee and his salt.

Harris helped her to her feet. She was blond, garishly blond, but that was just the effect of the bar marquee lights, which laid an orange tint over her hair. I SURVIVED CATHOLIC SCHOOL, the T-shirt said. "She told me to go home and let my mother have a good look at me. She called me a strumpet." The woman had not yet started to cry, but she was about to.

"She was once badly beaten by prostitutes." Harris was consoling. "Maybe this is a problem area for her." The beating happened in 1901, when the proprietor of a Texas bar, feeling it would unman him to attack Carry Nation himself, had hired a group of prostitutes to beat her with whips and chains. He had also persuaded his wife to take part. Harris had paid particular attention to the incident, because there was a vulnerability and he wondered if he could exploit it. He was not thinking of real prostitutes, of course. He was thinking of undercover vice cops. Beating was a common step in the creation of a zombie. The ti bon ange was thought less likely to return to a body that was being beaten.

Still, there was something distasteful about this strategy. Carry Nation had gone down like a wounded bear, surrounded by dogs. She might have been killed had her own temperance workers not finally rescued her. "There is a spirit of anarchy abroad in the land," Carry Nation was reported to have said, barely able to stand, badly cut and bruised. For the next two weeks she appeared at all speaking and smashing engagements with a large steak taped to the side of her face. She changed steaks daily.

Probably it had left her a little oversensitive on the subject of professional women. The woman in the street was obviously no strumpet. She was just a nice woman in a wet T-shirt. She seemed to be in shock. "It was ladies' night," she told Harris, over and over and over again.

Salt and gravel stuck to her face and the front of her shirt. Harris pulled out a handkerchief and cleaned her face. He heard twanging sounds inside, like a guitar being smashed. He put away his handkerchief and went back to his case. "I have to go in there," he said.

She didn't try to dissuade him. She didn't even stay. Apparently she had hurt his knee when she landed on him. He hadn't noticed at first, but now it was starting to throb. The agent in the car, part of his backup, showed the woman a badge and offered to take her out for coffee and a statement.

Harris watched the taillights until the car disappeared. He poured himself another whiskey and had sharp thoughts on the subject of heroines. It was easy for his wife to tell him women were hungry for heroines. She didn't work undercover among the drug lords in Latin America. Teaching women's literature didn't require exceptional courage, at least not on the junior college level where she taught. And when a woman did find herself in a tight spot as this one had just done—well, what happened then? Women didn't want heroines. Women wanted heroes, wanted heroes to be such an ordinary feature of their daily lives that they didn't even feel compelled to stay and watch their own rescue. Wanted heroes who came home and did the dishes at night.

Harris rubbed his knee and cautiously straightened it. He took the black toad from his case and slipped it into a pocket. He took a tranquilizer gun and, against all orders, a mayonnaise jar containing the doctored Shirley Temple. The ginger ale was laced with bufotenine rather than bufotoxin. Bufotoxin had proved difficult to obtain on short notice, even for a DEA agent who knew his way around the store, but bufotenine was readily available in South Carolina and Georgia, where the cane toad secreted it, and anyone willing to lick a toad the size of a soccer ball could have some. Perfectly legal, too, in some forms, although the two state legislatures had introduced bills to outlaw toad-licking.

"Touch not, taste not, handle not!" The voice was suddenly amplified and accompanied by feedback; perhaps the rap singer had left his mike on. The last time Harris had heard Voudon singing he had been in Haiti, sleeping in the house of a Haitian colonel the DEA suspected of trafficking. He had gotten up and crept into the colonel's study, and the voices came in the window with the moonlight.

Eh! Eh! Bomba! Heu! Heu! Canga, bafio te! Canga, moune de le! Canga, do ki la! Canga, li!

The song had frightened him back to his room. In the morning, he asked the cook about the voices. "A slave song," she said. "For children." She taught it to him, somewhat amused, he thought, at his rendition. Later he sang it to a friend, who translated. "'We swear to destroy the whites and all they possess; let us die rather than fail to keep this vow.'" The cook had served him eggs.

Harris felt no compulsion at this particular moment to be fair, but in his heart he knew that, had his wife been there, she would never have let him go into that bar alone.

The bar was dark; the overheads had all been smashed, and the only light came from something that lay in front of Harris. This something blocked the door so that he could open it just halfway, and he could identify the blockage as Super Mario Bros. 2 by the incessant little tune it was playing. It was tipped onto its side and still glowed ever so slightly. Situated as it was, its little light made things inside even harder to see.

Deep in the bar, there was an occasional spark, like a firefly. Harris squinted in that direction. He could just make out the vacant bandstand. A single chair for a soloist lay on its back under a keyboard that had been snapped in half. The keyboard was still plugged in, and this was what was throwing off sparks. Harris's eyes began to adjust. Above the keyboard, on the wall, about spark-high, was a nest of color-coded wires. The wall phone had been ripped out and stuffed into one of the speakers. Behind the speakers were rounded shapes he imagined to be cowering customers. The floor of the bar was shiny with liquor.

On the other side of the bar were the video games. Street Fighter, Cyberball, and Punch-Out!! all bore the marks of the hatchet. Over the tune of the video, Harris could hear someone sniffling. The mike picked it up. Otherwise the bar was quiet. Harris squeezed inside, climbing over Super Mario Bros. 2. His knee hurt. He bent and straightened it experimentally. Super Mario Bros. 2 played its music: *Dee, dee, dee, dee, dee.*

The loa charged, shrieking, from the corner. "Peace on Earth," she howled, as her hatchet cleaved the air by Harris's head, shattering the mayonnaise jar in his hand. The loa's stroke carried her past him.

A piece of broken glass had sliced across his palm. Harris was bleeding. But worse than that, ginger ale laced with bufotenine was soaking into the cut and into the skin around the cut and way down his wrist. He had dosed the Shirley Temple to fell a linebacker with a couple of sips.

Harris dropped the tranquilizer gun and groped blindly to his right until he located a wet T-shirt. He rubbed his hand with it, all in a panic. Someone slapped him. There was a scream. The hatchet sliced through the air above him and lodged itself into the bar's wood paneling. The tune from Super Mario Bros. 2 played on. The other singing started, in cacophonous counterpoint.

"An awful foe is in our land, drive him out, oh, drive him out! Donkey-faced bedmate of Satan," the loa shrieked. She struggled to remove the hatchet head from the wood. She was an enormous woman, a woman built to compete in the shotput event. She would have the hatchet loose in no time. Harris looked about frenziedly. His heart was already responding, either to bufotenine or to the threat of hatchetation. The tranquilizer gun was on top of Super Mario Bros. 2 and under the loa's very feet, but farther into the bar, at a safer distance, Harris saw his maraschino cherry on the floor. He dropped, ignoring the alarmed flash of pain from the injured knee, and groped with his uninjured hand. Something squished under his palm and stuck to him. He peeled it off to examine it.

It was a flattened cherry, a different cherry. Now Harris could see that the floor of the Gateway Bar was littered with maraschino cherries. One of them was injected with tetrodotoxin. There was no way to tell which just by looking.

Near him, under a table, a woman in a wet T-shirt sat with her hands over her ears and stared at him. NEVADA BOB'S, the T-shirt read. It struck Harris as funny. The word BOB. Suddenly Harris saw that BOB was a very funny word, especially stuck there like that between two large breasts whose nipples were as obvious as maraschino cherries. He started to say something, but a sudden movement to one side made him turn to look that way instead. He wondered what he had been going to say.

The loa brandished her hatchet. Harris retreated into the bar on his knees. The hatchet went wide again, smashed an enormous Crock-Pot that sat on the bar. Chili oozed out of the cracks.

"I shall pray for you," the loa said, carried by the momentum of her stroke into the video games. "I shall pray for all of you whose American appetites have been tempted with foreign dishes." She put her arms around the casing for Ghouls 'n Ghosts, lifted the entire thing from the floor, and piled it onto Super Mario Bros. 2. The music hiccoughed for a moment and then resumed.

There was now absolutely no exit from the bar through that door. Harris's backup was still out there, peering into manholes and washing windows, and the street was two video games away. Harris's amusement vanished. He wasn't likely to be at his best, alone, weaponless, with a hurt knee, and bufotenine pulsing through his body. Only one of these things could be rectified.

The bar was starting to metamorphose around him. The puddles of liquor on the floor sprouted into fountains, green liquid trees of crème de menthe, red trees of wine, gold trees of beer. The smell of liquor intensified as the trees bloomed. They grew flowers and dropped leaves in the liquid permanence of fountains, an infinite, unchanging season that was all seasons at once. A jungle lay between Harris and the loa. His tranquilizer gun was sandwiched between Super Mario Bros. 2 and Ghouls 'n Ghosts. The barrel protruded. Harris wrenched it free. It took three tries and the awesome properties of the lever to move the uppermost video game. Harris tried not to remember how the loa had picked it up off the floor with her hands. He retrieved his gun and went hunting.

She was coy now, ducking away from him, so that he only caught glimpses of her through the watery branches of liquor. A sound here and there indicated that she had stopped to smash a wooden keg or pound the cash register. Harris himself was stealthy, timing each footfall to coincide with the tones of Super Mario Bros. 2.

The fountains were endlessly mobile. They rose and diminished unpredictably so that at one moment they could be between him and the loa, screening her from him, and the next moment, without his taking a step, he and the loa could be face-to-face. This gave the hunt a sort of funhouse quality. The loa was likewise changeable now—a big and ugly woman one moment, a lovely young one in a wet T-shirt the next—and this, too, added to the fun. Harris much preferred hunting young women without bras to hunting old ones with hatchets. Harris approved the change until it suddenly occurred to him just what the loa's strategy was. She was fiendishly clever. The same way a maraschino cherry laced with tetrodotoxin could be hidden among other, innocent, maraschino cherries, a loa, assuming the shape of a young woman in a wet T-shirt, could hide among other young women in wet T-shirts. Harris would have to think of some way to identify her. Failing that, he would simply have to shoot everything in a wet T-shirt with the tranquilizer gun. This would probably require more tranquilizer darts than he had on him.

He would have to entice the loa out of hiding. He would have to make himself into bait.

Several overturned ashtrays were on the floor. It was the work of a moment to locate a cigarette butt, a matchbook with the Gateway Bar logo on it. The matches were damp and sticky. Harris put the butt in his mouth and tried to light one of the matches with his left, bloody hand, his right clenched on the trigger of the tranquilizer gun. He bent several matches before giving up. He switched the match to his right hand, still holding the gun, but not in a ready position, not with a finger on the trigger. He bent several matches before one flamed.

The loa charged immediately. "Filthy poison! Breath of hell!" she screamed. She was old and huge, and her hatchet wavered over her head. There was no time to shoot. Harris rolled.

Harris rolled through the many-colored puddles and fountains of drink and immediately to his feet, shaky on his hurt knee. Before she could transform, before she could regroup herself for another charge, Harris shot her.

She was in the middle of a scream. She stopped, looked down to her right hip where the tranquilizer dart had hit her. Super Mario Bros. 2 celebrated with a little riff: *Dee, dee, dee, dee, dee.* A fountain of red grenadine sprang up. The loa raised the hatchet, took a step into the fountain. The petals of red flowers exploded around her and fell onto her like rain. She threw the hatchet. Her aim was off; it clattered harmlessly a few feet behind him. She took a second step and then fell in his direction. One moment she was an enormous shadow and the grenadine fountain rose behind her like the distant fireworks of the Fourth of July and the smell of cherries was everywhere; the next she lay in a black heap on the floor, and the fountain had trickled to nothing. But in the tiny, invisible space between those moments, the loa left the body.

Her z'etoile rose from the black heap and spun above it. Harris could see it, like a star in the room. It came toward him slowly, backing him up until his heel touched the hatchet. Then it came faster, fast as falling, blazing larger and unbearably hot. His left hand found the black toad in his pocket so that, at the last possible moment, the moment before contact, when he threw up his hands to protect his face from the searing heat, the toad was in them. The z'etoile swerved and entered the toad instead of him.

Harris dropped the toad to the floor, grabbed the hatchet, and smashed with the blunt end. The toad skittered, and he followed it over the sticky floor among the maraschino cherries, smashing again and again, until the toad cracked in one long rent down the middle and went to pieces. The z'etoile tried to leap away, but it was in pieces too now, like the toad. It shot in many directions and entered video games and broken keyboards and customers and lounge rap singers and ashtrays, but only in subdued, confused sparkles. It was the best Harris could do. He lay down on the floor and imagined there were shoes, open-toed and pointy with nail polish on the toes, canvas and round-toed, leather and bootlike, all about him.

"Come on," someone said. It sounded like his mother, only she was speaking through a microphone. He must be late for school. The song from Super Mario Bros. 2 was playing in the background, but when wasn't it? Harris tried to open his eyes. He had no way of knowing if he'd succeeded or not. He didn't see his mother. He saw or imagined DEA agents attempting to lift the body of the huge woman from the floor. It took three of them. "Come on," someone said again, nudging him with a toe.

"I'm coming," said Harris, who refused to move.

MEANWHILE, in an abandoned inner-city warehouse . . .

The background is test tubes and microscopes and a bit of graffiti, visual, not verbal. A bald-headed man stands over a camp stove. He holds an eyedropper above a pot with green liquid inside. Steam rises from the pot. Three more drops, he thinks. He has a snake tattooed on his arm.

Knock, knock! "I said no interruptions," the man snarls. The liquid in the pot turns white.

The door opens. A shabby man enters, his clothes torn, his hair matted. "Give me some," the shabby man says.

The bald man laughs at him. "You can't afford this."

"I'll do anything," says the shabby man.

"This is special. This isn't for the likes of you."

"The likes of me?" The shabby man remembers a different life. There is a white house, a wife, two children, a boy and a girl. He is in a business suit, clean, carrying a briefcase. He comes home from work, and his children run to meet him. "Who made me into the likes of me?" the shabby man asks. There is a tear in the corner of one eye.

He lunges for the pot, takes a drink before the bald man can stop him. "Wha—?" the bald man says.

The shabby man clutches at his throat. "Arghh!" He falls to the ground.

The bald man tells him to get up. He kicks him. He takes his pulse. "Hmm. Dead," he says. He is thinking, I must have made it a little strong. Lucky I didn't try it myself. He goes back to his cooking. "Two drops," he says. He thinks, I'm going to need someone new to test it on.

Later that day . . .

The bald man is dressed in a winter coat. His tattoo is covered; he wears a hat. He enters a city park. A grandmotherly type drinks from the water fountain. She leans on a cane. Such a cold winter, she is thinking. A group of kids skateboard. "My turn!" one of them says.

The bald man in the hat approaches one of the kids. This kid is a little small, a little tentative. "Hey, kid," the bald man says. "Want to try something really great?"

The grandmother thinks, Oh, dear. She hobbles on her cane to a large tree, hides behind it.

"My mom says not to take anything from strangers," the kid says.

"Just a couple drops," the bald man wheedles. "It's as good as peppermint ice cream." He takes a little bottle from his pocket and uncorks it. He holds it out.

I shouldn't, the kid thinks, but he has already taken the bottle.

"Eeeagh!" Carry Nation emerges from behind the tree. Her cane has become a hatchet; her costume is a black dress with special pockets. "Son of Satan!" she screams, hurtling toward the bald man, hatchet up. *Whooosh!* The hatchet takes off the bald man's hat. *Kaboom!* Carry strikes him with her fist. *Kapow!*

COLORS HAPPENED ON the inside of Harris's eyelids. Harsh, unnatural, vivid colors. Colors that sang and danced in chorus like Disney cartoons, dark colors for the bass voices, bright neons for the high notes. Harris was long past enjoying these colors. Someone had put Harris to bed, but it was so long ago Harris couldn't quite remember who. It might have been his mother. Someone had bandaged his hand and cleaned him up, although his hair was still sticky with liquor. Someone had apparently thought Harris might be able to sleep, someone who had clearly never dosed themselves with bufotenine. Never licked a toad in their life. Someone brought Harris soup. He stared at it, abandoned on the nightstand, thinking what a silly word *soup* was. He closed his eyes, and the colors sang it for him with full parts. A full choral treatment. Soup. Soup. Souped up. In the soup. Soupçon.

The phone rang, and the colors splashed away from the

sound in an unharmonious babble of confusion. They recovered as quickly as the ringing stopped, re-formed themselves like water after a stone. Only one ring. Harris suddenly noticed other noises. The television in his room was on. There were visitors in the living room. His wife was sitting on the bed beside him.

"That was your superior," she said. Harris laughed. Soupe-rior. "He said to tell you, 'Package delivered.' He said you'd be anxious."

He wishes he worked for the CIA, the colors sang to Harris. Package delivered.

"Patrick." Harris's wife was touching his arm. She shook it a little. "Patrick? He's worried about you. He thinks you may have a drinking problem."

Harris opened his eyes and saw things with a glassy, weary clarity. Behind his wife was the *Oprah* show, her favorite. No wonder he hadn't noticed the television was on. Harris's mind was moving far too fast for television. Harris's mind was moving far too fast for him to be able to follow what his wife was saying. He had to force his mind back, remember where she thought he was in the conversation.

"I'm a moderate drinker," he said.

"He sent over a report. Last night. A report the government commissioned on moderate drinking. It's interesting. Listen." She had pages in her hand. Harris was pretty certain they hadn't been there before. They popped into her fingers before his very eyes. She riffled through them, read, with one finger underlining the words. "'To put it simply, people who drink a lot have many problems, but few people drink a lot.

"'People who only drink a little have fewer problems, but there are a great many people who drink a little.

"'Therefore, the total number of problems experienced by those who drink a little is likely to be greater than the total number experienced by those who drink a lot, simply because more people drink a little than a lot.'"

Harris was delighted with this. It made no sense at all. He was delighted with his wife for producing it. He was delighted with himself for hallucinating it. He would have liked to hear it again. He closed his eyes. The colors began singing obligingly. *To put it simply, people who drink a lot have many problems, but few people drink a lot.*

"All I had was a Shirley Temple," Harris told his wife. He remembered the voices in the living room. "Do we have company?"

"Just some women from my class," she answered. She put the report down uncertainly. "He's just worried about you, Patrick. As your supervisor, he's got to be worried. The stress of fieldwork. It's nothing to be ashamed of, if you have a problem. You've handled it better than most."

Harris skipped ahead in this conversation to the point where he explained to her that he didn't have a drinking problem and she was persuaded. She would be persuaded. She was a reasonable woman and she loved him. He was too tired to go through it step by step. Now he was free to change the subject. "Why are there women in the living room?"

"We're just doing a project," his wife said. "Are you going to drink your soup?" *Soup, soup, soup,* the colors sang. Harris didn't think so. "Would you like to see the project?" Harris didn't think he wanted this either, but apparently he neglected to say so, because now she was back and she had different papers. Harris tried to read them. They appeared to be a cartoon.

"It's for the women's center," his wife said. "It's a Carry Nation/Superhero cartoon. I thought maybe you could help advise us on the drug stuff. The underworld stuff. When you're feeling better. We think we can sell it."

Harris tried to read it again. Who was the man in the hat? What did he have in his bottle? He liked the colors. "I like the colors," he said.

"Julie drew the pictures. I did the words."

Harris wasn't able to read the cartoon or look at the pictures. His mind wasn't working that way. Harris's mind was reading right through the cartoon as if it were a glass through which he could read the present, the past, and the future. He held it between himself and the television. There was a group of women on *Oprah.* They were all dressed like Carry Nation, but they had masks on their faces like the Lone Ranger, to protect their real identities. They were postmenopausal terrorists in the war on drugs. A man in the audience was shouting at them.

"Do you know what I'm hearing? I'm hearing that the ends justify the means. I could hear that in Iraq. I could hear that in China."

The women didn't want to be terrorists. The women wanted to be DEA agents. Harris's supervisor was clearing out his desk, removing the pins from the map in his office as if casting some sort of reverse Voudon hex. He had lost his job for refusing to modify recruitment standards and implement a special DEA reentry training program for older women.

In a deserted field in Colombia, a huge woman gradually came to her senses. She stared at the clothing she was wearing. She stared around the Colombian landscape. "Where the hell am I?" her ti bon ange asked. "*¿Que pasa?*"

From the safety of his jail cell, Manuel Noriega mourned for his lost yachts.

A woman in a wet T-shirt played a new video game in the dark back room of a bar. MY MOTHER TOLD ME TO BE GOOD, BUT SHE'S BEEN WRONG BEFORE, the T-shirt read. Bar-Smasher was the name of the video game. A graphic of Carry Nation, complete with bonnet and hatchet, ran about evading the police and mobs of angry men. Five points for every bottle she smashed. Ten points a barrel. Fifty points for special items such as chandeliers and pornographic paintings. She could be sent to jail three times. The music was a video version of "Who Hath Sorrow, Who Hath Woe." The woman in the T-shirt was very good at this game. She was a young woman, and men approved of her. Her boyfriend helped her put her initials on the day's high score, although anyone who gets the day's high score probably doesn't need help with the initials. She let him kiss her.

Harris was back in Panama, dancing and raising a loa. The Harris in Panama could not see into the future, but even if he could, it was already too late. Raising a loa had not been his real mistake. By the time the loa came, everything here had already occurred. Harris had made his real mistake when he took the toad. Up until that moment, Harris had always played by the rules. Harris had been seduced by a toad, and in yielding to that seduction he created a whole new world for himself, a world without rules, just exactly the sort of world in which Harris himself was unlikely to be comfortable.

"Come on," his wife said. "What do you really think?" She was so excited. He had never seen her so animated.

She was going to be old someday. Harris could see it lurking in her. Harris would still love her, but what kind of a love would that be? How male? How sufficient? These things Harris was unsure of. For these things he had to look into himself, and the cartoon looking glass didn't go that way.

He held the cartoon panels between himself and his wife and looked into her instead. He had never understood why Carry Nation appealed to her so. His wife was not religious. His wife enjoyed a bit of wine in the evening and thought what people did in the privacy of their own homes was pretty much their own business. Now he saw that what she really admired about Carry Nation was her audacity. Men despised Carry Nation, and Harris's wife admired her for that. She admired the way Carry didn't care. She admired the way Carry carried on. "I always look a fool," Carry wrote. "God had need of me and the price He exacts is that I look a fool. Of course, I mind. Anyone would mind. But He suffered on the cross for me. It is little enough to ask in return. I do it gladly."

"I know it's not literature," Harris's wife said, a bit embarrassed. "We're trying to have an impact on the American psyche. Literature may not be the best way to do that anymore."

Harris's wife wanted to encourage other women not to care whether men approved of them or not, and she wanted and expected Harris to say he approved of this project.

He tried to focus again on the surface of the glass, on the cartoon panels. What nice colors.

"Kapow!" Harris said. "Kaboom!"

We come from the cemetery,
We went to get our mother,
Hello mother the Virgin,
We are your children,
We come to ask your help,
You should give us your courage.

—Voudon song

CONTENTION

Some of us are dreamers.

—Kermit

At dinner Claire's son asks her if she knows the name of the man who is on record as having grown the world's largest vegetable, not counting the watermelon, which may be a fruit, Claire's son is not sure. Claire says that she doesn't. Her son is eight years old. It is an annoying age. He wants her to guess.

"I really don't know, honey," Claire says.

So he gives her a hint. "It was a turnip."

Claire eliminates the entire population of Lapland. "Elliot," she guesses.

"Nope." His voice holds an edge of triumph, but no more than is polite. "Wrong. Guess again."

"Just tell me," Claire suggests.

"Guess first."

"Edmund," Claire says, and her son regards her with narrowing eyes.

"Guess the last name."

Claire remembers that China is the world's most populous country. "Edmund Li," she guesses, but the correct answer is Edmund Firthgrove and the world's most common surname is Chang. So she is not even close.

"Guess who has the world's longest fingernails," her son suggests. "It's a man."

Well, Claire is quite certain it's not going to be Edmund Firthgrove. Life is a bifurcated highway. She points this out to her son, turns to make sure her daughter is listening as well. "We live in an age of specialization," she tells them. "You can make gardening history or you can make fingernail history, but there's no way in hell you can make both. Remember this. This is your mother speaking. If you want to be great, you've got to make choices." And then immediately Claire wonders if what she has just said is true.

"We're having hamburgers again." Claire's husband makes this observation in a slow, dispassionate voice. Just the facts, ma'am. "We had hamburgers on Sunday and then again on Thursday. This makes three times this week."

Claire tells him she is going for a personal record. In fact it is a headline she read while waiting with the ground meat for the supermarket checker that is making her rethink this issue of choices now. "Meet the laziest man in the world," it said. "In bed since 1969 . . . his wife even shaves and bathes him."

Claire imagines that a case like this one begins when a man loses his job. He may spend weeks seeking new employment and never even make it to the interview. He's just not a self-starter. Thoroughly demoralized, on a Monday in 1969, at the height of the Vietnam War, he refuses to get out of bed. "What's the point?" he asks his wife. She is tolerant at first. He needs a rest. Fine. She leaves him alone for a couple of days, even brings in trays of food, changes the channel of the TV for him.

This is no bid for greatness, this is a modified suicide. "Man collapses watching game show." But staying in bed turns out to have pleasant associations for him. He begins to remember a bout of chicken pox he had as a child—how his mother would bring him glasses of orange juice. He feels warm and cared for; his despair begins to dissipate. "I've got such a craving for orange juice," he tells his wife.

Months pass; he has been in bed an entire year before he realizes what he has become. He's not just some schlub who can't find work. Suddenly he's a *contender.* With stamina, perseverance, and support he can turn tragedy into triumph. He tells his wife that the only thing they have to fear now is a failure of nerve.

How does she feel about this? In the picture which accompanied the story she was shown plumping up his pillow and smiling, a beefy sort of woman, a type that is never going to be fashionable. She may feel, like him, that this is her only shot. His greatness is her greatness. His glory is her glory.

Or her motives may be less pure. Out in the world more, she is bound to be more worldly than he is. He has a vision. He is extending the boundaries of human achievement. She is speculating on the possibility of a movie made for TV. She may suggest that, as long as he is just lying there, he could be growing his fingernails, too.

She is an ignorant woman. You don't just grow your fingernails because you happen to have time on your hands. It requires commitment, a special gelatinous diet, internal and external fortification. A person's nails are, in fact, most at risk during those precise hours a person spends in bed. She has her own motives, of course. She is tired of clipping his nails. "Why don't you grow your beard out?" she suggests, rouging her cheeks and donning a feathery hat before slipping out to a three-martini lunch with the network executives. She will order lobster, then sell the exclusive rights to the tabloids instead. "Why don't you make a ball out of twine?" The largest recorded string ball is more than twelve feet in diameter. *That* will keep him in bed for a while.

At the restaurant she meets Solero don Guillermo, the world's fastest flamenco dancer. She forgets to come home. Her husband grows hungrier and hungrier. He makes his way to the kitchen five days later, a smashed man. He contemplates slitting his wrists. Instead, while preparing his own breakfast, he manages, in twelve seconds, to chop a cucumber in 250 slices, besting Hugh Andrews of Blackpool by four cuts. The rounds of cucumber are so fine you could watch TV through them.

Forty-two years later—a good twenty-four years off the record—he gets his wife's note, placed in a bottle and tossed off the *Queen Mary*. "Kiss my ass," it says.

"You *know*"—Claire's son's voice is accusing—"how much I hate raw hamburgers. This is all pink in the middle. It's gross. I can't eat this."

"I'm tired of hamburgers," Claire's daughter says.

"Is there anything else to eat?" Claire's husband asks.

Claire smiles at them all. She sends them a message, tapping it out with her fork on the side of her plate. It may take years, but she imagines it will get there eventually.

SHIMABARA

The sea, the same as now. It had rained, and we can imagine that, too, just as we have ourselves seen it—the black sky, the ocean carved with small, sharp waves. At the base of each cliff would be a cloud of white water.

At the top of the cliffs was a castle and, inside the castle, a fifteen-year-old boy. Here is where it gets tricky. What is different and what is the same? The story takes place on the other side of the world. The boy has been dead more than three hundred and fifty years. There was a castle, but now there is a museum and a mall. A Japanese mall is still a mall; we know what a mall looks like. The sea is the same. What about a fifteen-year-old boy?

The boy's mother, Martha, was in a boat on the sea beneath the cliffs. Once a day she was taken to shore to the camp of Lord Matsudaira for interrogation. Then she could see the castle where her son was. The rest of the time she lay inside the boat with her two daughters, each of them bound by the wrists and the ankles, so that when she was allowed to stand, her legs, through disuse, could hardly hold her up. Add to that the motion of the boat. When she walked on land, on her way to interrogation, she shook and pitched. The samurai thought it was terror, and of course there was that, too.

Perhaps Martha was more concerned about her son in the castle than her daughters on the boat. Perhaps a Japanese mother three hundred and fifty years ago would feel this way. In any case, all their lives depended on her son now. As she lay on the boat, Martha passed the time by counting miracles. The first was that she had a son. On the day of Shiro's birth, the sunset flamed across the entire horizon, turning the whole landscape red, then black. Later, when Shiro was twelve, a large, fiery cross rose out of the ocean off the Shimabara Peninsula and he was seen walking over the water toward it. He could call birds to his hands; they would lay eggs in his palms. This year, the year he turned fifteen, the sunset of his birth was repeated many times. The cherry blossoms were early. These things had been foretold. Martha remembered; she summoned her son's face; she imagined the sun setting a fire each night behind Hara Castle. The worst that could happen was that her son prove now to be ordinary. The wind that had brought the rain rocked the boat.

Thirty-seven thousand Kirishitan rebels followed Shiro out of Amakusa to the Shimabara Peninsula and the ruin of Hara Castle. *Kirishitan* is a word that has been translated into Japanese and come back out again, as in the children's game of telephone. It goes in as Christian, comes out Kirishitan.

The rebels made the crossing in hundreds of small boats, each with a crucifix in the bow. A government spy stood in the cold shadow of a tree and watched the boats leave. He couldn't count the rebels. Maybe there were fifty thousand. Maybe twenty thousand. Of those, maybe twelve thousand were men of fighting age. The spy grew weak from hunger and fatigue. Just to stand long enough to watch them all depart required the discipline and dedication of a samurai.

General Itakura Shigemasa pursued the rebels through Amakusa, burning the villages they'd left behind. Many of the remaining inhabitants died in the fires. Those who survived, Itakura put to death anyway. He had the children tied to stakes and then burned alive. It was a message to the fifteen-year-old Kirishitan leader.

Although Hara Castle had been abandoned for many years, it was built to be defended. The east side of the castle looked over the sea; on the west was a level marsh, fed by tides, which afforded no footing to horses, no cover to attackers. North and south were cliffs one hundred feet high. Only two paths led in, one to the front, one to the rear, and neither was wide enough for more than a single man. On January 27, 1637, after ten days of repairs, the rebels occupied Hara Castle.

They hoisted a flag. It showed a goblet, a cross, a motto, and two angels. The angels were fat, unsmiling, and European; the motto was in Portuguese. LOVVAD SEIA O SACTISSIM SACRAMENTO: Praised be the most holy sacrament. In March, when Martha knelt in Lord Matsudaira's camp to write Shiro a letter, there were one hundred thousand Bakufu samurai between her and her son.

JANUARY, FEBRUARY, MARCH, and early April passed in a steady storm of negotiations. The air above Shimabara was full of words wound around the shafts of arrows. One landed in the camp outside the castle. "Heaven and earth have one root, the myriad things one substance. Among all sentient beings there is no such distinction as noble and base," the arrow said. An arrow flew back. "Surrender," it asked, but obliquely, politely, confining itself, in fact, to references to the weather.

January and February were muddy. General Itakura commanded the Bakufu forces. Government agents tried to dig a tunnel into the castle, but the digging was overheard. The rebels filled the tunnel with smoke and regular deposits of urine and feces until the diggers refused to dig farther.

Itakura planned to pummel the castle walls with cannonballs so large it took twenty-five sweating men to move each one to the front lines. The last days of January were spent pulling and pushing the cannonballs into place, but it proved a Sisyphean labor in the end since no cannon, no catapult, was large enough to launch them.

More letters flew across on arrow shafts. "The samurai in Amakusa cannot fight," the letters from inside the castle said. "They are cowards and only good at torturing unarmed farmers. The sixty-six provinces of Japan will all be Kirishitan, of that there is no doubt. Anyone who does doubt, the Lord Deus with His own feet will kick him down into Inferno; make sure this point is understood." "Surrender," said the arrows going in, but the penmanship was beautiful; the letters could almost have been framed. Meanwhile, Lord Matsudaira Nobutsuna and a fleet of sixty ships were moving up the coast from Kyushu, bringing Martha to her son.

General Itakura received a letter from his cousin in Osaka. "All is well. When Lord Matsudaira arrives, the castle, held as it is by mere peasants, will not last another day." Itakura translated this letter immediately as mockery. He decided to attack before the reinforcements arrived.

His first try was on February 3, a mousy, hilarious effort; his second on New Year's Day, February 14. Itakura himself led the bold frontal attack across the marsh and was killed by a rebel sharpshooter. After his death, he was much condemned for inappropriate bravura. He had laid the government open to more ridicule, dying as he had at the hands of farmers.

The night before his death Itakura wrote a poem.

When only the name remains of the flower that
bloomed on New Year's Day,
remember it as the leader of our force.

He attached it to an arrow and shot it out over the ocean in the direction of Lord Matsudaira's fleet and the moon.

On February 24, the Commissioner of Nagasaki transmitted Lord Matsudaira's request that the Dutch ship *de Ryp* begin a bombardment of the castle from the sea. The shelling lasted two weeks until, on March 12, the shogunate canceled the request. Two Dutch sailors had been killed; one, shot in the topmast, fell to the deck and landed on the other. A storm of arrows left the castle. "The government agents," these arrows said, "are better at squeezing taxes out of starving farmers, better at keeping account books, than at risking their lives on the field of battle. This is why they have to depend on foreigners to do their fighting. We in Hara Castle are armed with faith. We cannot be killed and we will slay all village magistrates and heathen bonzes without sparing even one; for judgment day is at hand for all Japan."

The Dutch commissioner, Nicolaus Coukebacker, sent a defensive letter by boat back to Holland. "We were, of course, reluctant to fire upon fellow Christians, even though the rebels in question are Roman Catholics and the damage the rebellion has done to trade conditions in Nagasaki has been severe. Our bombardment was, in any case, ineffectual." He was too modest. The outer defenses had been weakened.

On March 5, in the middle of the lull provided by the Dutch bombardment, a letter flew into the government camp from one Yamada Emonsaku of Hara Castle. Expressing his reverence for the rule of hereditary lords in particular and governments in general, Yamada assured them he had never been a sincere Kirishitan. He then outlined a lengthy plan in which he offered to deliver Shiro to the Bakufu alive. "Please give me your approval immediately, and I will overthrow the evil Kirishitans, give tranquillity to the empire, and, I trust, escape with my own life." An answer asking for further information was sent back, but Yamada did not respond.

The invisible men, the *ninjutsuzukai*, went into Hara Castle and returned with information. The rebel leader had a mild case of scabies. While he'd been playing a game of *go*, an incoming cannonball had ripped the sleeve of his coat. His divinity had never seemed more questionable. The letter to Yamada had been easily intercepted. He was bound in a castle room under a sentence of death.

Around their ankles, the invisible men wore leads which unwrapped as they walked. If they were killed, their bodies could be dragged back out. You might think such cords would have given them away, but you are more inclined to believe in the fabulous skills of the ninjutsuzukai than that a boy has walked on water. Not a single ninjutsuzukai was lost.

Lord Matsudaira judged that the rebel position was weakening. After the silly death of Itakura, he had settled on the inglorious strategy of blockade. The strategy appeared justified. The ninjutsuzukai said that the rebels were living in holes they had excavated under the castle. There was not enough to eat.

MATSUDAIRA WROTE A LETTER. The letter spoke of the filial piety owed to parents. It assured Shiro of Matsudaira's reluctance to hurt Shiro's family and said further that Matsudaira knew a fifteen-year-old boy couldn't possibly be leading such a large force. "I am pleased, therefore, to offer a full pardon to the boy, asking only that he surrender, recant, and identify the real leader of the rebellion. I look forward to a joyful family reunion."

Martha knelt in the mud beside Matsudaira and wrote as he directed. "We know that you have forced conversions on some of your followers. If you let those hostages go, Lord Matsudaira will allow your family to join you in Hara Castle. All who surrender may depend on the traditional magnanimity of the Bakufu; no one who freely recants will be punished. Indeed, rice lands will be given to those who surrender!" Matsudaira gestured with one hand that Martha was to finish the letter herself. "For myself, I ask only to see you again. Perhaps we could speak. Lord Matsudaira is willing. Don't forget your family on the outside who wish only to be with you."

These letters were carried into the castle by Shiro's young nephew and little sister. They had been dressed by the Bakufu in kimonos with purple bursts of chrysanthemums. They wore embroidered slippers brought up the coast by boat for the occasion.

Small as they were, the narrow path to the castle held them both, but the path was muddy from the rain, and the children wanted to save their shoes, so they stepped slowly and sometimes, when puddles narrowed the path even more, one did go before the other. Inside the shining kaleidoscope of armor and sunlight, Martha saw the small bobbing chrysanthemums and, high above them, the flag over Hara Castle. "Now we will know what kind of a son you have," Lord Matsudaira told her. "If you have the wrong kind, only you are to blame for what happens next."

Soon the tiny figures disappeared from view. Martha counted slowly, trying to guess at the exact moment they would enter the castle. The path was very long and their steps so small. The ocean sobbed behind her. The sun through the trees moved down her face to her hands. If she could send Shiro one more message, she would ask him to keep the children. She imagined the wish like a small, shining stone in Shiro's hand. He rubbed it with his fingers, feeling it, understanding it. He threw it into the air, as he would any other stone, but it became the bird whose shadow passed over Martha's face, the shadow Shiro's answer to her.

Martha struggled to keep her mind on the miracles. Left to itself, her memory immediately chose the most ordinary of moments. A little boy throwing stones. A pair of arms around her neck. A game of hiding. His face when he slept.

Matsudaira had tea prepared. He drank and attended to his mail. He discussed Hara Castle with several of his officers. They were all agreed that the rebellion could not have held out at any other spot. It was a wonderful castle, and after they had taken it they must be sure to destroy it completely. Fire, first, but then the stonework must be carefully dismantled. The unit from Osaka was charged with this.

Matsudaira decided to change the passwords. He sent out the new codes. Now the sentries were to inquire, "A mountain?" "A river" would be the correct reply. In an optimistic mood, he selected a password to signal the start of an attack. It, too, would be in the form of a question. "A province?" "A province!" was also the answer. He had a meal of rice balls and mullet. While he was eating, Martha heard a shout. The children were returning.

Shiro had written a letter, which his nephew gave to Matsudaira. "Frequent prohibitions have been published by the Shogun, which have greatly distressed us. Some among us there are who consider the hope of future life as of the highest importance. For these there is no escape. Should . . . the above laws not be repealed, we must incur all sorts of punishments and torture; we must, our bodies being weak and sensitive, sin against the infinite Lord of Heaven; and from solicitude for our brief lives incur the loss of what we highly esteem. These things fill us with grief beyond our capacity. There are no forced converts among us, only outside, among you. We are protected by Santa Maria-sama [Mary], Sanchiyago-sama [Jesus], and Sanfuranshisuko-sama [St. Francis]."

To his mother Shiro sent a large parcel of food containing honey, bean-jam buns, oranges, and yams. He had given his little sister his ring to wear.

The ninjutsuzukai had reported starvation. Scavengers from the castle had been seen on Oe beach, searching for edible seaweeds. The bodies of rebel dead had been cut open and their stomachs contained only seaweed and barley. The unexpected sight of bean-jam buns sent Matsudaira into a rage. "Your son thinks very little of you," he said. "Very little of his sisters. All you ask is to speak with him. What kind of a son is this?"

Martha was filled with grief beyond her capacity. The largest part of it was only the fact that her daughter and her grandson had been allowed to see Shiro and she had not. In Shiro's presence she would have endured anything. "God is feeding him," she told Matsudaira. "He is stronger than you can imagine. God will change him into a bird to fly away from your soldiers. You will never kill my son."

This display angered Matsudaira even more. "Take her back to the boat," Matsudaira told the soldiers. "Take her and bind her below where she can't watch the sun set or see the castle. Her son doesn't love her enough to see her. What kind of a mother is this?"

WHEN IT CAME, the final attack was a mistake. On April 12 a fire was misread as a signal. The Nabeshima division rushed forward, soon joined by others. The rebels were completely out of ammunition and the sentries too weak from hunger to hold their posts. The agents easily penetrated the outer perimeter. In the inner rings, the women and children defended themselves with stones and cooking pots. They held out for two more days and nights of steady fighting. On April 15, the defenses collapsed.

By nightfall the government had set up tables to count and collect heads. The count was at 10,869. Headless bodies covered the fields about the castle, clogged the nearby rivers. By April 16, only one person from the castle had survived. As a reward for his letter of March 5, Yamada Emonsaku was spared. Eventually he would be taken back to Edo to serve in Lord Matsudaira's house as his assistant.

The *kubi-jikken*, or head inspection scene, is a traditional element of feudal literature. Martha saw Shiro one more time. The soldiers collected every head that might belong to a fifteen-year-old boy and summoned Martha to identify her son. "He is not here," she told them. Her daughters had been killed and her grandson. Their heads would be displayed in Nagasaki. Her own death was very close now. "He was sent by Heaven and Heaven has protected him. God has transformed him to escape you." There were many possible heads. She rejected them all. Finally Lord Sasaemon held up a recent victim. The boy had been dressed in silks.

Martha began to weep at once, and once she began there was no reason to stop. She thought of her son throwing stones, playing hiding games, his face when he slept. She took the head and held it in her lap. We can imagine this moment, if we let ourselves, as a sort of Japanese pietà, the pietà translated, like the word Kirishitan, into Japanese and out again. "Can he really have become so thin?" Martha asked.

EVERY MOTHER CAN easily imagine losing a child. Motherhood is always half loss anyway. The three-year-old is lost at five, the five-year-old at nine. We consort with ghosts, even as we sit and eat with, scold and kiss, their current corporeal forms. We speak to people who have vanished and, when they answer us, they do the same. Naturally, the information in these speeches is garbled in the translation.

I myself have a fifteen-year-old son who was once nine, once five, once fit entirely inside me. At fifteen, he speaks in monotones, sounds chosen deliberately for their minimal content. "Later," he says to me, leaving the house, and maybe he means that he will see me later, that later he will sit down with me, we will talk. At fifteen, he has a whole lot of later.

Me, not so much. To me, later is that time coming soon, when he will be made up almost entirely of words: letters in the mailbox, conversations on the phone, stories we tell about him, plans he tells to us. And you probably think I would have trouble imagining that thirty-seven thousand people could follow him to their deaths, that this is the hard part, but you would be wrong. No other part of the story, except for the sea, is so easy to imagine.

Isn't it really just a matter of walking on water? To me, today, this seems a relatively insignificant difference, but of course it is the whole point—along with starvation and persecution, peasant messianism and ronin discontent. Was the boy in the castle God, or wasn't he? Who saw him walking on water? Who says the sunsets were his?

The story comes to us over time, space, and culture, a game of telephone played out in magnificent distances. Thirty-seven thousand Kirishitans and one hundred thousand Bakufu samurai were willing to die, arguing over the divinity of Amakusa

Shiro. But what does this mean to us? Nothing is left now but the flag and the words.

"An angel was sent as messenger and the instructions he transmitted must therefore be passed on to the villagers," the rebels wrote to someone and, eventually, to us. "And the august personage named Lord Shiro who has these days appeared in Oyano of Amakusa is an angel from Heaven."

Within one moment, anything is possible. Only the passage of time makes our miraculous lives mundane. For a single moment any boy can walk on water. An arrow can hang in the sky without falling. Martha kneels to write a letter. The sun is in her face. Negotiations continue. CNN is filming. The compound will never be taken. There are children inside.

THE ELIZABETH COMPLEX

Love is particularly difficult to study clinically.

—*Nancy J. Chodorow*

Fathers love as well
—Mine did, I know,—but still with heavier brains.

—*Elizabeth Barrett Browning*

There is no evidence that Elizabeth ever blamed her father for killing her mother. Of course, she would hardly have remembered her mother. At three months, Elizabeth had been moved into her own household with her own servants; her parents became visitors rather than caretakers. At three years, the whole affair was history—her mother's head on Tower Green, her father's remarriage eleven days later. Because the charge was adultery and, in one case, incest, her own parentage might easily have come into question. But there has never been any doubt as to who her father was. "The lion's cub," she called herself, her father's daughter, and from him she got her red hair, her white skin, her dancing, her gaiety, her predilection for having relatives beheaded, and her sex.

Her sex was the problem, of course. Her mother's luck at cards had been bad all summer. But the stars were good, the child rode low in the belly, and the pope, they had agreed, was powerless. They were expecting a boy.

After the birth, the jousts and tournaments had to be canceled. The musicians were sent away, except for a single piper, frolicsome but thin. Her mother, spent and sick from childbirth, felt the cold breath of disaster on her neck.

Her father put the best face on it. Wasn't she healthy? Full weight and lusty? A prince would surely follow. A poor woman gave the princess a rosemary bush hung all with gold spangles. "Isn't that nice?" her mother's ladies said brightly, as if it weren't just a scented branch with glitter.

Elizabeth had always loved her father. She watched sometimes when he held court. She saw the deference he commanded. She saw how careful he was. He could not allow himself to be undone with passion or with pity. The law was the law, he told the women who came before him. A woman's wages belonged to her husband. He could mortgage her property if he liked, forfeit it to creditors. That his children were hungry made no difference. The law acknowledged the defect of her sex. Her father could not do less.

He would show the women these laws in his books. He would show Elizabeth. She would make a little mark with her fingernail in the margin beside them. Some night when he was asleep, some night when she had more courage than she had ever had before, she would slip into the library and cut the laws she had marked out of the books. Then the women would stop weeping and her father would be able to do as he liked.

Her father read to her *The Taming of the Shrew.* He never seemed to see that she hated Petruchio with a passion a grown woman might have reserved for an actual man. "You should have been a boy," he told her, when she brought home the prize in Greek, ahead of all the boys in her class.

Her older brother died when she was a small girl. Never again was she able to bear the sound of a tolling bell. She went with her father to the graveyard, day after day. He threw himself on the grave, arms outstretched. At home, he held her in his arms and wept onto her sleeve, into her soft brown hair. "My daughter," he said. His arms tightened. "If only you had been a boy."

She tried to become a boy. She rode horseback, learned Latin. She remained a girl. She sewed. She led the Presbyterian Girls' Club. The club baked and stitched to earn the money to put a deserving young man through seminary. When he graduated, they went as a group to see him preach his first sermon. They sat in the front. He stood up in the clothes they had made for him. "I have chosen my text for today," he said from the pulpit. "First Timothy, chapter two, verse twelve: 'I suffer not a woman to teach, nor to usurp authority over the man, but be in silence.'"

Elizabeth rose. She walked down the long aisle of the church and out into the street. The sun was so fiery it blinded her for a moment. She stood at the top of the steps, waiting until she could see them. The door behind her opened. It opened again and again. The Presbyterian Girls' Club had all come with her.

She had, they said, a pride like summer. She rode horseback, learned Latin and also Greek, which her father had never studied. One winter day she sat with all her ladies in the park, under an oak, under a canopy, stitching with her long, beautiful, white fingers. If the other ladies were cold, if they wished to be inside, they didn't say so. They sat and sewed together, and one of them sang aloud and the snowflakes flew about the tent like moths. Perhaps Elizabeth was herself cold and wouldn't admit it, or perhaps, even thin as she was, she was not cold and this would be an even greater feat. There was no way to know which was true.

Perhaps Elizabeth was merely teasing. Her fingers rose and dipped quickly over the cloth. From time to time, she joined her merry voice to the singer's. She had a strong animal aura, a force. Her spirits were always lively. John Knox denounced her in church for her fiddling and flinging. She and her sister both, he said, were incurably addicted to joyosity.

Her half brother had never been lusty. When he died, some years after her father, long after his own mother, hail the color of fire fell in the city, thunder rolled low and continuous through the air. This was a terrible time. It was her time.

Her father opposed her marriage. It was not marriage itself he opposed; no, he had hoped for that. It was the man. A dangerous radical. An abolitionist. A man who would never earn money. A man who could then take her money. Hadn't she sat in his court and seen this often enough with her very own eyes?

For a while she was persuaded. When she was strong enough, she rebelled. She insisted that the word *obey* be stricken from the ceremony. Nor would she change her name. "There is a great deal in a name," she wrote her girlfriend. "It often signifies much and may involve a great principle. This custom is founded on the principle that white men are lords of all. I cannot acknowledge this principle as just; therefore I cannot bear the name of another." She meant her first name by this. She meant Elizabeth.

Her family's power and position went back to the days when Charles I sat on the English throne. Her father was astonishingly wealthy, spectacularly thrifty. He wasted no money on electricity, bathrooms, or telephones. He made small, short-lived exceptions for his youngest daughter. She bought a dress; she took a trip abroad. She was dreadfully spoiled, they said later.

But spinsters are generally thought to be entitled to compensatory trips abroad, and she had reached the age where marriage was unlikely. Once men had come to court her in the cramped parlor. They faltered under the grim gaze of her father. There is no clear evidence that she ever blamed him for this, although there is, of course, the unclear evidence.

She did not get on with her stepmother. "I do not call her mother," she said. She herself was exactly the kind of woman her father esteemed—quiet, reserved, respectful. Lustless and listless. She got from him her wide beautiful eyes, her sky-colored eyes, her chestnut hair.

When Elizabeth was one year old, her father displayed her, quite naked, to the French ambassadors. They liked what they saw. Negotiations began to betroth her to the Duke of Angoulême, negotiations that foundered later for financial reasons.

She was planning to address the legislature. Her father read it in the paper. He called her into the library and sat with her before the fire. The blue and orange flames wrapped around the logs, whispering into smoke. "I beg you not to do this," he said. "I beg you not to disgrace me in my old age. I'll give you the house in Seneca Falls."

She had been asking for the house for years. "No," Elizabeth said.

"Then I'll disinherit you entirely."

"If you must."

"Let me hear this speech."

As he listened his eyes filled with tears. "Surely, you have had a comfortable and happy life," he cried out. "Everything you could have wanted has been supplied. How can someone so tenderly brought up feel such things? Where did you learn such bitterness?"

"I learnt it here," she told him. "Here, when I was a child, listening to the women who brought you their injustices." Her own eyes, fixed on his unhappy face, spilled over. "Myself, I am happy," she told him. "I have everything. You've always loved me. I know this."

He waited a long time in silence. "You've made your points clear," he said finally. "But I think I can find you even more cruel laws than those you've quoted." Together they reworked the speech. On toward morning, they kissed each other and retired to their bedrooms. She delivered her words to the legislature. "You are your father's daughter," the senators told her afterward, gracious if unconvinced. "Today, your father would be proud."

"Your work is a continual humiliation to me," he said. "To me, who's had the respect of my colleagues and my country all my life. You have seven children. Take care of them." The next time she spoke publicly he made good on his threats and removed her from his will.

"Thank God for a girl," her mother said when Elizabeth was

born. She fell into an exhausted sleep. When she awoke she looked more closely. The baby's arms and shoulders were thinly dusted with dark hair. She held her eyes tightly shut, and when her mother forced them open, she could find no irises. The doctor was not alarmed. The hair was hypertrichosis, he said. It would disappear. Her eyes were fine. Her father said that she was beautiful.

It took Elizabeth ten days to open her eyes on her own. At the moment she did, it was her mother who was gazing straight into them. They were already violet.

When she was three years old, they attended the silver jubilee for George V. She wore a Parisian dress of organdie. Her father tried to point out the royal ladies. "Look at the King's horse!" Elizabeth said instead. The first movie she was ever taken to see was *The Little Princess* with Shirley Temple.

Her father had carried her in his arms. He dressed all in joyous yellow. He held her up for the courtiers to see. When he finally had a son, he rather lost interest. He wrote his will to clarify the order of succession. At this point, he felt no need to legitimize his daughters, although he did recognize their place in line for the throne. He left Elizabeth an annual income of three thousand pounds. And if she ever married without sanction, the will stated, she was to be removed from the line of succession, "as though the said Lady Elizabeth were then dead."

She never married. Like Penelope, she maintained power by promising to marry first this and then that man; she turned her miserable sex to her advantage. She made an infamous number of these promises. No other woman in history has begun so many engagements and died a maid. "The Queen did fish for men's souls and had so sweet a bait that no one could escape from her network," they said at court. She had a strong animal aura.

A muskiness. When she got married for the first time, her father gave her away. She was only seventeen years old and famously beautiful, the last brunette in a world of blondes. Her father was a guest at her third wedding. "This time I hope her dreams come true," he told the reporters. "I wish her the happiness she so deserves." He was a guest at her fifth wedding, as well.

Her parents had separated briefly when she was fourteen years old. Her mother, to whom she had always been closer, had an affair with someone on the set; her father took her brother and went home to his parents. Elizabeth may have said that his moving out was no special loss. She has been quoted as having said this.

She never married. She married seven different men. She married once and had seven children. She never married. The rack was in constant use during the latter half of her reign. Unexplained illnesses plagued her. It was the hottest day of the year, a dizzying heat. She went into the barn for Swansea pears. Inexplicably the loft was cooler than the house. She said she stayed there half an hour in the slatted light, the half coolness. Her father napped inside the house.

"I perceive you think of our father's death with a calm mind," her half brother, the new king, noted.

"It was a pleasant family to be in?" the Irish maid was asked. Her name was Bridget, but she was called Maggie by the girls, because they had once had another Irish maid they were fond of and she'd had that name.

"I don't know how the family was. I got along all right."

"You never saw anything out of the way?"

"No, sir."

"You never saw any conflict in the family?"

"No, sir."

"Never saw the least—any quarreling or anything of that kind?"

"No, sir."

The half hour between her father settling down for his nap and the discovery of murder may well be the most closely examined half hour in criminal history. The record is quite specific as to the times. When Bridget left the house, she looked at the clock. As she ran, she heard the city hall bell toll. Only eight minutes are unaccounted for.

After the acquittal she changed her name to Lizbeth. "There is one thing that hurts me very much," she told the papers. "They say I don't show any grief. They say I don't cry. They should see me when I am alone."

Her father died a brutal, furious, famous death. Her father died quietly of a stroke before her sixth wedding. After her father died, she discovered he had reinserted her into his will. She had never doubted that he loved her. She inherited his great fortune, along with her sister. She found a sort of gaiety she'd never had before.

She became a devotee of the stage, often inviting whole casts home for parties, food, and dancing. Her sister was horrified; despite the acquittal they had become a local grotesquerie. The only seemly response was silence, her sister told Lizbeth, who responded to this damp admonition with another party.

The sound of a pipe and tabor floated through the palace.

Lord Semphill went looking for the source of the music. He found the queen dancing with Lady Warwick. When she had become queen, she had taken a motto, SEMPER EADEM, it was. ALWAYS THE SAME. This motto had first belonged to her mother.

She noticed Lord Semphill watching her through the drapes. "Your father loved to dance," he said awkwardly, for he had always been told this. He was embarrassed to be caught spying on her.

"Won't you come and dance with us?" she asked. She was laughing at him. Why not laugh? She had survived everything and everyone. She held out her arms. Lord Semphill was suddenly deeply moved to see the queen—at her age!—bending and leaping into the air like the flame on a candle, twirling this way and then that, like the tongue in a lively bell.

GO BACK

I spent the first eleven years of my life in Bloomington, Indiana, but I don't remember it as eleven years. In fact, I couldn't tell you in what year or in what sequence anything happened, only in what season. It is as if in my mind my whole childhood is collapsed into one crowded year. And me, I grow, I shrink; I am three years old, ten, five; I am eight again and it is summer.

In the summer the tar on the streets turned liquid and bubbled. We popped the bubbles with our shoes on our way to the pool and came home smelling of tar and chlorine. In the evenings we chased fireflies and played long games of Capture the Flag. I was fast and smart and usually came home covered in glory.

The Rabinowitzes, our next-door neighbors, had a brief bat infestation in their upstairs closet. Stevie showed them to me during the day, hanging from the rod, sleeping among Mrs. Rabinowitz's print dresses. You could see their teeth, and the closet smelled of mothballs. At dusk the bats streamed into the sky through an attic grate, which Mr. Rabinowitz then screened over. You might have thought they were birds, except for the way they shrieked.

Above the Rabinowitzes' bed hung a star of David made of straw. Mrs. Rabinowitz's wedding ring was of tin. They came from Germany and spoke with accents. Mrs. Rabinowitz was much calmer than my mother would have been about the bats.

Stevie Rabinowitz was my best friend. He moved in next door when we were both four years old. Stevie could already read. He learned off the sports page. He would come over in the morning for toast and juice and to tell my father the baseball standings. We played Uncle Wiggily and he read both his own cards and mine. When I played with Stevie, we drew cards I never drew with anyone else. After I could read for myself, the cards were ordinary again. But when Stevie read them, Uncle Wiggily said that he would play for the Pirates when he grew up. He went ahead two spaces. I would play for the Dodgers. I would be the first girl to bat leadoff in the majors. I went ahead three spaces. Uncle Wiggily said Stevie would have a baby sister and his parents would pay her all the attention. He went back three spaces. Uncle Wiggily said I was too bossy. I was supposed to go back three spaces, but I wouldn't.

"Sometimes going back is better," my mother told me when I complained about it to her. "Sometimes it only looks like you're losing when really it's the only way to win."

Uncle Wiggily said that we would meet movie stars, and in the summer Jayne Mansfield came to the Indianapolis 500. We went to the airport to get her autograph. She signed pictures of herself, dotting the *i* in Mansfield with a heart. Her husband was furious with her, but it probably didn't have anything to do with us. She looked like no woman I had ever seen.

In the spring my brother entered the science fair with a project on Euclidean principles in curved space. He took second prize. Spring was the season for jacks and baseball. My father bought an inflatable raft for fishing trips. When I came home from school, it was fully inflated, filling our living room. "How did I get it in here?" my father asked, tickling me under the chin like a cat. "It's a boat in a bottle. How did I do it, Yvette? How will I get it out again?"

In the winter he bought us skis, although there was nowhere in Indiana to go skiing. One snowy morning I looked outside and saw a blue parrot in the dogwood tree. My mother went out to it and coaxed it onto her finger. We put an ad in the paper, but no one ever called. My own parakeet was an albino who could talk. "Yvette is pretty," it said. "Pretty, pretty, pretty." And sometimes, "Yvette, be quiet!"

In the winter we went sledding on Ballentine Hill. When we came inside again, the heat would make our fingers ache. There was an ice storm that closed Elm Heights Elementary for a whole day since no one could keep their footing. I stayed home with my mother and brother and father, as if it were Christmas already.

Uncle Wiggily said the Kinsers' house would burn down and this happened in the winter. One Sunday morning, my mother answered the door. She was already up, cooking breakfast; I was lying in bed waiting for the house to get warm. I couldn't hear what she said, but the tone of her voice made me get up and I met my brother in the hallway. The five Kinser children were crying in our kitchen. They were all in their pajamas, their slippers wet with snow, holding toys and books in their laps.

There'd been a fire in Meg's closet, Barbara, the oldest, said.

Barbara found it and then she had to hunt for Meg, who was hiding under her bed and didn't answer for a long time. And then her mother wouldn't let her go back and get Tweed.

"Where is the dog?" my father asked.

"She sleeps on the back porch," said Barbara.

We could hear the sirens coming now. "I think you should wait," my mother said, but my father went into the snow, his pipe in his mouth, sending streams of smoke around his face. We all watched him from the kitchen window.

He passed the Kinser parents, who were standing in the street watching for the fire trucks. They spoke to him briefly. The Kinser adults didn't like my father, who didn't go to church. The rest of my family didn't go to church either—my brother and I considered it a great gift our parents had given us, our Sunday mornings—but my father drank and was noisy about it. Bobby Kinser, Stevie Rabinowitz, and I argued religion. Bobby's family believed in God and Christ, Stevie's in God but not Christ; my family didn't believe in either one. Also, my father wouldn't go to the local barbershop, because they wouldn't take black customers. The barber was a friend of the Kinsers'. My father went up the steps of the Kinser house and in through the front door.

The fire trucks arrived and began unrolling the hoses. My father did not come back. Flames were visible through the glass of the upstairs windows. A net curtain burned, browning and curling at the edges as if it were newspaper. The glass cracked and black smoke came out, thick as oatmeal. The firemen spoke to the Kinsers; there were gestures and shouting. The ladder went up. And then, finally, Tweed bolted into the front yard with my father behind her.

My father had burned his hand, but not badly. The firemen were very angry at him. "You're not just risking your own life," one of them shouted. "Someone has to go in after you. You have children. Did you think about them?"

My father hardly paused. He came through the kitchen with Tweed. Tweed checked for each of the Kinser children in turn. My father went to my mother. He was still smoking his pipe. She put his hand under the water faucet. "You're proud of me," my father said to her. "You might as well admit it."

"I shouldn't be," she said, holding on to his hand, smiling back at him. "Sometimes I just can't help myself," and suddenly, just like that, I was in love with fires and storms, thunder and wind. I can remember a lot of fires and storms in Indiana when I was growing up, but what I remember is that they were never big enough. No matter how much damage they did, I was never satisfied.

In the spring there was a green sky and a tornado watch. "A tornado sounds like a train," our teacher, Miss Radcliffe, told us. "But by the time you hear it, it's too late for you."

"Then how do you know it sounds like a train?" asked Stevie. When the tornado came it picked up a horse trailer and carried it seven miles, dumping it finally in Bryan's Park just six blocks from where I lived.

In the fall the Imperial Theater was struck by lightning and set afire. I'd seen *Ben-Hur* there and *Old Yeller.* Stevie and I biked over. We were unlikely to get permission to go to a fire so we didn't ask. This was my first fire in the rain. The insides of the theater were gutted, but the outside was untouched. The police wouldn't let us get near enough to see anything.

In the fall Elm Heights held a Halloween carnival. I wore a red cape with a hood and carried a basket for treats. My brother bought me a cake I wanted with his very own money. There was a booth where you could win a goldfish by throwing a ring over its bowl, and I won at this, too. Barbara Kinser organized all her brothers and her sister to spend their money at this booth. By the end of the evening they'd won thirty-three goldfish, all of which boiled to death in the winter when their house caught fire.

In the spring the nursery school where my mother taught held a picnic at Converse Park. Converse was forty minutes out of town, heavily wooded and big. It contained the Tulip Tree Trace, a twenty-two-mile hike my father took me and my brother and the Kinser and Rabinowitz children on in the summer. We weren't very old, but we all made it, even Julia Rabinowitz, Stevie's little sister. I remember my mother sitting on the hood of the car, waiting for us, smiling and waving when she finally saw us all walking in.

My father didn't come to the nursery school picnic. He was fly-fishing on the Wabash River. He was camping out. He was to be gone the whole weekend. Stevie came to the picnic so I'd have someone my own age to play with.

Stevie said if we walked down the trace, but not all the way down to the sycamores, if we took a turn off to the right and went downhill again, there was a cabin his father had shown him. We went looking for it. My father was a botanist at the university and had been teaching me the names of trees and wild plants. I walked and named things for Stevie.

It took us a while to find it and then it wasn't really a cabin, just the remnant of a cabin. The front door was gone, if there had ever been a front door. Weeds grew up around the windows, blocking the light. Inside was ghastly, a webby, musty place with one dim little room, a jumble of bad-smelling clothing on the floor, plates and cups and silverware for four on the table. The plates were of tin, the clothes old-fashioned. There was a black dress with a bustle.

"They left in the middle of dinner," Stevie told me. "Without packing or anything. They left everything."

I thought there must have been something awful to make them leave like that, something that really frightened them, but Stevie said no. It was gold. A wagon train came by and told them there was gold in California, and they left without even eating their dinner. The food got cold and spoiled and bugs ate it and eventually it just dissolved away, leaving only the chicken bones on the tin plates.

"The historical society keeps the cabin up," Stevie said, but it didn't look kept up to me. My mother's parents lived in California. My grandfather was a dentist and he put gold into people's teeth. Stevie didn't have any grandparents at all.

It started to rain. We had about twenty minutes back down the trace to the picnic. The rain was light at first, then so heavy it was hard to walk in it. Water streamed down the trace over our feet, up to our ankles.

The nursery school party was gathered by the picnic tables, which were sheltered and on a hill. I found my mother. She dried my face with a paper napkin, never really looking at me, looking instead down to the gravel parking lot where we'd left our cars. Water covered the lot, deep and deeper. While we watched, our cars began to move, only jostled at first, but then lifted. They floated away, fifty, sixty feet downhill and piled up on each other in a big metal dam.

The city sent a bus and some firemen to pick us up. They stretched a rope across the gravel lot and carried the children, including me and Stevie, across the water. The adults and my brother came next, holding on to the rope. My mother was worried about my father, out on the Wabash in his inflatable boat.

He didn't come home that night, but he did manage to call. My mother spoke to him and told my brother and me to go to the Rabinowitzes and tell them we were having dinner with them. Mrs. Rabinowitz made me a peanut butter sandwich, because she knew I didn't like fish. She talked to my mother on the phone and said my brother and I were to spend the night.

In the morning it was still raining. I went home before anyone else was up. My mother and father were in the living room. My mother was in her robe. She was crying. My father was drunk. "I love her more than I ever loved anyone," my father said in a strangled, slurred voice. "Nobody will believe it because nobody wants to believe it. They prefer it ugly."

"How can you say that?" my mother asked. She was holding his hand. "Tell me how you have the nerve to say that to me."

"I just can't help myself," my father answered. He saw me and his voice rose. "Go back to the Rabinowitzes. Do as you're told."

By the time I got back, I was crying hard. Mrs. Rabinowitz heard me. She came down from the bedroom and held me in her lap. Mr. Bush, the milkman, came to the door. He had just been to my house. He spoke to Mrs. Rabinowitz in a whisper while he handed her their milk. "Cynthia Marciti drowned," he told her.

"I know," Mrs. Rabinowitz said.

"Her parents thought she was at a slumber party. She was out on the Wabash."

"I know," Mrs. Rabinowitz said. Cynthia Marciti baby-sat for me occasionally. She was a student of my father's. My brother and I stayed with the Rabinowitzes for four more days.

On Friday, my mother came walking across the lawn, dressed in a black dress. "No one expects this of you," Mr. Rabinowitz told her. "You don't have to."

"She was eighteen years old," my mother said. "Do you think I could blame her for any of this?"

Stevie told me that my father paid for the gravestone. He said it was very big and had an angel on it. I didn't see how this could be possible. My father didn't believe in angels.

The Rabinowitzes drove my mother to the funeral. I hadn't seen my father in four days. When I tried to talk to my brother about the angel he told me to shut up. "I wish everybody would just leave me alone," he said, which was unnecessary because pretty much everybody was.

Stevie and I got out the Uncle Wiggily board. I couldn't read my first card, because of the tears in my eyes. "Read it to me," I said, handing it to Stevie.

"Uncle Wiggily says you are moving to California," Stevie said. "Go ahead three spaces."

I put the card in my pocket. At some point I must have used it as a bookmark, because seven years later I found it again, stuck in a book in my grandparents' house, in the bedroom my mother had slept in as a child, which was now my room. There were no seasons in California. In seven years I had had to learn to remember things differently.

I had been eleven years old the last time I saw Stevie. Now I was eighteen, the same age as Cynthia Marciti.

The card had Uncle Wiggily's picture on it, a rabbit gentleman farmer in a top hat, collar, and cuffs. "Uncle Wiggily says you will marry a man who is a lot like you are. You will have two children, a boy and a girl. You turn out very ordinary," it said. "Go back three spaces."

THE TRAVAILS

Inspired by John Kessel's story
"Gulliver at Home."

I hope I may with Justice pronounce
myself an Author perfectly blameless;
against whom the Tribes of Answerers,
Considerers, Observers, Reflectors,
Detectors, Remarkers, will never be able to
find Matter for exercising their Talents.
—*Lemuel Gulliver*

September 28, 1699

Dear Lemuel,

When you think of us, think of us missing you. As Betty cleared the Table from Breakfast this morning, she burst into Tears. "There is Papa," she said, pointing to a Crumb of Bread. And I perfectly comprehended her. I saw you in my Mind, your Speck of a Boat, no bigger than a Crumb on the whole of the Kitchen Table. God speed you back to us.

And then we sat no longer, because of all the daily Work to be done. Now it is Evening and I take Time to write. I hope you received my Letter of July 3rd. Our Betty is Ten Years today and, though only Months have passed since your Departure, I believe she is much altered and not the little Girl you left. I feel the Passage of Years more acutely in the Children's Lives than in my own. With a ten year Daughter, I cannot be accounted young. Already she is more than half as old as I when you came courting. I imagine therefore that she is already half done with being mine. A melancholy Thought.

But the Days grow ever more beautiful, so I shall look outside rather than in. How do you endure a Day at Sea with no Trees about you? The Elm at our Window is all turned, its Leaves as golden as Egg Yolks. The Moon tonight is as big as a Tea Tray, but of course you have that too, wherever you are.

Johnny is growing out of all his Clothes, and Betty and I are kept forever sewing. I never pass Mrs. Nardac in the Shops but that she informs me that the Islands where you are sailing are filled with Women who wear no Stitch of Clothing. If they cover their Bodies at all, she says, they do it with their Hair, which is longer and thicker and more lustrous than anything any Woman in London can do with Wigs. Mermaids then, I say, teazing. No, no, they are quite real, she assures me. She thinks you will not come Home this time and she wishes me to know she thinks this.

But I know otherwise! And such an Adventure we had when the Weather first chilled. Suddenly we were overrun with Ants. What you now picture, double. Ants poured into the House from every Crack in every Wall. Not just the Kitchen, they assaulted us in the Parlour and even the Bed Chambers. Oh, it was War and went on for three whole Days. I plotted and laid Traps. You would imagine we had every Advantage, from Size to Cunning, and yet we could not win through. In truth, they seemed uncannily clever at times. Johnny even made use of a Weapon I must leave you to imagine. His Face when I came upon him! "I washed away great Hordes of them," he insisted, but I took him to Bed by his Ear and it has taken me many Days of scrubbing to see the Humour in it. And then, with no more Warning than we had at the Beginning, they vanished and we are at Peace again.

Mrs. Nardac thinks that Johnny should be sent away to School, but of course he is far too young still. I know I anticipate your Wishes in the Matter by keeping him at Home for now. When you return, you will find us all,
Your loving Family and,
Your Mary

Yuletide, 1701

Dearest, dearest,
I have received Word today from a dear Mrs. Biddle that you are recovered from the fast Grip of the Sea and safe aboard her Husband's Ship. What joyous Tidings! What Joy to write a Letter I know you will receive! I ran all the

way Home and shouted the News without pausing to every Soul I passed. Then Betty and I wore ourselves out with the Weeping and Relief. You are on your way Home to us and we are anxious to see you healthy and unchanged in your Regard. In truth, something in Mrs. Biddle's Letter betrayed Concern regarding your State of Mind, although I remind myself that she has also written here, *twice* in one Letter, that you are well. Eat and rest now, my Darling. Take care of your Dear Self.

We are all healthy here. Carolers came to the Window last Night. They sang of good King Wenceslas and Bethlehem. Snow fell, but gently, on their Scarves and Caps, while their Voices rose into the Air. Tonight all is Snow-Silent and I cannot choose which it is I like best, the Silence or the Noise of the World. Greedily, I would have them both. The Whole of it is the only thing that will suit me tonight. Mrs. Biddle said that you have such Stories to tell us. And we, you!

Such a Merry Christmas God has given us!

Your Mary

August 8, 1702

Dear Lemuel,

I have been melancholy since you left. I so wanted you Home, and then nothing matched my Hopes. I am sorry for the Quarrels and sorry, too, that you made your Departure while we were still quarrelling.

You have made fine Provision for us and left me no Fear that we shall ever fall upon the Parish. The little

Flock of Sheep you left has already increased its Number by Five. For this I am grateful. The new House is Tight and Warm, in spite of being so Large. Since you spent so little Time in it, it often feels entirely mine. I cannot picture you at the Table or in the Bed. I never see you, sleeping under a Book in the Parlour, as I did in our old, damp Cottage. And since you chose, much against my Wishes, to send Johnny to School—really, he is not nearly so grown as you think him—it is a quiet House with me sometimes in one End of it, and Betty far away in the other. I find myself missing even Mrs. Nardac.

But I do confess I often enjoy the Size of it. Not when I am dusting, perhaps! But I like a Room up the Stairs. As I write this, from my Desk I look down on the Fields and Lanes and Gardens as if I had the Eyes of the Trees. I look down on all the other tiny Nests of the tiny People. They love, they fight, they dispute, they cheat, they betray, but I am far above it and absolutely untouched. And then Betty comes, with a Scrape or a Slight to suffer over. A Letter arrives from Johnny, and between those Words the Headmaster has allowed him to send, I can read his Misery. I am part of the World again, with all its Hurts and Affections. And I cannot remember why I ever thought it best to be otherwise.

Yesterday Betty found a Fledgling blown from its Nest. She has brought it inside and made the softest Box, but its Wing is damaged and I fear we can never release it. She is kept up constantly, even at night, with feeding. No one is more tender with Small Creatures than a Young

Girl, and yet my Heart rebels against a Wild Thing kept forever in a Box.

We complete our Menagerie with Rats! Large as Dogs they sound as they pound over the Roof, but I have engaged a Man to deal with them. Money can buy Men for many but perhaps not all Purposes.
Mary

October 5, 1706

Dear Lemuel,
Where does this find you? This is a Letter I shall have to send in a Bottle with a Cork, by a strong Arm. It will wash ashore some months hence in Paradise and the Natives will read it, wondering if such a Place as green as England can really exist.

I fear my last Letter was uncharitable. I meant to be generous, but forgot. You know my Temper, little as you have seen it over the Years. I wished the Letter back as soon as I had sent it. Likely you did not receive it and are reading this in Wonder of what I might have written.

So I will only repeat that I was disappointed by your hasty Departure, but this time I was not surprized. We no longer seem to fit together, you and I. When you are Meditative, I wish to be Doing: when I am larkish, you choose that Moment to be sober. You are so credulous, I must learn again each time not to teaze. We are two Magnets, with an attractive but also a repulsive Power over one another. I fear the closer we stand, the more the Latter is evident.

"You married a Dreamer," Mrs. Balnibarb said to me in the Lanes but yesterday, "and no Woman can live in the Clouds." Yet I think I am one Woman who could, and wait only the Invitation. Time would teach us to mesh again, but Time is the one thing I never have from you.

Betty has a Beau in Mrs. Balnibarb's middle boy, William. Are you pleased? He calls each Thursday and is as clean and polite as you could ask. He is a Farmer's Son and I count his Prospects tolerable. Her Feelings are more difficult to discern. She colours if his Name is spoken but makes no effort in his Presence to delight him. She is still so young and I will counsel Delays if my Counsel is sought. I am sure this is as you would wish.

We shall at least want him a more sensible Man than his Father. Mr. Balnibarb often walks the Lanes so lost in Thought, I have seen William forced to cuff him soundly on the Ear, lest he walk into a Tree! And he has now given up that Farming proved over the Centuries, in favour of new Methods of Planting and Irrigation designed by a Scientist in London and circulated in our little County by Pamphlet. This Pamphlet argues the Water will have more Vitality if it is Pumped uphill before being spread downhill. Its Author has surely never seen a Field in his Life. As a result, all the Farms but Balnibarb's enjoyed a most bountiful Harvest.

Our own Walnut Tree was so loaded with Fruits this

year, it was dangerous to walk beneath. Nuts, like missiles, rained down at the slightest Breeze. We sit in front of the Fire and have our Pleasure, picking out the Meats and dreaming away the Evenings.

I do request that you discourage Johnny from going to Sea. I fear your Stories have had the opposite Effect. This is most unfair to me.

Rats on the Roofs, again, but I know just the Man to engage for it.
Mary

February 7, 1708

Dear Lemuel,
A short Letter today, and sad, to inform you of the Death of your Father. Betty and I were able to wait on him in his final Days. I know it is Customary to assure the Bereaved that the Sufferings were slight and not of long Duration. I wish I could, in Honesty, tell you this. Betty wept and wished him back, but I do not. He had already outlived his Health and Happiness, and if ever Death came as a Release, it came so to him. He missed you deeply and spoke of you often.

The Night after his Death he came to me in a Dream. He told me with great Clarity of his Willingness to be shed of a World he had always seen as Wicked. I was greatly impressed by the Vividness of this Dream, but as I have spoken of it, I have learnt that such Dreams are common on the Night of a Death. Whimsical Mr. Lugg believes the Dead have the one Night to return and tell us what needs to be said. I wish I had known to expect him. What Questions you could ask the Dead with a little Forewarning!

There were many at his Funeral, and all so respectful and sorry for your Loss. Johnny stood for you.

Our own Health, mine and our Children's, continues good. Betty and William have reached an Understanding. They will be married when the Year's Mourning is over and Johnny, young as he is, will give her to William.

Your own,
Mary

January 23, 1710

Dear Lemuel,

Your last Visit has finally borne its Fruit. I send this Letter to let you know your new Son, Samuel, has arrived. He came somewhat earlier than we anticipated. More than a Month has passed since his Birth, and I am only now able to take up Pen to tell you so. The Passage was perilous this time, but we are in Safe Harbour. Betty insists he favours me, but perhaps your Face is not so familiar to her. For my Part, his Face is exactly that of our dearest Johnny at the same age.

Betty, too, expects her second Child, so Son and Grandchildren will all grow up cozy together. Her little Anne grows daily. I will write again in the New Year when I hope to be stronger and more at Leisure.

Your loving,
Mary

July 5, 1712

Dear Lemuel,

I cannot know if my last Letter arrived, scrawled as it was in my Haste and Panic. But I send this one quickly after to let you know that Samuel's Fever has ended and his Recovery seems assured. I could not bear to think of a Day without him or to imagine that he might pass from this World to the Next without you once setting Eyes upon his Face. How could you risk it?

I am too Joyous to scold, but I wonder at your Willingness to be so much away. There is something unnatural and inhuman about such Detachment, as if you cared no more for us than for the Sheep or the Horses.

Here we live in the Dailiness of each other, that Dailiness that you have fled. Enough. Betty is preparing a Feast, as Johnny arrives today from London. He set out at once on hearing of our Distress, but we were able to reach him by Post with our Joy. When he is finally here, my Joy will be Complete.

Your loving wife,

Mary

November 13, 1715

Dear Lemuel,

So much Time has passed since I had any Word of you, I fear the Worst. I console myself that you have never come to me in such a Dream as I had of your dear, departed Father. Perhaps this Letter will find you yet.

All is not as well as I could wish. I am sorely troubled for our darling Daughter's sake. She comes to the House with her Children much against William's Desires. Much against my Desires she returns to him. I have seen Marks upon her Wrists and Neck and wish, before I consented to the Marriage, that I had heeded the way he whips his Horses. They are the noblest of Animals and so mild little Anne herself can ride. Yet all have long, deep Scars along their Flanks.

I long to undress Anne and examine her own Legs but have not yet had a Moment to do so. Dearest Annie, who once bubbled like a Brook, has fallen silent and sucks on her Fingers. She hides in the Stables, preferring Beasts to People.

William was able to govern his Temper well enough when Johnny was at Home. He is, of course, within his Rights and so thinks us defenseless against him. He will find otherwise. A Man can be engaged for almost any Purpose, as I have had every Occasion to learn.

It is a wicked World. Your Father told me so when he was most in a Position to know. The more I see of it, the more I wonder at your Desire to see so much of it. We are a wicked Race, we People, and it is better to be acquainted with as few of us as possible.

Do I sound here like your own Mary? I feel quite altered. Johnny has gone to Sea at last and all is Desolation. He sailed for the Indies in September.

I once saw something in William's Face that surprized me. That something was your Face. And I thought, then, of your Father and wondered if he had ever told you of the World's Wickedness, had ever made you feel a Part of it. It has always been too easy to persuade you, my Love. All these Years, all these Voyages—were you protecting us from yourself?

If you will be persuaded by someone, let it be me. First, I would have you believe that every Man and every Woman has a Kingdom of Evil somewhere in their Hearts. Yours is no bigger than some, and smaller than most. You are a Good Man and we are not afraid of you.

Second, you love us. Confess it, you are haunted by us. You can never go far enough to escape. We fill your Thoughts in spite of yourself. You mold your Memories about us, as if you had been here all along.

And now I will turn my Persuasions on myself; I will reason myself out of this Morbid Humour. My Life has not been a hard one. Perhaps I might have asked to be sheltered more. Perhaps I might have asked to live an Arm away from the Wicked World.

But I did not ask this. I asked to see the World, just as you did, so I will make no Complaint at seeing it. There are far worse things to be endured than an absent Husband, as Betty brings me constant Proof. And I am finished forever with blaming you for your Absence. I am hard at work to not blame you for Johnny's.

Indeed, I pray for your Return. Come Home to us now, surprize us just when everyone has said that this Time you are surely lost. Let us embrace again. We will find a way to live together, you and I, your Children and

Grandchildren. Stay with us as long as you will, a valued Guest.

And then go. We have no Wish to hold you. We have become the People you would have us be, and you need never fear hurting us again. We will rejoice at your Coming; your Going will cause us no Moment of Suffering. More than this, I think, no Man can ask of his Family.

As always,
Mary

LIESERL

Einstein received the first letter in the afternoon post. It had traveled in bags and boxes all the way from Hungary, sailing finally through the brass slit in Einstein's door. *Dear Albert,* it said. *Little Lieserl is here. Mileva says to tell you that your new daughter has tiny fingers and a head as bald as an egg. Mileva says to say that she loves you and will write you herself when she feels better.* The signature was Mileva's father's. The letter was sent at the end of January, but arrived at the beginning of February, so even if everything in it was true when written, it was entirely possible that none of it was true now. Einstein read the letter several times. He was frightened. Why could Mileva not write him herself? The birth must have been a very difficult one. Was the baby really as bald as all that? He wished for a picture. What kind of little eyes did she have? Did she look like Mileva? Mileva had an aura of thick, dark hair. Einstein was living in Bern, Switzerland, and Mileva had returned to her parents' home in Titel, Hungary, for the birth. Mileva was hurt because Einstein sent her to Hungary alone, although she had not said so. The year was 1902. Einstein was twenty-two years old. None of this is as simple as it sounds, but one must start somewhere even though such placement inevitably entails the telling of a lie.

Outside Einstein's window, large star-shaped flakes of snow swirled silently in the air like the pretend snow in a glass globe. The sky darkened into evening as Einstein sat on his bed with his papers. The globe had been shaken and Einstein was the still ceramic figure at its swirling heart, the painted Father Christmas. Lieserl. How I love her already, Einstein thought, dangerously. Before I even know her, how I love her.

THE SECOND LETTER arrived the next morning. *Liebes Schatzerl,* Mileva wrote. *Your daughter is so beautiful. But the world does not suit her at all. With such fury she cries! Papa is coming soon, I tell her. Papa will change everything for you, everything you don't like, the whole world if this is what you want. Papa loves Lieserl. I am very tired still. You must hurry to us. Lieserl's hair has come in dark and I think she is getting a tooth.* Einstein stared at the letter.

A friend of Einstein's will tell Einstein one day that he, himself, would never have the courage to marry a woman who was not absolutely sound. He will say this soon after meeting Mileva. Mileva walked with a limp, although it is unlikely that a limp is all this friend meant. Einstein will respond that Mileva had a lovely voice.

Einstein had not married Mileva yet when he received this letter, although he wanted to very badly. She was his *Lieber*

Dockerl, his little doll. He had not found a way to support her. He had just run an advertisement offering his services as a tutor. He wrote Mileva back. *Now you can make observations*, he said. *I would like once to produce a Lieserl myself, it must be so interesting. She certainly can cry already, but to laugh she'll learn later. Therein lies a profound truth.* On the bottom of the letter he sketched his tiny room in Bern. It resembled the drawings he would do later to accompany his gedanken, or thought experiments, how he would visualize physics in various situations. In this sketch, he labeled the features of his room with letters. Big B for the bed. Little b for a picture. He was trying to figure a way to fit Mileva and Lieserl into his room. He was inviting Mileva to help.

In June he will get a job with the Swiss Civil Service. A year after Lieserl's birth, the following January, he will marry Mileva. Years later when friends ask him why he married her, his answer will vary. Duty, he will say sometimes. Sometimes he will say that he has never been able to remember why.

A THIRD LETTER arrived the next day. *Mein liebes böse Schatzerl!* it said. *Lieserl misses her Papa. She is so clever, Albert. You will never believe it. Today she pulled a book from the shelf. She opened it, sucking hard on her fingers. Can Lieserl read? I asked her, joking. But she pointed to the letter E, making such a sweet, sticky fingerprint beside it on the page. E, she said. You will be so proud of her. Already she runs and laughs. I had not realized how quickly they grow up. When are you coming to us? Mileva.*

His room was too small. The dust collected over his books and danced in the light with Brownian-like movements. Einstein went out for a walk. The sun shone, both from above him and also as reflected off the new snowbanks in blinding white sheets. Icicles shrank visibly at the roots until they cracked, falling from the eaves like knives into the soft snow beneath them. Mileva is a book, like you, his mother had told him. What you need is a housekeeper. What you need is a wife.

Einstein met Mileva in Zurich at the Swiss Federal Polytechnical School. Entrance to the school required the passage of a stiff examination. Einstein himself failed the General Knowledge section on his first try. She will ruin your life, Einstein's mother said. No decent family will have her. Don't sleep with her. If she gets a child, you'll be in a pretty mess.

It is not clear what Einstein's mother's objection to Mileva was. She was unhappy that Mileva had scholastic ambitions and then more unhappy when Mileva failed her final examinations twice and could not get her diploma.

FIVE DAYS PASSED before Einstein heard from Mileva again. *Mein Liebster. If she has not climbed onto the kitchen table, then she is sliding down the banisters,* Mileva complained. *I must watch her every minute. I have tried to take her picture for you as you asked, but she will never hold still long enough. Until you come to her, you must be content with my descriptions. Her hair is dark and thick and curly. She has the eyes of a doe. Already she has outgrown all the clothes I had for her and is in proper dresses with aprons. Papa, papa, papa, she says. It is her favorite word. Yes, I tell her. Papa is coming. I teach her to throw kisses. I teach her to clap her hands. Papa is coming, she says, kissing and clapping. Papa loves his Lieserl.*

Einstein loved his Lieserl, whom he had not met. He loved Mileva. He loved science. He loved music. He solved scientific puzzles while playing the violin. He thought of Lieserl while solving scientific puzzles. Love is faith. Science is faith. Einstein could see that his faith was being tested.

Science feels like art, Einstein will say later, but it is not. Art involves inspiration and experience, but experience is a hindrance to the scientist. He has only a few years in which to invent, with his innocence, a whole new world that he must live in for the rest of his life. Einstein would not always be such a young man. Einstein did not have all the time in the world.

EINSTEIN WAITED FOR the next letter in the tiny cell of his room. The letters were making him unhappy. He did not want to receive another so he would not leave, even for an instant, and risk delaying it. He had not responded to Mileva's last letters. He did not know how. He made himself a cup of tea and stirred it, noticing that the tea leaves gathered in the center of the cup bottom, but not about the circumference. He reached for a fresh piece of paper and filled it with drawings of rivers, not the rivers of a landscape but the narrow, twisting rivers of a map.

The letter came only a few hours later in the afternoon post, sliding like a tongue through the slit in the door. Einstein caught it as it fell. *Was treibst Du, Schatzerl?* it began. *Your little Lieserl has been asked to a party and looks like a princess tonight. Her dress is long and white like a bride's. I have made her hair curl by wrapping it over my fingers. She wears a violet sash and violet ribbons. She is dancing with my father in the hallway, her feet on my father's feet, her head only slightly higher than his waist. They are waltzing. All the boys will want to dance with you, my father said to her, but she frowned. I am not interested in boys, she answered. Nowhere is there a boy I could love like I love my Papa.*

In 1899 Einstein began writing to Mileva about the electrodynamics of moving bodies, which became the title of his 1905 paper on relativity. In 1902 Einstein loved Mileva, but in 1916 in a letter to his friend Besso, Einstein will write that he would have become mentally and physically exhausted if he had not been able to keep his wife at a distance, out of sight and out of hearing. You cannot know, he will tell his friends, the tricks a woman such as my wife will play.

Mileva, trained as a physicist herself, though without a diploma, will complain that she has never understood the special theory of relativity. She will blame Einstein who, she will say, has never taken the time to explain it properly to her.

Einstein wrote a question along the twisting line of one river. Where are you? He chose another river for a second question. How are you moving? He extended the end of the second river around many curves until it finally merged with the first.

LIEBES SCHATZERL! the next letter said. It came four posts later. *She is a lovely young lady. If you could only see her, your breath would catch in your throat. Hair like silk. Eyes like stars.*

She sends her love. Tell my darling Papa, she says, that I will always be his little Lieserl, always running out into the snowy garden, caped in red, to draw angels. Suddenly I am frightened for her, Albert. She is as fragile as a snowflake. Have I kept her too sheltered? What does she know of men? If only you had been here to advise me. Even after its long journey, the letter smelled of roses.

Two friends came for dinner that night to Einstein's little apartment. One was a philosophy student named Solovine. One was a mathematician named Habicht. The three together called themselves the Olympia Academy, making fun of the serious bent of their minds.

Einstein made a simple dinner of fried fish and bought wine. They sat about the table, drinking and picking the last pieces of fish out with their fingers until nothing remained on their plates but the spines with the smaller bones attached like the naked branches of winter trees. The friends argued loudly about music. Solovine's favorite composer was Beethoven, whose music, Einstein suddenly began to shout, was emotionally over-charged, especially in C minor. Einstein's favorite composer was Mozart. Beethoven created his beautiful music, but Mozart discovered it, Einstein said. Beethoven wrote the music of the human heart, but Mozart transcribed the music of God. There is a perfection in the humanless world which will draw Einstein all his life. It is an irony that his greatest achievement will be to add the relativity of men to the objective Newtonian science of angels.

He did not tell his friends about his daughter. The wind outside was a choir without a voice. All his life, Einstein will say later, all his life he tried to free himself from the chains of the *merely personal.* Einstein rarely spoke of his personal life. Such absolute silence suggests that he escaped from it easily or, alternatively, that its hold was so powerful he was afraid to ever say it aloud. One or both or neither of these things must be true.

LET US TALK about the merely personal. The information received through the five senses is appallingly approximate. Take sight, the sense on which humans depend most. Man sees only a few of all the colors in the world. It is as if a curtain has been drawn over a large window, but not drawn so that it fully meets in the middle. The small gap at the center represents the visual abilities of man.

A cat hears sounds that men must only imagine. It has an upper range of 100,000 cycles per second as opposed to the 35,000 to 45,000 a dog can hear or the 20,000 which marks the upper range for men. A cat can distinguish between two sounds made only eighteen inches apart when the cat itself is at a distance of sixty feet.

Some insects can identify members of their own species by smell at distances nearing a mile.

A blindfolded man holding his nose cannot distinguish the taste of an apple from an onion.

Of course man fumbles about the world, perceiving nothing, understanding nothing. In a whole universe, man has been shut into one small room. Of course, Einstein could not begin to know what was happening to his daughter or to Mileva, deprived even of these blundering senses. The postman was careless with Mileva's next letter. He failed to push it properly through the door slit so that it fell back into the snow, where it lay all night and was ice the next morning. Einstein picked the envelope up on his front step. It was so cold it burned his fingers. He breathed on it until he could open it.

Another quiet evening with your Lieserl. We read until late and then sat together, talking. She asked me many questions tonight about you, hoping, I think, to hear something, anything, I had not yet told her. But she settled, sweetly, for the old stories all over again. She got out the little drawing you sent just after her birth; have I told you how she treasures it? When she was a child she used to point to it. Papa sits here, she would say, pointing. Papa sleeps here. I wished that I could gather her into my lap again. It would have been so silly, Albert. You must picture her with her legs longer than mine and new gray in the black of her hair. Was I silly to want it, Schatzerl? Shouldn't someone have warned me that I wouldn't be able to hold her forever?

Einstein set the letter back down into the snow. He had not yet found it. He had never had such a beautiful daughter. Perhaps he had not even met Mileva yet, Mileva whom he still loved, but who was not sound and who liked to play tricks.

Perhaps, he thought, he will find the letter in the spring when the snow melts. If the ink has not run, if he can still read it, then he will decide what to do. Then he will have to decide. It began to snow again. Einstein went back into his room for his umbrella. The snow covered the letter. He could not even see the letter under the snow when he stepped over it on his way to the bakery. He did not want to go home where no letter was hidden by the door. He was twenty-two years old and he stood outside the bakery, eating his bread, reading a book in the tiny world he had made under his umbrella in the snow.

Several years later, after Einstein has married Mileva and neither ever mentions Lieserl, after they have had two sons, a colleague will describe a visit to Einstein's apartment. The door will be open so that the newly washed floor can dry. Mileva will be hanging dripping laundry in the hall. Einstein will rock a baby's bassinet with one hand and hold a book open with the other. The stove will smoke. How does he bear it? the colleague will ask in a letter which still survives, a letter anyone can read. That genius. How can he bear it?

The answer is that he could not. He will try for many years and then Einstein will leave Mileva and his sons, sending back to them the money he wins along with the Nobel Prize.

When the afternoon post came, the postman had found the letter again and included it with the new mail. So there were two letters, only one had been already opened.

EINSTEIN PUT the new letter aside. He put it under his papers. He hid it in his bookcase. He retrieved it and opened it clumsily because his hands were shaking. He had known this letter was coming, known it perhaps with Lieserl's first tooth, certainly with her first dance. It was exactly what he had expected, worse than he could have imagined. *She is as bald as ice and as mad as a goddess, my Albert,* Mileva wrote. *But she is still my Lieber Dockerl, my little doll. She clings to me, crying if I must leave her for a minute. Mama, Mama! Such madness in her eyes and her mouth. She is toothless and soils herself. She is my baby.*

And yours, Schatzerl. Nowhere is there a boy I could love like my Papa, she says, lisping again just the way she did when she was little. She has left a message for you. It is a message from the dead. You will get what you really want, Papa, she said. I have gone to get it for you. Remember that it comes from me. She was weeping and biting her hands until they bled. Her eyes were white with madness. She said something else. The brighter the light, the more shadows, my Papa, she said. My darling Papa. My poor Papa. You will see.

The room was too small. Einstein went outside where his breath rose in a cloud from his mouth, tangible, as if he were breathing on glass. He imagined writing on the surface of a mirror, drawing one of his gedanken with his finger into his own breath. He imagined a valentine. *Lieserl,* he wrote across it. He loved Lieserl. He cut the word in half, down the s, with the stroke of his nail. The two halves of the heart opened and closed, beating against each other, faster and faster, like wings, until they split apart and vanished from his mind.

LETTERS FROM HOME

I wish you could see me now. You would laugh. I have a husband. I have children. Yes. I drive a station wagon. I would laugh, too. Our turn to be the big kids, the grown-ups. Our turn to be over thirty. It astonishes me whenever I stop and think about it. It has to be a joke.

I miss you. I've always missed you. I want us to understand each other. I want to tell you what I did after you left. I want to tell you what I did during the war. Most of all, I want to tell you the truth. This is what makes it so difficult. I have learned to distrust words, even my own. Words can be made to say anything. I know this. Do you?

Much of what I will tell you actually happened. You will be able to identify these parts, or you can ask me. This does not mean, of course, that any of it is true. Even among the people who were there with me are some who remember it differently. Gretchen said something once that echoed my own feelings. "We were happy, weren't we?" she said. "In spite of everything. We made each other happy. Ill-advised, really, this putting your happiness into other people's hands. I've tried it several times since, and it's never worked again."

But when I repeated this to Julie she was amazed. "Happy?" she asked. "How can you say that? I was so fat. I was being screwed by that teaching assistant. And 'screwed' is the only word that applies. There was a war. Don't you remember?"

Can I tell you what I remember about the war? I remember the words. Vietnam was the language we spoke—secret bombing, the lottery, Vietnamization, self-immolation, Ho-Ho-Ho Chi Minh, peace with honor, peace at any price, peace, peace, peace. Somewhere, I imagine, on the other side of the world, these words meant something. Somewhere they had physical counterparts. Except for the last set, of course. If peace has ever had a physical value anywhere, none of us has been able to find it. But the other words corresponded to something. There was a real war going on, and in many ways we were untouched by it. This is what I'm trying to say: If the words alone were powerful enough to shape us and our lives as they did, what kind of an impact must the real war have had on its people?

I remember sitting on our sofa watching television. Julie is on the floor at my feet. She's the red-haired Jewish one. She's studying set design and is busy gluing together a tiny throne, part of a mock-up for the set of *Saint Joan*. "Women have fought in wars before," she reminds us, "but only when God tells them to."

Lauren is next to me. She's black, light-skinned, and freckled. Her dog is on her lap, giving the television the same studied attention the rest of us are. Gretchen is standing in the doorway to the kitchen drinking a diet soda. She has short brown hair and heavy bangs, a white Catholic though not a practicing one. She clings to Catholicism because it protects her from being a WASP. This unpleasant designation is applicable only to me. You know me. I'm the plain white one on the end there with my legs drawn up to my chest and my arms around them. And that ten-inch figure on the screen with his hands in motion before him and the map of Cambodia behind him, that's President Nixon. The Quaker. He is busy redrawing the Cambodian border and explaining to us that we are not really invading Cambodia, because the border is not where we have always thought it was. Gretchen swallows the last of her soda. "My God," she says. "The man may be right. Just now, just out of the corner of my eye, I saw the border jump."

Nixon is impervious to our criticism. He is content; he feels it is enough merely to have found something to say. I am twenty years old. I believe nothing I hear.

I was not always like that. Here is an earlier memory. We are standing on my parents' front porch and you have your arms around me. You have driven all the way down from San Francisco to tell me you have been drafted. I find this incomprehensible. I know you could have avoided it. Isn't Allen in Manhattan Beach, getting braces put on his teeth? Hasn't Greg moved three times in three months, burying his induction notice in the U.S. mails? Hasn't Jim joined VISTA, taking advantage of the unspoken agreement that if you are reluctant to burn villages and bomb children, your country will accept two years of urban volunteerism instead?

You are so thin I feel your bones inside your arms. If you fasted, you could fall below the required weight. Why will you do none of these things? I can't help feeling betrayed.

You try to explain and I try to listen. You tell me that the draft is unfair because you could evade it. You say if you don't go, they will just send someone else. (Yes, I say. Yes.) You say that perhaps you can have some impact from within. That an evasion won't realistically affect the war effort at all, but maybe if you were actually there . . . "Hey." You are holding your arms about me so tightly, helping me to hold myself so tightly inside. "Don't cry. I'm going to subvert every soldier I meet. The war will be over by Christmas." And I don't cry. Remember? I don't cry.

You disappeared into the real war and you never got one word back out to me. I never heard from you or of you again. So that is what I remember about the war. The words over here. The war over there. And increasingly little connection between the two.

YOU ARE PUT on a bus and sent to basic training. You take the last possible seat, left rear corner. The bus fills with young men, their white necks exposed by new haircuts, their ears open and vulnerable.

It reminds you of going to camp. You suggest a game of telephone. You whisper into the ear closest to you. You whisper, "The Geneva Accords." The man next to you leans across the aisle. The message travels over the backs of the seats and crisscrosses the bus. When it comes out at the front, it is "the domino theory."

You try again. "Buddhist barbecues," you whisper. You think the man next to you has it right, repeats it just the way you said it. You can hear the *b*'s and the s's even over the bus motor. But the large man at the front of the bus, the one whose pink scalp is so vivid you can't even guess what color the fuzz of his hair might be, claims to have heard "strategic hamlets." Someone is changing the words.

"Body bags!" You have shouted it accidentally. Everyone turns to look at you. Fifty faces. Fifty selected faces. Already these men are different from the men they were yesterday, a difference of appearance, perhaps, and nothing else. It may stay this way. It may be the first hint of the evolution of an entirely new person. You turn to the tinted window, surprised by your own face staring at you.

The other men think you have said, "Operation Rolling Thunder." Even so, nobody smiles.

When you leave the bus, you leave the face in the window. You go and it stays. So it cannot have been your face after all.

AFTER YOU LEFT I went to Berkeley. I lived in the student dorms for a year, where I met Gretchen and Julie. When we moved out, we moved together, into a fairly typical student apartment. It had a long shag carpet—even the rugs were hairy then—of a particularly putrid green, and the appliances were avocado. The furniture had been stapled together. There were four beds, and the rent clearly had been selected with four in mind. We advertised for a roommate in the *Daily Cal.* Although taking a stranger into our home entailed a definite risk, it seemed preferable to inviting someone we actually knew.

I remember that we flipped a coin to see which of us would have to share the bedroom with the newcomer, and Julie lost. She had some procedural objection she felt was sufficiently serious to require a second toss, but Gretchen and I refused. The new roommate hadn't even appeared and was already making things sticky.

Lauren was the first respondent to our ad—a beautiful, thin, curly-haired girl with an elegant white curly-haired dog. They made a striking pair. Julie showed Lauren the apartment; the conversation was brisk and businesslike. Gretchen and I petted the dog. When Lauren left, Julie had said we would take her.

I was unsettled by the speed of the decision and said so. I had no objections to Lauren, but I'd envisioned interviewing several candidates before making a selection.

"I'm the one who has to room with her. I should get to choose." Julie held out one long strand of her own red hair and began methodically to split the ends. Julie was artistic and found the drab apartment painful. Initially, I believe she wanted Lauren mostly for decor. Lauren moved in the next day.

Immediately, objectionable characteristics began to surface. If I'd had your address, I would have written long complaints. "She dresses with such taste," I would have said. "Who would have guessed she'd be such a slob?" Lauren's messiness was epic in its proportions. Her bed could hardly be seen under the pile of books, shoes, combs, and dirty dishes she left on it. She had to enter it gingerly at night, finding small empty spaces where she might fit an arm or a leg. She would sleep without moving, an entire night spent in the only position possible.

"She's late wherever she goes," I would have written, "not by minutes or quarter hours, but by afternoons. On her night to cook, we eat in front of Johnny Carson."

Then I would have divulged the worst complaint of all: "She talks baby talk: to the dog, which is tolerable; to her boyfriend, which is not." Lauren's boyfriend was a law student at Boalt. He was older than us, big, and wore his hair slicked back along his head. Of course, no one wore their hair like that then. There was a sort of mafioso cut to his clothes, an intensity in his eyes. I never liked being alone with him, but Lauren called him Owlie and he called her his Sugarbear. "It is absolutely sickening the way you two go on," I told her, and she was completely unabashed. She suggested that, although we didn't have the guts to be as up front about it as she was, we probably all talked baby talk to our boyfriends, an accusation we strenuously denied. We had no boyfriends, so the point was academic. Owlie studied judo as well as the law, and there was always a risk, opening some door, that you might find him demonstrating some hold to Lauren. Sickening, like I said.

I would have finished my letter by telling you, if you could only meet her, you would love her. Well, we all did. She was vivacious, imaginative, courageous. She removed some previously unnoticed tensions from our relationships—somehow with four the balance was better. By the spring of 1970, when the war of the words achieved its most intense pitch ever, this balance had become intricate and effortless.

I had gone out to protest the Cambodian invasion and come home in a cast. The police had removed their badges, donned their gas masks, and chased us down, catching me just outside Computer Sciences. They had broken my ankle. Owlie was gone. His birthday had been drawn seventeenth in the lottery, and he'd relocated to a small town in Oregon rumored to have a lenient draft board. Gretchen had acquired a boyfriend whose back had been injured in a high school wrestling match, rendering him 4-F with no tricks. He went off to Europe and was, consequently, very little trouble. Julie had switched her major from set design to Chicano studies. We heard that the National Guard was killing people on the campus of Kent State. I heard nothing from you.

YOU ARE IN a small room, a cell. It is cold and the walls are damp stone. You sit cross-legged like a monk on the thin mattress and face the wall. There is so much moisture you can imprint your hand in it. By 10 a.m. the prints disappear. The sun has reached the wall, but it still is not warm. If you were sure no one would come to look, you would levitate yourself into the sunshine. You are thinking of me.

How much I expected of you. How stupid I am. I probably believed you could end the war by Christmas. You can imagine me believing that. Even now I am probably working out long chain-letter calculations: If you subvert four soldiers every day and they subvert four soldiers and they subvert four soldiers, how many days will the war last? When will you come home?

Do I expect miracles from a prison cell? Why should you provide them? You make a decision. You decide to be warm. You exhale your warmth into the air. It rises to the ceiling, it seems to disappear, but as you repeat this, over and over, the layers eventually drop to where they surround you. When you leave the cell, you will leave it filled with your heat.

It is a small room. Any man can accomplish a small task.

IN RESPONSE TO the invasion of Cambodia and the deaths at Kent State (Can I say murders? Will you object? Will you compare those four deaths to the body count in Vietnam on any single day or on 4 May itself and believe you have made some point?) UC Berkeley suspended classes. When they recommenced, they had been reconstituted; they were now supposed to be directly relevant to the single task of ending the war in Southeast Asia. I will not pretend to you that there was no opposition within the university to this. But a large segment of the campus made this commitment together—we would not continue with our lives until the war was over.

At the same time Nixon made his own pledge to the American people. He promised them that nothing we could do would affect policy in any way.

The war of the words took on a character which was at once desperate and futile, a soul-dampening combination we never shook free of. We did the work because it seemed right to us. We had no illusions of its potency. It began to feel like a game.

Julie and I had volunteered for a large committee whose purpose was to compile a list of war profiteers so that their products could be boycotted. We researched mergers and parent companies; the list grew like a chain letter. It would have been quicker to list those companies *not* turning a profit in Vietnam. I remember Lauren perusing our list one day with great dissatisfaction. "The counterculture makes roach clips," she said. "It makes liquid sculptures you can plug in and they change shape."

"Lava lamps," I told her.

"Whatever. It makes hash pipes. I need a raincoat. What am I supposed to do?"

"Get wet," Julie suggested.

"Get stoned," said Gretchen. "And then get wet. You'll hardly notice."

Lauren had volunteered herself for the university's media watchdog committee. Her job was to monitor three news shows daily and report on the coverage they gave to the war and to the student movement. The idea was that we would apply whatever pressure we could on those stations whose coverage seemed slanted in favor of the administration. The fallacy was that we had any meaningful pressure that could be brought to bear. We wrote letters. We added their sponsors to the boycott. Nobody cared.

I know that Nixon felt undermined and attacked by the media. We did not see it this way. None of the major networks met with our approval. Only the local public station reported the news in Berkeley the way we saw it happening. One of their reporters was a young man who covered those stories felt to be of particular interest to the black community. He was handsome, mustached, broad-shouldered. He had the same dark, melting eyes as Lauren's dog. His name was Poncho Taylor. Lauren fell in love with him.

Well, you didn't expect us to give up love, did you? Just because there was a war on? I never expected you to.

Poncho was politically impeccable. He was passionate, he was committed. He was gorgeous. Any one of us could have fallen in love with him. But Lauren was the first to announce her passion, and we were content to provide support. We took turns with her transcribing duties during his airtime so she wouldn't miss a moment of his face. We listened patiently while she droned on about his cheekbones, his hair, the sexy tremor in his voice when a story had an unhappy conclusion, and we agreed. We saw it all. He was wonderful.

I remember a night when we made chocolate chip cookies and ate the dough. Nestlé had just made the boycott list, but the chips were old. "The sooner we eat them, the better," Julie had suggested.

Gretchen had just returned from an organizational meeting with new instructions for us. We had been told to band together into small groups like the revolutionaries in *The Battle of Algiers*. These were to be called affinity groups, and we were to select for them people we trusted absolutely. We were to choose those people we would trust with our lives. We smiled at one another over the bowl of dough as it suddenly occurred to us that, for us, this choice had already been made. Just as Gretchen said, when we could find our happiness nowhere else, we were able to put it into each other's hands and hold it there.

"There's more," Gretchen continued. "We're supposed to arm ourselves." Julie took another spoonful of dough, heavy on the chips. I used the handle of my spoon to reach inside my cast and scratch myself. Nobody said anything for a long time.

Finally Julie indicated the boycott list. "The pen is mightier than the sword," she suggested. She didn't sound sure.

Gretchen did. "The boycott list is liberal bullshit," she said. "It's too easy. What good will it possibly do?"

Lauren cleared her throat and tapped the air with the back of her spoon. "It's a capitalist country. Money matters."

"You can't destroy the system from within the system." Gretchen was very unhappy. "We're too safe."

We sent Nixon a telegram. Gretchen composed it. END THIS OBSCENE WAR AT ONCE STOP PULL OUT THE WAY YOUR FATHER SHOULD HAVE STOP It didn't make us feel better.

We should have done more. I look back on those years, and it's clear to me that we should have done more. It's just not clear to me what more we should have done.

Perhaps we lacked imagination. Perhaps we lacked physical courage. Perhaps our personal stakes were just not high enough. We were women. We were not going to Vietnam. We were privileged. Our brothers, our lovers, were not going to Vietnam. But you do us an injustice if you doubt our sincerity. Remember that we watched the news three times a day. Three times a day we read the body count in the upper right-hand corner of the screen like the score of a football game. This is how many of them we killed today. They killed this many of us. Subtract one figure from the other. Are we winning?

Could anyone be indifferent to this? Always, I added the two numbers together. My God, I would think. Dear God. Look how many people died today! (What if one of them was you?)

YOU ARE ON A PLANE, an ordinary plane. You could be en route to Denver from Chicago or going home for Christmas if you just close your eyes and believe only your ears. But you are really between Japan and Vietnam. The plane has a stewardess dressed in a bathing suit like Miss America. This is designed as a consolation for you. If you are very, very frightened, she may agree to wear rabbit ears and a tail when she brings you your drink. But you must not touch her. She is a white woman and looks familiar to you—her height, her build quite ordinary. This will change. When you remember her later she will seem exotic. It will seem odd to you that a woman should be so big. You will remember that she came and tightened your seat belt as if she were your mother. What was she keeping you safe for? Whose body is it anyway? You look at your legs, at your hands, and wonder what your body will be like when it is returned to you. You wonder who will want it then.

The immediate threat is the plane's descent. You make a sudden decision not to descend with it. You spread your arms to hold yourself aloft. You hover near the top of the plane. But it is hopeless. If they have to shoot you down, they will. Friendly fire. You return to your seat. The plane carries your body down into Vietnam.

You think of me. How I will hate you if you don't live through this. How you must protect me. And during your whole tour, every time you meet someone returning home, you will give him a message for me. You will write your message on the casts of the wounded. You will print it on the foreheads of those who return walking, on the teeth of those who return bagged. *I am here, I am here, I am here.* So many messages. How are you to know that none will get through?

MY AFFINITY GROUP was very kind about you. I would tell them frequently how the war would be over by Christmas, how you were responsible for the growing dissatisfaction among servicemen. Vets against the war, I said to them, was probably one of your ideas. They never mentioned how you never wrote. Neither did I. You were my wound. I had my broken ankle and I had you. It was so much more than they had. It made them protective of me.

They didn't want me at any more demonstrations. "When you could run," Lauren pointed out, "look what happened to you." But I was there with them when the police cordoned off Sproul Plaza, trapping us inside, and gassed us from the air. You don't want to believe this. Governor Ronald Reagan and all the major networks assured you that we had been asked to disperse but had refused. Only Poncho Taylor told the truth. We had not been allowed to leave. Anyone who tried to leave was clubbed. A helicopter flew over the area and dropped tear gas on us. The gas went into the hospital and into the neighboring residential areas. When the police asked the city to buy them a second helicopter so that they could enlarge operations, many people not of the radical persuasion objected. A committee was formed to prevent this purchase, a committee headed by an old Bay Area activist. She happened to be Poncho Taylor's grandmother. Lauren took it as a sign from God.

Lauren's passion for Poncho had continued to grow, and we had continued to feed it. It's difficult to explain why Poncho had become so important to us. Partly it was just that Lauren loved him and we loved Lauren. Whatever Lauren wanted she should have. But partly it was the futility of our political work. We continued to do it but without energy, without hope. Poncho began to seem attainable when peace was not. Poncho began to represent the rest of our lives, outside the words.

Lauren told everyone how she felt. Our friends all knew and soon their friends knew and then the friends of their friends. It was like a message Lauren was sending to Poncho. And if it didn't reach him, Lauren could combine useful political effort with another conduit. She called Poncho's grandmother and volunteered us all for the Stop the Helicopter campaign.

We went to an evening organizational meeting. (We did more organizing than anything else.) Though now I remember that Julie did not come with us, but stayed at home to rendezvous in the empty apartment with her teaching assistant.

The meeting was crowded, but eventually we verified Poncho's absence. After interminable discussion we were told to organize phone trees, circulate petitions, see that the city council meeting, scheduled for the end of the month, was packed with vocal opponents. Lauren couldn't even get close to Poncho's grandmother.

When we returned home, Julie was drunk. Her lover had failed to show, but Mike, a friend of mine, had come by with a bottle of wine. Julie had never known Mike very well or liked him very much, but he had stayed the whole evening and they had gotten along wonderfully. Julie had a large collection of Barbra Streisand records we refused to let her play. Mike had not only put them on but actually cried over them. "He's a lot more sensitive than I thought," Julie told me.

Mike denied it all. He was so drunk he wove from side to side even sitting down. He tried to kiss me and landed on my shoulder. "How did the meeting go?" he asked, and snorted when we told him. "Phone trees." He lifted his head to grin at me, red-faced, unshaven, wine-soaked breath. "The old radicals are even less ballsy than the young ones."

I picked up one of his hands. "Do you think it's possible," I asked him, "for a revolution to be entirely personal? Suppose we all concentrated on our own lives, filled them with revolutionary moments, revolutionary relationships. When we had enough of them, it would be a revolution."

"No." Mike removed his hand from mine. "It wouldn't. That's

cowardice talking. That's you being liberal. That's you saying, 'Let's make a revolution, but let's be nice about it.' People are dying. There's a real war going on. We can't be incremental."

"Exactly," said Gretchen. "Exactly. Time is as much the issue as anything else."

"Then we should all be carrying guns," said Julie. "We should be planning political assassinations."

"We should be robbing banks," said Mike. "Or printing phony bills." Mike had been known to pass a bad check or two, though he never needed the money. He was an auto mechanic by day, a dope dealer by night. He was the richest person we knew. "Lauren," he called, and Lauren appeared in the doorway to the kitchen. "I came here tonight because I have a surprise for you." He was grinning.

"If it's dope, I'm not interested," said Lauren. "Nor am I solvent."

"What would you say," Mike asked, "if I told you that right now, right at this very moment, I have Poncho Taylor's car sitting in my garage waiting for repairs?" Lauren said we would go right over.

Poncho had a white convertible. Lauren loved it. She sat in the driver's seat, because Poncho had sat there. She sat on the passenger side, because that was where she would be sitting herself. I discovered an old valentine in the glove compartment. Lauren was torn between the despair of thinking he already had a girlfriend and the thrill of finally discovering something personal. She opened it.

"*Love and a hundred smooches, Deborah.*" Lauren read it aloud disapprovingly. "This Deborah sounds like a real sap."

"Poncho seems more and more to be the perfect match for you," I added. The valentine had one feature of incontrovertible value. It had Poncho's address on it. Lauren began to copy it, then looked at us.

"What the hell," she said and put the whole thing in her purse.

I had no address for you, you know. I mean, in the beginning I did, and I probably should have written you first. Since I hardly talked to you when you came to say good-bye. Since I didn't cry. I did miss you. I kept thinking you would write me. And then later, when I saw you wouldn't, it was too late. Then I had no address. I couldn't believe you would never write me. What happened to you?

Even our senators sent me form letters. More than I got from you.

> Dear (fill in name),
> Well, here I am in Vietnam! The people are little and the bugs are big, but the food is Army and that means American. As far as I can see, Saigon has been turned into one large brothel. I go there as often as I can. It beats my other way of interacting with the locals, which is to go up in planes and drop Willie Peter on them. Man, those suckers burn forever! I made my first ground kill yesterday. Little guy in a whole lot of pieces. You have to bring the body for the body count and the arm came off right in my hand. We were able to count him six times, which everybody said was really beautiful. Hey, he's in so many pieces he's never going to need any

company but his own again. The dope is really heavy-duty here, too. I've lost my mind.

Listen, I got to go. We're due out tonight on a walk-through with ARVN support, and you know what they say here about the ARVN—with friends like these . . . Ugly little buggers.

Dust off the women. I'll be home by Christmas. Love you all.

(fill in name)

Now you're angry. I hope. Who am I to condemn you? What do I know about the real war? Absolutely nothing. Gretchen says you're a running-dog imperialist. She thinks she met you once before you left, before she knew me, at a party at Barbara Meyer's. In Sausalito? I don't think it was you. She waited a long time to tell me about it. I was married before she told me. I don't think it was you.

So it took Lauren two days to formalize her final plan. It was audacious. It was daring. It had Lauren's stamp all over it. Mike called when Poncho came in and picked up his car. This was our signal to start.

It was Lauren's night to cook dinner, and she saw no reason to change this. She had bought the ingredients for cannelloni, a spectacular treat she made entirely from scratch. It required long intervals, she claimed, when the dough must be allowed to rest. During one of these rest periods, she fixed herself up and Julie drove her to San Francisco, where Poncho lived. Julie returned in forty minutes. She had only stayed long enough to see Lauren safely inside.

Lauren came home perhaps a half an hour later. She changed her clothes again, dropping the discarded ones onto the living room floor, and went into the kitchen to roll out the cannelloni dough. We sat around her at the kitchen table, chopping the onions, mixing the filling, stuffing the rolls while she talked. She was very high, very excited.

"I knocked on the door," she said. "Poncho's roommate let me in. Poncho was lying on the couch, reading. Poncho Taylor! He was there!"

"Can I come in?" Lauren had asked. She made her voice wobble. She showed us how. "A man in a car is following me."

"What was the roommate like?" Julie asked hopefully. "Pretty cute?"

"No. He wears big glasses and his hair is very short. James. His name is James. He asked me why I came to their apartment since they live on the second floor."

"Good question," I admitted. "What did you say?"

"I said I saw their Bobby Seale poster and thought they might be black."

"Good answer," said Julie. "Lauren thinks on her feet. All right!"

"There's nothing wrong with glasses," Gretchen objected. "Lots of attractive people wear glasses." She cut into an onion with determined zeal. "Maybe he's gay," she said.

"No," said Lauren. "He's not. And it wasn't the glasses. It was the competition. Poncho is so . . ." We waited while she searched for the word worthy of Poncho. "Magnetic," she concluded.

Well, who could compete with Poncho? Gretchen let the issue drop.

Lauren had entered the apartment and James and Poncho had gone to the window. "What make was the car?" James had asked. "I don't see anybody."

"Green VW bug," said Lauren.

"My car," said Julie. "Great."

"They wanted me to call the police," Lauren said. "But I was too upset. I didn't even get the license."

"Lauren," said Gretchen disapprovingly. Gretchen hated women to look helpless. Lauren looked back at her.

"I was distraught," she said evenly. She began picking up the finished cannelloni and lining the pan with neat rows. Little blankets. Little corpses. (No. I am being honest. Of course I didn't think this.)

Poncho had returned immediately to the couch and his books. "Chicks shouldn't wander around the city alone at night," he commented briefly. Lauren loved his protectiveness. Gretchen was silent.

"Then I asked to use the phone," Lauren said. She wiped her forehead with her upper arm since her hands were covered with flour. She took the pan to the stove and ladled tomato sauce into it. "The phone was in the kitchen. James took me in; then he went back. I put my keys on the floor, very quietly, and I kicked them under the table. Then I pretended to phone you."

"All your keys?" Julie asked in dismay.

Lauren ignored her. "I told them no one was home. I told them I'd been planning to take the bus, but by now, of course, I'd missed it."

"All your keys?" I asked pointedly.

"James drove me home. Damn! If he hadn't been there . . ."

Lauren slammed the oven door on our dinner and came to sit with us. "What do you think?" she asked. "Is he interested?"

"Sounds like James was interested," said Gretchen.

"You left your name with your keys?" I said.

"Name, address, phone number. Now we wait."

We waited. For two days the phone never rang. Not even our parents wanted to talk to us. In the interest of verisimilitude, Lauren had left all her keys on the chain. She couldn't get into the apartment unless one of us had arranged to be home and let her in. She couldn't drive, which was just as well since every gas company had made the boycott list but Shell. Shell was not an American company, but we were still investigating. It seemed likely there was war profiteering there somewhere. And, if not, we'd heard rumors of South African holdings. We were looking into it. But in the meantime we could still drive.

"The counterculture is going to make gas from chicken shit," said Julie.

"Too bad they can't make it from bullshit," Lauren said. "We got plenty of that."

Demonstrators had gone out and stopped the morning commuter traffic to protest the war. It had not been appreciated. It drove something of a wedge between us and the working class. Not that the proletariat had ever liked us much. I told our postman that more than two hundred colleges had closed. "BFD," he said, handing me the mail. Nothing for me.

YOU ARE ON the surface of the moon and the air itself is a poison. Nothing moves, nothing grows, there is nothing but ash. A helicopter has left you here and the air from its liftoff made the ash fly and then resettle into definite shapes, like waves. You don't move for fear of disturbing these patterns, which make you think of snow, of children lying on their backs in the snow until their arms turn into wings. You can see the shadows of winged people in the ash.

Nothing is alive here, so you are not here, after all, on this man-made moon where nothing can breathe. You are home and have been home for months. Your tour lasted just over a year and you only missed one Christmas. You have a job and a wife and you eat at restaurants, go to baseball games, commute on the bus. The war is over and there is nothing behind you but the bodies of angels flying on their backs in the ash.

PONCHO NEVER CALLED. We went to the city meeting on the helicopter, all four of us, to help the city make this decision. The helicopter was item seven on the agenda. We never got to it. Child care had been promised but not provided. Angry parents dumped their children on the stage of the Berkeley Community Theatre to sit with the council members. A small girl with a sun painted on her forehead knocked over a microphone. The conservative council members went home. Berkeley.

Lauren found Poncho and James in the dress circle. Poncho was covering the meeting. Lauren introduced us all. "By the way," she said carefully, "you didn't find a set of keys at your house, did you? I lost mine, and that night is the last I remember having them."

"Keys?" asked Poncho. "No." Something in his smile told me

Lauren must have overplayed herself that evening. He knew exactly what was going on.

"If you do find them, you will call me?"

"Of course."

Julie drove us home, and I made Lauren a cup of tea. She held my hand for a moment as she took it from me. Then she smiled. "I thought we were boycotting Lipton's," she said.

"It's a British tea." I stirred some milk into my own cup. "That should be all right, shouldn't it?"

"Have you ever heard of Bernadette Devlin?" Gretchen asked.

We never saw Poncho again except on TV. On 29 June he told us all American forces had been withdrawn from Cambodia. Your birthday, so I remember the date. Not a bad lottery number either. So I always wondered. Were you really drafted? Did you enlist?

Poncho lost his job about the same time Nixon lost his. Some network executive decided blacks didn't need special news, so they didn't need special reporters to give it to them. Let them watch the same news as the rest of us. And apparently Poncho's ability to handle generic news was doubtful. The network let him go. Politically we regretted this decision. Privately we thought he had it coming.

God, it was years ago. Years and years ago. I got married. Lauren went to Los Angeles and then to Paris, and now she's in Washington writing speeches for some senator. Hey, we emerged from the war of the words with some expertise. Gretchen and Julie had a falling-out and hardly speak to each other now. Only when I'm there. They make a special effort for me.

Julie asked me recently why I was so sure there ever had been a real war. What proof did I have, she asked, that it wasn't a TV movie of the decade? A miniseries? A maxiseries?

It outraged Gretchen. "Don't do that," she snapped. "Keep it real." She turned to me. She said she saw you about a month ago at Fisherman's Wharf in San Francisco. She said you had no legs.

It doesn't alarm me as much as you might think. I see you all the time, too. You're in the park, pushing your kids on the swings and you've got one hand and one hook. Or you're sitting in a wheelchair in the aisle of the movie theater watching *The Deer Hunter*. Or you're weighing vegetables at the supermarket and you're fine, you're just fine, only it's never really you. Not any of them.

SO WHAT DO you think of my war? At the worst I imagine you're a little angry. "My God," I can imagine you saying. "You managed a clean escape. You had your friends, you had your games. You were quite happy." Well, I promised you the truth. And the truth is that some of us went to jail. (Damn few. I know.) Some of us were killed. (And the numbers are irrelevant.) Some of us went to Canada and to Sweden. And some of us had a great time. But it wasn't a clean escape, really, for any of us.

Look at me. I'm operating all alone here with no affinity group and it seems unnatural to me. It seems to me that I should be surrounded by people I'd trust with my life. Always. It makes me cling to people, even people I don't care for all that much. It makes me panic when people leave. I'm sure they're not coming back. The war did this to me. Or you did. Same thing. What did the war do to you?

Look how much we have in common, after all. We both lost. I lost my war. You lost your war. I look today at Vietnam and Cambodia and Laos and I feel sick inside. Do you ever ask yourself who won? Who the hell won?

Your war. I made it up, of course. It was nothing, nothing like that. Write me. Tell me about it. Please. If I have not heard from you by Christmas, I have decided to ask Lauren to go to the monument and look for your name. I don't want to do this. Don't make me do this. Just send me some word.

I am thirty-five years old. I am ready to believe anything you say.

DUPLICITY

They took Alice out every single day. Sometimes she was crying when she came back. Sometimes she was limp and had to be carried. This was not much like Alice.

Alice had been Alice the day she and Tilly had returned to the base camp and found it violated. The tent had been ransacked. The camp lantern had been taken and some of their more brightly colored clothes were gone. A box of tampons had been opened and several unwrapped. Alice picked one up, holding it by its long tail like a dead mouse. She laughed. "What do you suppose they made of these?" she asked Tilly. She stuck the tampon into one of her ears, plugging the other ear with her finger. "Very useful," she said. "Yes? Sleep late in the mornings. Miss the birds."

Alice's cheerfulness was so marked it required explanation. Alice, who was an artist and amateur cartographer, had told Tilly that the blank spaces in maps were often referred to as sleeping beauties. This surprised Tilly, who had never given it any thought. She could not imagine anyone actually functioning with this optimistic attitude toward the unknown. Not without a lot of effort. Here be dragons, was Tilly's philosophy. Expect the worst and you'll still be disappointed. Her reaction to the intrusion into their camp had been one of barely controlled alarm. She had known this trip would be dangerous. They had come so casually. They had been very stupid.

But Alice had been Alice. "It was clearly investigative," she told Tilly calmly. "And not malicious. Nothing was broken. If they had wanted us to go, they would have found an unambiguous way to suggest it. This was just curiosity. Though I do wish they hadn't taken our light." Alice had been sitting outside the tent in the sun, since she could no longer work at night. Propped open on her knees, she'd had a lap desk which folded and unfolded; she'd been penciling a curve in the Nhamundá River onto her graph.

The map Alice and Tilly had brought was based on high-altitude infrared pictures. The maps Alice was doing would be much more detailed. On that day she had been working on something whimsical, partly map, partly picture. She had noted the turn in the river and then, in the water, had added the head of a large river turtle—the *tracaja.* On the day of their arrival, a turtle like this had watched them for hours while they emptied the boat and set up camp. Alice had sung the turtle song from *Sesame Street* to it, bringing civilization, she said, to the backwards turtles of Brazil, who could have no knowledge of the advances other turtles had made globally. Alice had nieces and nephews and a predilection for information there was no reasonable way she could know anyhow. Tilly didn't know that song.

Two untidy brown braids rested on Alice's shoulders. A slight breeze blew the unrestrained wisps of hair into her face. She held them back with her left hand, added an arrow to the map with her right. "You are here," she'd said to Tilly. Brightly. You are here.

THE SUN WAS UP. Dim green light filtered through the walls of the tent, which smelled of sleeping bags and hiking boots and moisture. They opened the flaps every day but the tent never lost its hothouse feel. Tilly woke this morning missing Steven. Not memories; she wasn't thinking. The surface of her body missed him. Her skin. Where's Steven? it asked. Where's his mouth? Where're his hands? She substituted her own hands, but her body knew the difference. And there was another difference, which she recognized, that she would do this in front of Alice now. As if Alice had become part of her like an arm, like Tilly's left arm, less intimate than the right but part of her all the same.

Although really she believed Alice was still asleep. Sleep was the only escape for Alice now. Tilly would have felt very guilty if she woke Alice from it early. She listened to Alice breathe and tried to guess if Alice were awake or not. Alice moved so seldom; her body was landscape.

Tilly would have liked to get up, but this would have woken Alice for sure, and anyway the tent was clogged with the sleeping mats and bags, with the unused stove, with Tilly's camera cases, and with Alice's maps. Tilly could only stand up straight in the very middle of the tent. She had bouts of claustrophobia.

Everything Tilly knew, everything Tilly could imagine, was either inside or outside this tent. The two sets were infinitely inclusive. The two sets were mutually exclusive. Except for Alice. Alice could belong to both.

The size of the tent had never bothered her before, when she could come and go as she pleased. In actual fact the tent was probably no smaller than the bedroom she had had as a child, and it had never seemed small to her either, although you couldn't even open the bedroom door completely; the chest of drawers was behind it. The bedroom was a safe place, a place where you were cared for and protected. You could depend on this so confidently you didn't even notice it. As Tilly grew older she began to see the shapes and shadows of another world. A girl in the sixth grade at Tilly's school was followed home by a man in a white car. Tilly was told at the dinner table that she mustn't talk to strangers. Angela Ruiz, who lived next door, had heard from her cousin in Chicago how some boy she knew was beaten with a pair of pliers by his own father while his mother watched. In *Life* magazine Tilly saw a picture of a little boy and his two sisters, but there was something wrong about the way they looked, and the article said that their mother hadn't wanted anyone to know she had children so she'd hidden them in the basement for five years. Without sunshine, without exercise, their growth had been stunted. They were bonsai children. In the last week their vaguely misshapen bodies had returned to Tilly's dreams.

In Óbidos, where children at twelve play soccer and have sex, the man who sold them supplies had told them a story. A cautionary tale—Tilly could see this in retrospect. It involved the freshwater dolphin called the *boto.* The boto could take a woman, penetrating her in the water, or in human male form on shore, or even in her dreams. She would grow pale and die in childbirth, if she lasted that long, and her child would be deformed—having the smooth face of the father, his rubber skin, a blowhole on the top of the head where the fontanel should be.

Tilly had moved her pad so that it was, in relation to the door, in the same spot as her bed was in her bedroom. Alice never mentioned it, though she'd had to move Alice's pad, too. Alice was gone at the time. They took Alice out every single day. It was hard not to envy Alice for this, no matter how she looked when she came back.

An unseen bird, a trogon, began to shriek nearby. The sound rose above the other rain-forest noises in the same way a police siren always buries the sounds of normal traffic. *Shhh.* The door was a curtain of nylon which whispered when the wind blew. The faint smell of mimosa, just discernible over the smell of sleep and sweat and last night's urine, passed through the tent and was gone. Alice's pad was as far away from the door as it could be. Tilly propped herself on one elbow to look at Alice, who was staring up at the ceiling. "Alice," Tilly said. Any word you spoke in this little room was spoken too loudly. *Shhh* said the door.

"I'm still here," said Alice. "Did you think I might not be?" She moved and caught herself in mid-movement. Her hair was snarled in the back. She had stopped braiding it weeks ago when her last rubber band had snapped. "My back is sore," she said. "I ache all over." She looked directly at Tilly. "I thought of another one. The boy in the bubble."

This was a game Alice had made up to pass the time. She and Tilly were making a list of famous prisoners. The longer the game went on, the more flexible the category became. Tilly wanted to count Howard Hughes. You could be self-imprisoned, Tilly argued. But Alice said no, you weren't a prisoner if there wasn't a jailer, and the jailer had to be someone or something on the outside. Outside the tent something shifted and coughed.

When the camp was violated, Alice and Tilly had assumed the trespassers were Indians—what else could they think?—although it had surprised them. A number of the local tribes were considered low contact but hardly untouched. There were the Hixkaryana, the Kaxuiana, the Tirio. They had shotguns and motorboats. They had been to the cities. If you mentioned Michael Jackson to them they would nod and let you know you were not the first. The man who advised them on supplies in Óbidos had been from the Tirio tribe. His advice, though lengthy, had been essentially indifferent; the spectacle of two women on holiday in the rain forest had aroused less comment than they expected. He had made one ominous observation in Portuguese. "It is quite possible," he had said, "to go into the forest as a young woman and come out very old."

Alice and Tilly should have gone to FUNAI for permission to visit the Indians, who were protected by the Brazilian government from curious tourists. But Alice was only interested in the terrain. She had hardly given the Indians a thought when she planned the trip. Steven had asked about them, but then Steven asked about everything. He was in New York City riding the subways and worrying about Tilly out here with the savages. Steven had been mugged twice last year.

Tilly had insisted on moving the camp after the intrusion, back from the river but not too far, since they still needed water and Alice was still taking measurements. It was a lot of work for nothing. Tilly was setting up the tent again when she realized she was being watched.

From a distance they still looked like Indians. Tilly saw shadows of their shapes between the trees. They paced her when she went to the river for water. She wondered how she'd ever be able to bathe again, knowing or not knowing they were there. She wouldn't even brush her teeth. She went back to camp and argued with Alice about setting a watch at night.

By then it was afternoon. Alice had made lunch. "We can decide that later," she said. "There will be plenty of time to decide that later." But later they came right into the camp, and they didn't look like Indians at all. Their heads were hairless and flattened uniformly in the back. The features on their faces were human enough to be recognizable: two eyes deep set into pockets of puffy skin and two nostrils flush with the rest of the face, expanding and contracting slightly when they breathed. Their mouths were large and mobile. They had a human mix of carnivorous and herbivorous teeth. If Tilly had only seen one she might have thought it a mutation of some sort, or the result of disease or accident. In books she had seen pictures of humans deformed to a similar degree. But these were all the same. They were aliens. She told Alice so.

Alice was not sure. There was nothing off-world about their clothing, drapes of an undyed loose weave, covering the same parts of the body that humans felt compelled to conceal. She pointed to the tampons, which dangled by their strings from cloth belts. "They've taken trophies," said Alice. "They've got our scalps. Doesn't that strike you as rather primitive for a race with interstellar capabilities?" Alice invited them into the tent.

Tilly did not follow. Tilly had the sense to be terrified. She was ready to run, had a clear path to the river, hardly stopped to notice that flight would have meant abandoning Alice. But there were more and more of them. She never had the chance. On the way into the tent one veered toward Tilly. She ducked away, but the arm was longer than she expected; the hand landed on her shoulder. There was an extra flexibility in the fingers, an additional joint, but Tilly didn't notice it then. The hand was cooler than her own skin. She could feel it through her cotton shirt and it pulsed, or else that was her own heartbeat she felt. She was so frightened she fainted. It was a decision she made; she remembered this later. A blackening void behind her eyes and her own voice warning her that she was going to faint. Shall we stop? the voice asked, and Tilly said, No, no, let's do it, let's get out of here.

The clasps of the tent door clicked together like rosary beads as it was brushed to one side. Breakfast had arrived. The dishes were from Tilly's and Alice's own kits. Tilly's was handed to her. Alice's was set on the floor by the door. One of them stayed to watch as Alice and Tilly ate.

Tilly's plate had a tiny orange on it, porridge made of their own farinha, and a small cooked fish. There were crackers from their own store. Alice was given only the crackers and fewer of them. From the very first there had been this difference in their treatment. Of course, Tilly shared her food with Alice. Tilly had to move onto Alice's pad to do this; Alice would never come to Tilly. She made Tilly beg her to eat some of Tilly's breakfast, because there was never enough food for two people. "What kind of fish do you think this is?" Tilly asked Alice, taking a bit of it and making Alice take a bite.

"It's a dead fish," Alice answered. Her voice was stone.

Tilly was very hungry afterward. Alice was hungry, too, had to be, but she didn't say so. "Thank you, Tilly," Alice would say. And then two more would come, and the three of them would take Alice.

Tilly was always afraid they would not bring her back. It was a selfish thing to feel, but Tilly could not help it. Tilly cared about Alice, and Alice should belong to the set of things inside the tent. Everything else Tilly cared about did not. Like Steven. She missed Steven. He was so nice. That's what everyone said about Steven. Alice was always pointing this out to Tilly. The thing about Steven, Alice was always saying, was that he was just so nice. Alice didn't quite believe in him. "And women don't want nice men anyway," said Alice. "Let's be honest."

"I do," said Tilly.

"Then why aren't you married to Steven?" Alice asked. "Why are you here in the rain forest instead of home married to your nice man? Because there's no adventure with Steven. No intensity. The great thing about men, the really appealing thing, is that you can't believe a word they say. They fascinate. They compel." Alice knew a variety of men. Some of them had appeared to be nice men initially. Alice always found them out, though. Occasionally they turned out to be married men. "I don't know why so many women complain that they can't find men willing to commit," Alice said. "Mine are always overcommitted."

Steven must be just starting to wonder if everything was all right. A small worry at first, but it would grow. No sight of them in Óbidos, he would hear. Where they were expected four weeks ago. Perhaps the boat would be found, covered by then in the same purple vines that choked the rest of the riverbank. Would Steven come himself to look for her? Steven had taken her to the plane, and at just the last minute, with his arms around her, he had asked her not to go. Tilly could feel his arms around her arms if she tried very hard. He could have asked earlier. He could have held her more tightly. He had been so nice about the trip. Tilly thought of him all day long, and it made her lonely. She never dreamed of him at night, though; her dreams had shadows with elongated arms and subtly distorted shapes. Steven had no place in that world. And even without him, even with the dreams, night was better.

A storm of huge green dragonflies battered themselves against the walls of the tent, but they couldn't get in. It sounded like rain. All around her, outside, her jailers grunted as they drove the insects away with their hands. They were in front of the tent and they were behind the tent; there would be no more escape attempts. Alice was no longer even planning any. Alice was no longer planning anything. To convince herself that Alice would be coming back, Tilly played Alice's game. She sat still with her legs crossed, combing out her hair with her fingers, and tried to think of another prisoner for their list. Her last suggestion had come from a story she suddenly remembered her father telling her. It was about a mathematician who'd been sentenced to death for a crime Tilly didn't recall. On the night before his execution he'd tried to write several proofs out, but very quickly. The proofs were hard to read and sometimes incomplete. Generations of mathematicians had struggled with them. Some of these problems were still unsolved. Tilly's father had been a mathematician. Steven was an industrial artist.

Alice had told Tilly she had the story wrong. "He wasn't a prisoner and he wasn't sentenced to death," Alice said. "He was going to fight a duel and he was very myopic so he knew he'd lose." She wouldn't count Tilly's mathematician. The last prisoner of Tilly's whom Alice had been willing to count was Mary, Queen of Scots. This was way back when they were first detained. Tilly was just the tiniest bit irritated by this.

The river drummed, birds cried, and far away Tilly heard the roaring of the male howler monkeys, like rushing water or wind at this distance. Bugs rattled and clicked. Each ordinary sound was a betrayal. How quickly the forest accepted an alien presence. It was like plunging a knife into water; the water re-formed instantly about the blade, the break was an illusion. Of course, the forest had responded to Tilly and Alice in much the same way. And now they were natives, local fauna to an expedition from the stars. Or so Tilly guessed. "Our only revenge," she had told Alice, "is that they're bound to think we're indigenous. We're going to wreak havoc with their data. Centuries from now a full-scale invasion will fail because all calculations will have been based on this tiny error."

Alice had offered two alternative theories. Like Tilly's, they were straight from the tabloids. The first was that their captors were the descendants of space aliens. Marooned in the forest here, they had devolved into their current primitive state. The second was that Tilly and Alice had stumbled into some Darwinian detour on the evolutionary ladder. Something about this particular environment favored embedded eyes and corkscrew fingers. It was a closed gene pool. "And let's keep it closed," Alice had added. She smiled and shook her head at Tilly. Her braids flew. "South American Headshrinking Space Aliens Forced Me to Have Elvis's Baby," Alice said.

At first Alice had kept diary entries of their captivity. She did a series of sketches, being very careful with the proportions. She told Tilly to take pictures but Tilly was afraid, so Alice took them herself with Tilly's cameras. The film sat curled tightly in small dark tubes, waiting to make Alice and Tilly's fortunes when they escaped or were let go or were rescued. Alice had tallied the days in the tent on her graphs and talked as if they would be released soon. There was no way to guess how soon because there was no way to guess why they were being held. Alice fantasized ways to escape. Tilly would have liked to ink the days off on the wall of the tent; this would have been so much more in the classical tradition. Four straight lines and then a slash. A hieroglyphic of the human hand. A celebration of the opposable thumb. Anne Boleyn had six fingers. Tilly wondered how she had marked the walls of her cell.

The door clicked to the side. Tilly sat up with a start. One of them was entering, bent over, her dish in its hands. It was one of the three who had taken Alice. There was no mistaking it, because it wore Tilly's green sweater, the two arms tied round its neck in mock embrace, the body of the sweater draped on its back. The face belonged to a matinee horror monster, maybe the Phantom of the Opera. From the neck to the waist, largely because of her sweater, it could have been any freshman at any eastern university. From the waist down Tilly saw the rest of the sacklike gown, bare legs, bare feet. Monklike, only the legs were hairless. On the dish was a duplication of Tilly's breakfast. She stared at it, hardly able to believe in it. She had never been offered additional food before. The door rattled again as she was left alone. She took a tiny bit of the fish in her fingers. She looked at it. She put it in her mouth. She took another bite. And then another. The food was here, after all. Why shouldn't she eat it just because Alice was so hungry? How would it help Alice not to eat this food? Alice would want her to eat it. She ate faster and faster, licking her fingers. She ate the rind and seeds of the orange. She scraped the fish bones under her sleeping pad.

Alice was pale and tearful when she came back. She lay down, and her breath was a ragged series of quick inhalations. There were no marks on her. There never were. Just an agony about her face. "What did they do to you?" Tilly asked her, and Alice closed her eyes. "I mean, was it different today?" Tilly said. She sat beside Alice and stroked her hair until Alice's breathing had normalized.

Alice had her own question. "Why are they doing this?" Alice asked. Or she didn't ask it. The question was still there. "They don't try to talk to me. They don't ask me anything. I don't know what they want. They just hurt me. They're monsters," said Alice.

And then there was a silence for the other questions they asked only deep inside themselves. Why to me and not to you? Why to you and not to me?

When dinner came that night, there was nothing but crackers for both of them. Alice was given more than Tilly. This had never happened before. "Look at that," she said with the first lilt Tilly had heard in her voice in a long time. "Why do you suppose they are doing that?" She equalized the portions. "They will see that we always share," she told Tilly. "No matter what they do to us."

"I don't want any," Tilly said. "Really. After what they did to you today I'm sure you need food more than I do. Please. You eat it."

It made Alice angry. "You've always shared with me," Alice insisted. "Always. We share." She directed these last words toward the one who stayed to watch them eat. Tilly took the crackers. The sun went down. The birds quieted and the bugs grew louder. Tree frogs sang, incessantly alto. The world outside maintained a dreadful balance. Inside, the tent walls darkened, and they were left alone. Alice lay still. Tilly undressed completely. She climbed into her bag, which smelled of mildew, and missed Steven.

She had to urinate during the night. She waited and waited until she couldn't wait anymore, afraid she would wake Alice. Finally she slid out of her bag and crawled to the empty bucket that sat by the tent door. She tried to tilt the bucket so that the urine would make less noise hitting the bottom, but every sound she made was too loud in this room. Of course Alice would hear her and wonder. Alice rarely used the bucket at all now. Tilly wished she could empty the bucket before Alice saw it. She got back into her sleeping bag and missed Steven until she finally fell asleep, sometime in the morning.

When she woke up, she missed him again. Alice's eyes were

open. "That teacher who killed that doctor," Tilly said. "The diet doctor."

"Jean Harris," said Alice. "I already said her."

"No, you didn't," said Tilly.

"I don't want to play anymore. It was a stupid game and it just upsets me. Why can't you forget it?" Of course the mornings were always tense for Alice. The day's ordeal was still ahead of her. Tilly tried not to mind anything Alice said in the mornings. But the truth was that Alice was often rather rude. Maybe that was why she was treated the way she was. Tilly was not rude, and nobody treated Tilly the way they treated Alice.

"I have another one," said Tilly. There was already a film of sweat on her forehead; the day was going to be hot. She climbed out of her sleeping bag and lay on top of it, wiping her face with the back of her hand. "And you certainly haven't said her. I can't remember her name, but she lived in Wales in the 1800s and she was famous for fasting. She lived for two years without eating food and without drinking water and people said it was a miracle and came to be blessed and brought her family offerings."

Alice said nothing.

"She was a little girl," Tilly said. "She never left her bed. Not for two years."

Alice looked away from her.

"There was a storm of medical controversy. A group of doctors finally insisted that no one could live for two years without food and water. They demanded a round-the-clock vigil. They hired nurses to watch every move the little girl made. Do you know this story?"

Alice was silent.

"The little girl began to starve. It was obvious that she had been eating secretly all along. I mean, of course she had been eating. The doctors all knew this. They begged her to eat now. But they wouldn't go away and let her do it in secret. They were not really very nice men. She refused food. She and her parents refused to admit that it had all been a hoax. The little girl starved to death because no one would admit it had all been a hoax," said Tilly. "What was she a prisoner of? Ask me. Ask me who her jailers were."

Shhh said the door.

"You must be very hungry," said Alice. "Diet doctors and fasting girls. I'm hungry, too. I wish you'd shut up." It wasn't a very nice thing for Alice to say.

Alice was given crackers for breakfast. Tilly had a Cayenne banana and their own dried jerky and some kind of fruit juice. Tilly sat beside Alice and made Alice take a bite every time Tilly took a bite. Alice didn't even thank her. When they finished breakfast, two more of them came and took Alice.

They brought Tilly coffee. There were sugar and limes and tinned sardines. There was a kind of bread Tilly didn't recognize. The loaf was shaped in a series of concentric circles from which the outer layers could be torn one at a time until the loaf was reduced to a single simple circle. It was very beautiful. Tilly was angry at Alice so she ate it all, and while she was eating it she realized for the first time that they loved her. That was why they brought her coffee, baked bread for her. But they didn't love Alice. Was this Tilly's fault? Could Tilly be blamed for this?

Tilly was not even hungry enough to eat the seeds of the

limes. She lifted her pad to hide them with the fish bones. Many of the tiny bones were still attached to the fish's spine, even after Tilly had slept on them all night. It made her think of fairy tales, magic fish bones, and princesses who slept on secrets, and princes who were nice men or maybe they weren't; you really never got to know them at home. She could imagine the fish alive and swimming, one of those transparent fish with their feathered backbones and their trembling green hearts. No one should know you that well; no one should see inside you like that, Tilly thought. That was Alice's mistake, wearing her heart outside the way she did. Telling everybody what she thought of everything. And she was getting worse. Of course she didn't speak anymore, but it was easier and easier to tell what she was thinking. She felt a lot of resentment for Tilly. Tilly couldn't be blind to this. And for what? What had Tilly ever done? This whole holiday had been Alice's idea, not Tilly's. It was all part of Alice's plan to separate Tilly from Steven.

Tilly got out Alice's papers, looking to see if she'd written anything about Tilly in them. But Alice hadn't written anything for a couple of weeks. PD, the last entry ended. PD. Tilly traced it with her index finger. What did that mean?

When Alice came back, Tilly was shocked by the change in her. She was carried in and left, lying on her back on Tilly's mat, which was closer to the door, and she didn't move. She hardly looked like Alice anymore. She was fragile and edgeless, as if she had been rubbed with sandpaper. The old Alice was all edges. The new Alice was all bone. Her bones were more and more evident. It was a great mistake to show yourself so. "What does PD mean?" Tilly asked her.

"Get me some water," Alice whispered.

They kept a bucket full by the door next to the empty bucket which functioned as the toilet. A bug was floating in the drinking water, a large white moth with faint circles painted on its furry wings. If Tilly had seen it fall she would have rescued it. She doubted that Alice would have bothered. Alice was so different now. Alice would have enjoyed seeing the moth drown. Alice wanted everyone to be as miserable as she was. It was the only happiness Alice had. Tilly scooped the dead moth into the cup of water for Alice, to make Alice happy. She held the cup just out of Alice's reach. "First tell me what it means," she said.

Alice lay with her head tilted back. The words moved up and down the length of her throat. Her voice was very tired and soft. *Shhh* said the door. "It's a cartographer's notation." Her eyes were almost closed. In the small space between the lids, Tilly could just see her eyes. Alice was watching the water. "It means position doubtful." Tilly helped her sit up, held the cup so she could drink. Alice lay back on the mat. "Prospects doubtful," said Alice. "Presumed dead," said Alice.

Outside Tilly heard the howler monkeys, closer today. She could almost distinguish one voice from the rest, a dominant pitch, a different rhythm. She had once stood close enough to a tribe of howler monkeys to connect each mouth with its own deafening noise. This was at the zoo in San Diego. In San Diego, Tilly had been the one on the outside.

It was so like Alice to just give up, thought Tilly. Not like Alice before, but certainly like Alice now. Alice now was completely different from Alice before. Living together like this had shown her what Alice was really like. This was probably what the South

American Headshrinking Space Alien Children of the Boto had wanted all along, to see what people were really like.

Well, what did they know now? On the one hand, they had Alice. Alice was completely exposed. No wonder they didn't love Alice.

But on the other hand, they had Tilly. And there was no need to change Tilly. They loved Tilly.

THE FAITHFUL COMPANION AT FORTY

This One Is Also for Queequeg, for Kato, for Spock,

for Tinker Bell, and for Chewbacca.

His first reaction is that I just can't deal with the larger theoretical issues. He's got this new insight he wants to call the Displacement Theory and I can't grasp it. Your basic, quiet, practical minority sidekick. The *limited* edition. Kato. Spock. Me. But this is not true.

I still remember the two general theories we were taught on the reservation which purported to explain the movement of history. The first we named the Great Man Theory. Its thesis was that the critical decisions in human development were made by individuals, special people gifted in personality and circumstance. The second we named the Wave Theory. It argued that only the masses could effectively determine the course of history. Those very visible individuals who appeared as leaders of the great movements were, in fact, only those who happened to articulate the direction which had already been chosen. They were as much the victims of the process as any other single individual. Flotsam. Running Dog and I used to be able to debate this issue for hours.

It is true that this particular question has ceased to interest me much. But a correlative question has come to interest me more. I spent most of my fortieth birthday sitting by myself, listening to Pachelbel's *Canon*, over and over, and I'm asking myself: Are some people special? Are some people more special than others? *Have I spent my whole life backing the wrong horse?*

I mean, it was my birthday and not one damn person called.

Finally, about four o'clock in the afternoon, I gave up and I called him. "Eh, Poncho," I say. "What's happening?"

"Eh, Cisco," he answers. "Happy birthday."

"Thanks," I tell him. I can't decide whether I am more pissed to know he remembered but didn't call than I was when I thought he forgot.

"The big four-o," he says. "Wait a second, buddy. Let me go turn the music down." He's got the *William Tell Overture* blasting on the stereo. He's always got the *William Tell Overture* blasting on the stereo. I'm not saying the man has a problem, but the last time we were in Safeway together he claimed to see a woman being kidnapped by a silver baron over in frozen foods. He pulled the flip top off a Tab and lobbed the can into the ice cream. "Cover me," he shouts, and runs an end pattern with the cart through the soups. I had to tell everyone he was having a Vietnam flashback.

And the mask. There are times and seasons when a mask is useful; I'm the first to admit that. It's Thanksgiving, say, and you're an Indian so it's never been one of your favorite holidays, and you've got no family because you spent your youth playing the supporting role to some macho creep who couldn't commit, so here you are, standing in line to see *Rocky IV*, and someone you know walks by. I mean, I've been there. But for every day, for your ordinary life, a mask is only going to make you *more* obvious. There's an element of exhibitionism in it. A large element. If you ask me.

So now he's back on the phone. He sighs. "God," he says. "I miss those thrilling days of yesteryear."

See? We haven't talked twenty seconds and already the subject is *his* problems. *His* ennui. *His* angst. "I'm having an affair," I tell him. Two years ago I wouldn't have said it. Two years ago he'd just completed his est training and he would have told me to take responsibility for it. Now he's into biofeedback and astrology. Now we're not responsible for anything.

"Yeah?" he says. He thinks for a minute. "You're not married," he points out.

I can't see that this is relevant. "She is," I tell him.

"Yeah?" he says again, only this "yeah" has a nasty quality to it; this "yeah" tells me someone is hoping for sensationalistic details. This is not the "yeah" of a concerned friend. Still, I can't help playing to it. For years I've been holding this man's horse while he leaps onto its back from the roof. For years I've been providing cover from behind a rock while he breaks for the back door. I'm forty now. It's time to get something back from him. So I hint at the use of controlled substances. We're talking peyote *and* cocaine. I mention pornography. Illegally imported. From Denmark. Of course, it's not really *my* affair. Can you picture me? My affair is quiet and ardent. I borrowed this affair from another friend. It shows you the lengths I have to go to before anyone will listen to me.

I may finally have gone too far. He's really at a loss now. "Women," he says finally. "You can't live with them and you can't live without them." Which is a joke, coming from him. He had that single-man-raising-his-orphaned-nephew-all-alone schtick working so smoothly the women were passing each other on the way in and out the door. Or maybe it was the mask and the leather. What do women want? Who has a clue?

"Is that it?" I ask him. "The sum total of your advice? She won't leave her husband. Man, my *heart* is broken."

"Oh," he says. There's a long pause. "Don't let it show," he suggests. Then he sighs. Again. "I miss that old white horse," he tells me. And you know what I do? I hang up on him. And you know what he *doesn't* do? He doesn't call me back.

It really hurts me.

So his second reaction, now that I don't want to listen to him explaining his new theories to me, is to say that I seem to be sulking about something, he can't imagine what. And this is harder to deny.

The day after my birthday I went for a drive in my car, a little white Saab with personalized license plates, KEMO, they say. Maybe the phone is ringing, maybe it's not. I feel better when I don't know. So, he misses his horse. Hey, *I've* never been the same since that little pinto of mine joined the Big Roundup, but I try not to burden my friends with this. I try not to burden my friends with *anything*. I just nurse them back to health when the Cavendish gang leaves them for dead. I just come in the middle of the night with the medicine man when little Britt has a fever and it's not responding to Tylenol. I just organize the surprise party when a friend turns forty.

You want to bet even Attila the Hun had a party on his fortieth? You want to bet he was one hard man to surprise? And who blew up the balloons and had everyone hiding under the rugs and in with the goats? This name is lost forever.

I drove out into the country, where every cactus holds its memory for me, where every outcropping of rock once hid an outlaw. Ten years ago the terrain was still so rough I would have had to take the International Scout. Now it's a paved highway straight to the hanging tree. I pulled over to the shoulder of the road, turned off the motor, and just sat there. I was remembering the time Ms. Peggy Cooper stumbled into the Wilcox bank robbery looking for her little girl who'd gone with friends to the swimming hole and hadn't bothered to tell her mama. We were on our way to see Colonel Davis at Fort Comanche about some cattle rustling. We hadn't heard about the bank robbery. Which is why we were taken completely by surprise.

My pony and I were eating the masked man's dust, as usual, when something hit me from behind. Arnold Wilcox, a heavyset man who sported a five o'clock shadow by eight in the morning, jumped me from the big rock overlooking the Butterfield trail, and I went down like a sack of potatoes. I heard horses converging on us from the left and the right and that hypertrophic white stallion of his took off like a big bird. I laid one on Arnold's stubbly jaw, but he cold-cocked me with the butt of his pistol and I couldn't tell you what happened next.

I don't come to until it's after dark and I'm trussed up like a turkey. Ms. Cooper is next to me, and her hands are tied behind her back with a red bandanna and there's a rope around her feet. She looks disheveled but pretty; her eyes are wide and I can tell she's not too pleased to be lying here next to an Indian. Her dress is buttoned up to the chin so I'm thinking, At least, thank God, they've respected her. It's cold, even as close together as we are. The Wilcoxes are all huddled around the fire, counting money, and the smoke is a straight white line in the sky you could see for miles. So this is more good news, and I'm thinking the Wilcoxes were always a bunch of dumb-ass honkies when it came to your basic woodlore. I'm wondering how they got it together to pull off a bank job, when I hear a horse's hooves and my question is answered. Pierre Cardeaux, Canadian French, hops off the horse's back and goes straight to the fire and stamps it out.

"Imbeciles!" he tells them, only he's got this heavy accent so it comes out "Eembeeceels."

Which insults the Wilcoxes a little. "Hold on there, hombre," Andrew Wilcox says. "Jes' because we followed your plan into the bank and your trail for the getaway doesn't make you the boss here." Pierre pays him about as much notice as you do an ant your horse is about to step on. He comes over to us and puts his hand under Ms. Cooper's chin, sort of thoughtfully. She spits at him and he laughs.

"Spunk," he says. "I like that." I mean, I suppose that's what he says, because that's what they always say, but the truth is, with his accent, I don't understand a word.

Andrew Wilcox isn't finished yet. He's got this big chicken leg he's eating and it's dribbling onto his chin, so he wipes his arm over his face. Which just spreads the grease around more, really, and anyway, he's got this hunk of chicken stuck between his front teeth, so Pierre can hardly keep a straight face when he talks to him. "I understand why we're keeping the woman," Andrew says. "Cause she has—uses. But the Injun there. He's just going to be baggage. I want to waste him."

"Mon ami," says Pierre. "Even *pour vous,* thees stupiditee lives me spitchless." He's kissing his fingers to illustrate the point as if he were really French and not just Canadian French and has probably never drunk really good wine in his life. I'm lying in the dust, and whatever they've bound my wrists with is cutting off the circulation so my hands feel like someone is jabbing them with porcupine needles. Even now, I can remember smelling the smoke which wasn't there anymore and the Wilcoxes who were and the lavender eau de toilette that Ms. Cooper used. And horses and dust and sweat. These were the glory days, but *whose* glory? you may well ask, and even if I answered, what difference would it make?

Ms. Cooper gets a good whiff of Andrew Wilcox, and it makes her cough.

"He's right, little brother," says Russell Wilcox, the runt of the litter at three-hundred-odd pounds and a little quicker on the uptake than the rest of the family. "You ever heared tell of a man who rides a white horse, wears a black mask, and shoots a very pricey kind of bullet? This here Injun is his compadre."

"Oui, oui, oui, oui," says Pierre agreeably. The little piggie. He indicates me and raises his eyebrows one at a time. "*Avec le sauvage* we can, how you say? Meck a deal."

"Votre mère," I tell him. He gives me a good kick in the ribs and he's wearing those pointy-toed kind of cowboy boots, so I feel it, all right. Finally I hear the sound I've been waiting for, a hoot owl over in the trees behind Ms. Cooper, and then *he* rides

up. He hasn't even gotten his gun out yet. "Don't move," he tells Pierre, "or I'll be forced to draw," but he hasn't finished the sentence when Russell Wilcox has his arm around my neck and the point of his knife jabbing into my back.

"We give you the Injun," he says. "Or we give you the girl. You ain't taking both. You comprendez, pardner?"

Now, if he'd *asked* me I'd have said, Hey, don't worry about *me*, rescue the woman. And if he'd hesitated, I would have insisted. But he didn't ask and he didn't hesitate. He just hoisted Ms. Cooper up onto the saddle in front of him and pulled the bottom of her skirt down so her legs didn't show. "There's a little girl in Springfield who's going to be mighty happy to see you, Ms. Cooper," I hear him saying, and I've got a suspicion from the look on her face that they're not going straight to Springfield anyway. And that's it. Not one word for me.

Of course, he comes back, but by this time the Wilcoxes and Pierre have fallen asleep around the cold campfire and I've had to inch my way through the dust on my side like a snake over to Russell Wilcox's knife, which fell out of his hand when he nodded off, whittling. I've had to cut my own bonds, and my hands are behind me so I carve up my thumb a little, too. The whole time I'm right there beneath Russell, and he's snorting and snuffling and shifting around like he's waking up so my heart nearly stops. It's a wonder my hands don't have to be amputated, they've been without blood for so long. And then there's a big shoot-out and I provide a lot of cover. A couple of days pass before I feel like talking to him about it.

"You rescued Ms. Cooper first," I remind him. "And that was the right thing to do, I'm not saying it wasn't; don't misunderstand me. But it seemed to me that you made up your mind kind of quickly. It didn't seem like a hard decision."

He reaches across the saddle and puts a hand on my hand. Behind the black mask the blue eyes are sensitive and caring. "Of course I wanted to rescue you, old friend," he says. "If I'd made the decision based solely on my own desires, that's what I would have done. But it seemed to me I had a higher responsibility to the more innocent party. It was a hard choice. It may have felt quick to you, but, believe me, I struggled with it." He withdraws his hand and kicks his horse a little ahead of us because the trail is narrowing. I duck under the branch of a prairie spruce. "Besides," he says, back over his shoulder, "I couldn't leave a woman with a bunch of animals like Pierre Cardeaux and the Wilcoxes. A pretty woman like that. Alone. Defenseless."

I start to tell him what a bunch of racists like Pierre Cardeaux and the Wilcoxes might do to a lonely and defenseless Indian. Arnold Wilcox wanted my scalp. "*I* remember the Alamo," he kept saying, and maybe he meant Little Big Horn; I didn't feel like exploring this. Pierre kept assuring him there would be plenty of time for trophies later. And Andrew trotted out that old chestnut about the only good Indian being a dead Indian. None of which were pleasant to lie there listening to. But I never said it. Because by then the gap between us was so great I would have had to shout, and anyway the ethnic issue has always made us both a little touchy. I wish I had a nickel for every time I've heard him say that some of his best friends are Indians. And I know there are bad Indians; I don't deny it and I don't mind fighting them. I just always thought I should get to decide which ones were the bad ones.

I sat in that car until sunset.

But the next day he calls. "Have you ever noticed how close the holy word 'om' is to our Western word 'home'?" he asks. That's his opening. No hi, how are you? He never asks how I am. If he did, I'd tell him I was fine, just the way you're supposed to. I wouldn't burden him with my problems. I'd just like to be asked, you know?

But he's got a point to make, and it has something to do with Dorothy in *The Wizard of Oz*. How she clicks her heels together and says, over and over like a mantra, "There's no place like home, there's no place like home" and she's actually able to travel through space. "Not in the book," I tell him.

"I *know*," he says. "In the movie."

"I thought it was the shoes," I say.

And his voice lowers; he's that excited. "What if it was the *words*?" he asks. "I've got a mantra."

Of course, I'm aware of this. It always used to bug me that he wouldn't tell me what it was. Your mantra, he says, loses its power if it's spoken aloud. So by now I'm beginning to guess what his mantra might be. "A bunch of people I know," I tell him, "all had the same guru. And one day they decided to share the mantras he'd given them. They each wrote their mantra on a piece of paper and passed it around. And you know what? They all had the *same* mantra. So much for personalization."

"They lacked faith," he points out.

"Rightfully so."

"I gotta go," he tells me. We're reaching the crescendo in the background music, and it cuts off with a click. Silence. He doesn't say good-bye. I refuse to call him back.

The truth is, I'm tired of always being there for him.

So I don't hear from him again until this morning when he calls with the great Displacement Theory. By now I've been forty almost ten days, if you believe the birth certificate the reservation drew up; I find a lot of inaccuracies surfaced when they translated moons into months, so that I've never been too sure what my rising sign is. Not that it matters to me, but it's important to him all of a sudden; apparently you can't analyze personality effectively without it. He thinks I'm a Pisces rising; he'd love to be proved right.

"We can go *back*, old buddy," he says. "I've found the way back."

"Why would we want to?" I ask. The sun is shining and it's cold out. I was thinking of going for a run.

Does he hear me? About like always. "I figured it out," he says. "It's a combination of biofeedback *and* the mantra 'home.' I've been working and working on it. I could always leave, you know; that was never the problem; but I could never *arrive.* Something outside me stopped me and forced me back." He pauses here, and I think I'm supposed to say something, but I'm too pissed. He goes on. "Am I getting too theoretical for you? Because I'm about to get more so. Try to stay with me. The key word is *displacement.*" He says this like he's shivering. "I couldn't get back because there was no room for me there. The only way back is through an exchange. Someone else has to come forward."

He pauses again, and this pause goes on and on. Finally I grunt. A redskin sound. Noncommittal.

His voice is severe. "This is too important for you to miss just because you're sulking about God knows what, pilgrim," he says. "This is travel through space *and* time."

"This is baloney," I tell him. I'm uncharacteristically blunt, blunter than I ever was during the primal-scream-return-to-the-womb period. If nobody's listening, what does it matter?

"Displacement," he repeats, and his voice is all still and important. "Ask yourself, buddy, *what happened to the buffalo?*"

I don't believe I've heard him correctly. "Say *what?*"

"Return with me," he says, and then he's gone for good and this time he hasn't hung up the phone; this time I can still hear the *William Tell Overture* repeating the hoofbeat part. There's a noise out front so I go to the door, and damned if I don't have a buffalo, shuffling around on my ornamental strawberries, looking surprised. "You call this grass?" it asks me. It looks up and down the street, more and more alarmed. "Where's the plains, man? Where's the railroad?"

So I'm happy for him. Really I am.

But I'm not going with him. Let him roam it alone this time. He'll be fine. Like Rambo.

Only then another buffalo appears. And another. Pretty soon I've got a whole herd of them out front, trying to eat my yard and gagging. And whining. "The water tastes funny. You got any water with locusts in it?" I don't suppose it's an accident that I've got the same number of buffalo here as there are men in the Cavendish gang. Plus one. I keep waiting to see if any more appear; maybe someone else will go back and help him. But they don't. This is it.

You remember the theories of history I told you about, back in the beginning? Well, maybe somewhere between the great men and the masses, there's a third kind of person. Someone who listens. Someone who tries to *help*. You don't hear about these people much, so there probably aren't many of them. Oh, you hear about the failures, all right, the shams: Brutus, John Alden, Rasputin. And maybe you think there aren't any at all, that nobody could love someone else more than he loves himself. Just because *you* can't. Hey, I don't really care what you think. Because I'm here and the heels of my moccasins are clicking together and I couldn't stop them even if I tried. And it's okay. Really. It's who I am. It's what I do.

I'M GOING TO LEAVE YOU with a bit of theory to think about. It's a sort of riddle. There are good Indians, there are bad Indians, and there are dead Indians. Which am I?

There can be more than one right answer.

THE BREW

I spent last Christmas in The Hague. I hadn't wanted to be in a foreign country and away from the family at Christmastime, but it happened. Once I was there I found it lonely but also pleasantly insulated. The streets were strung with lights and it rained often, so the lights reflected off the shiny cobblestones, came at you out of the clouds like pale, golden bubbles. If you could ignore the damp, you felt wrapped in cotton, wrapped against breaking. I heightened the feeling by stopping in an ice cream shop for a cup of tea with rum.

Of course it was an illusion. Ever since I was young, whenever I have traveled, my mother has contrived to have a letter sent, usually waiting for me, sometimes a day or two behind my arrival. I am her only daughter and she was not the sort to let an illness stop her, and so the letter was at the hotel when I returned from my tea. It was a very cheerful letter, very loving, and the message that it was probably the last letter I would get from her and that I needed to finish things up and hurry home was nowhere on the page but only in my heart. She sent some funny family stories and some small-town gossip, and the death she talked about was not her own but belonged instead to an old man who was once a neighbor of ours.

After I read the letter I wanted to go out again, to see if I could recover the mood of the mists and the golden lights. I tried. I walked for hours, wandering in and out of the clouds, out to the canals and into the stores. Although my own children are too old for toys and too young for grandchildren, I did a lot of window shopping at the toy stores. I was puzzling over the black elf they have in Holland, St. Nicholas's sidekick, wondering who he was and where he came into it all, when I saw a music box. It was a glass globe on a wooden base, and if you wound it, it played music, and if you shook it, it snowed. Inside the globe there was a tiny forest of ceramic trees and, in the center, a unicorn with a silver horn, corkscrewed, like a narwhal's, and one gaily bent foreleg. A unicorn, tinted blue and frolicking in the snow.

What appealed to me most about the music box was not the snow or the unicorn but the size. It was a little world, all enclosed, and I could imagine it as a real place, a place I could go. A little winter. There was an aquarium in the lobby of my hotel, and I had a similar reaction to it. A little piece of ocean there, in the dry land of the lobby. Sometimes we can find a smaller world where we can live, inside the bigger world where we cannot.

Otherwise the store was filled with items tied in to *The Lion King*. Less enchanting items to my mind—why is it that children always side with the aristocracy? Little royalists, each and every one of us, until we grow up and find ourselves in the cubicle or the scullery. And even then there's a sense of injustice about it all. Someone belongs there, but surely not us.

I'm going to tell you a secret, something I have never told anyone before. I took an oath when I was seventeen years old and have never broken it, although I cannot, in general, be trusted with secrets and usually try to warn people of this before they confide in me. But the oath was about the man who died, my old neighbor, and so I am no longer bound to it. The secret takes the form of a story.

I should warn you that parts of the story will be hard to believe. Parts of it are not much to my credit, but I don't suppose you'll have trouble believing those. It's a big story, and this is just a small piece of it, my piece, which ends with my mother's letter and The Hague and the unicorn music box.

It begins in Bloomington, Indiana, the year I turned ten. It snowed early and often that year. My friend Bobby and I built caves of snow, choirs of snowmen, and bridges that collapsed if you ever tried to actually walk them.

We had a neighbor who lived next door to me and across the street from Bobby. His name was John McBean. Until that year McBean had been a figure of almost no interest to us. He didn't care for children much, and why should he? Behind his back we called him Rudolph, because he had a large purplish nose, and cold weather whitened the rest of his face into paste so his nose stood out in startling contrast. He had no wife, no family that we were aware of. People used to pity that back then. He seemed to us quite an old man, grandfather age, but we were children, what did we know? Even now I have no idea what he did for a living. He was retired when I knew him, but I have no idea of what he was retired from. Work, such as our fathers did, was nothing very interesting, nothing to speculate on. We thought the name McBean rather funny, and then he was quite the skinflint, which struck us all, even our parents, as delightful, since he actually was Scottish. It gave rise to many jokes, limp, in retrospect, but pretty rich back then.

One afternoon that year Mr. McBean slipped in his icy yard. He went down with a roar. My father ran out to him, but as my father was helping him up, McBean tried to hit him in the chin. My father came home much amused. "He said I was a British spy," my father told my mother.

"You devil," she said. She kissed him.

He kissed her back. "It had something to do with Bonnie Prince Charlie. He wants to see a Stuart on the throne of England. He seemed to think I was preventing it."

As luck would have it, this was also the year that Disney ran a television episode on the Great Pretender. I have a vague picture in my mind of a British actor—the same one who appeared with Hayley Mills in *The Moon-Spinners.* Whatever happened to him, whoever he was?

So Bobby and I gave up the ever popular game of World War II and began instead, for a brief period, to play at being Jacobites. The struggle for the throne of England involved less direct confrontation, fewer sound effects, and less running about. It was a game of stealth, of hiding and escaping, altogether a more adult activity.

It was my idea to break into the McBean cellar as a covert operation on behalf of the prince. I was interested in the cellar, having begun to note how often and at what odd hours McBean went down there. The cellar window could be seen from my bedroom. Once I rose late at night, and in the short time I watched, the light went on and off three times. It seemed a signal. I told Bobby that Mr. McBean might be holding the prince captive down there and that we should go and see. This plan added a real sense of danger to our imaginary game, without, we thought, actually putting us into peril.

The cellar door was set at an incline, and such were the times that it shocked us to try it and find it locked. Bobby thought he could fit through the little window, whose latch could be lifted with a pencil. If he couldn't, I certainly could, though I was desperately hoping it wouldn't come to that—already at age ten I was more of an idea person. Bobby had the spirit. So I offered to go around the front and distract Mr. McBean long enough for Bobby to try the window. I believe that I said he shouldn't actually enter, that we would save that for a time when McBean was away. That's the way I remember it, my saying that.

And I remember that it had just snowed again, a fresh white powder and a north wind, so the snow blew off the trees as if it were still coming down. It was bright, one of those paradoxical days of sun and ice, and so much light everything was drowned in it so you stumbled about as if there were no light at all. My scarf was iced with breath and my footprints were as large as a man's. I knocked at the front door, but my mittens muffled the sound. It took several tries and much pounding before Mr. McBean answered, too long to be accounted for simply by the mittens. When he did answer, he did it without opening the door.

"Go on with you," he said. "This is not a good time."

"Would you like your walk shoveled?" I asked him.

"A slip of a girl like you? You couldn't even lift the shovel." I imagine there is a tone, an expression, that would make this response affectionate, but Mr. McBean affected neither. He opened the door enough to tower over me with his blue nose, his gluey face, and the clenched set of his mouth.

"Bobby would help me. Thirty cents."

"Thirty cents! And that's the idlest boy God ever created. Thirty cents?"

"Since it's to be split. Fifteen cents each."

The door was closing again.

"Twenty cents."

"I've been shoveling my own walk long enough. No reason to stop."

The door clicked shut. The whole exchange had taken less than a minute. I stood undecidedly at the door for another minute, then stepped off the porch, into the yard. I walked around the back. I got there just in time to see the cellar light go on. The window was open. Bobby was gone.

I stood outside, but there was a wind, as I've said, and I couldn't hear and it was so bright outside and so dim within, I could hardly see. I knew that Bobby was inside, because there were no footprints leading away but my own. I had looked through the window on other occasions so I knew the light was a single bulb, hanging by its neck like a turnip, and that there were many objects between me and it, old and broken furniture, rusted tools, lawn mowers and rakes, boxes piled into stairs. I waited. I think I waited a very long time. The light went out. I waited some more. I moved to a tree, using it as a windbreak until finally it was clear there was no point in waiting any longer. Then I ran home, my face stinging with cold and tears, into our living room, where my mother pulled off my stiff scarf and rubbed my hands until the pins came into them. She made me cocoa with marshmallows. I would like you to believe that the next few hours were a very bad time for me, that I suffered a good deal more than Bobby did.

That case being so hard to make persuasively, I will tell you instead what was happening to him.

BOBBY DID, INDEED, manage to wiggle in through the window, although it was hard enough to give him some pause as to how he would get out again. He landed on a stack of wooden crates, conveniently offset so that he could descend them like steps. Everywhere was cobwebs and dust; it was too dark to see this, but he could feel it and smell it. He was groping his way forward, hand over hand, when he heard the door at the top of the stairs. At the very moment the light went on, he found himself looking down the empty eye slit of a suit of armor. It made him gasp; he couldn't help it. So he heard the footsteps on the stairs stop suddenly and then begin again, wary now. He hid himself behind a barrel. He thought maybe he'd escape notice—there was so much stuff in the cellar and the light so dim—and that was the worst time, those moments when he thought he might make it, much worse than what came next, when he found himself staring into the cracked and reddened eyes of Mr. McBean.

"What the devil are you doing?" McBean asked. He had a smoky, startled voice. "You've no business down here."

"I was just playing a game," Bobby told him, but he didn't seem to hear.

"Who sent you? What did they tell you?"

He seemed to be frightened—of Bobby!—and angry, and that was to be expected, but there was something else that began to dawn on Bobby only slowly. His accent had thickened with every word. Mr. McBean was deadly drunk. He reached into Bobby's hiding place and hauled him out of it, and his breath, as Bobby came closer, was as ripe as spoiled apples.

"We were playing at putting a Stuart on the throne," Bobby told him, imagining he could sympathize with this, but it seemed to be the wrong thing to say.

He pulled Bobby by the arm to the stairs. "Up we go."

"I have to be home by dinner." By now Bobby was very frightened.

"We'll see. I have to think what's to be done with you," said McBean.

They reached the door, then moved on into the living room, where they sat for a long time in silence while McBean's eyes turned redder and redder and his fingers pinched into Bobby's arm. With his free hand, he drank. Perhaps this is what kept him warm, for the house was very cold and Bobby was glad he still had his coat on. Bobby was both trembling and shivering.

"Who told you about Prince Charlie?" McBean asked finally. "What did they say to you?" So Bobby told him what he knew, the Disney version, long as he could make it, waiting of course, for me to do something, to send someone. McBean made the story longer by interrupting with suspicious and skeptical questions. Eventually the questions ceased and his grip loosened. Bobby hoped he might be falling asleep. His eyes were lowered. But when Bobby stopped talking, McBean shook himself awake, and his hand was a clamp on Bobby's forearm again. "What a load of treacle." His voice filled with contemptuous spit. "It was nothing like that."

He stared at Bobby for a moment and then past him.

"I've never told this story before," he said, and the pupils of his eyes were as empty and dark as the slit in the armor. "No doubt I shall regret telling it now."

IN THE DAYS of the bonnie prince, the head of the McBane clan was the charismatic Ian McBane. Ian was a man with many talents, all of which he had honed and refined over the fifty-odd years he had lived so far. He was a botanist, an orientalist, a poet, and a master brewer. He was also a godly man, a paragon, perhaps. At least in this story. To be godly is a hard thing and may create a hard man. A godly man is not necessarily a kindly man, although he can be, of course.

Now in those days, the woods and caves of Scotland were filled with witches; the church waged constant battle. Some of them were old and haggish, but others were mortally beautiful. The two words go together, mind you, mortal and beautiful. Nothing is so beautiful as that which will fade.

These witches were well aware of Ian McBane. They envied him his skills in the brewery, coveted his knowledge of chemistry. They themselves were always boiling and stirring, but they could only do what they knew how to do. Besides, his godliness irked them. Many times they sent the most beautiful among them, tricked out further with charms and incantations, to visit Ian McBane in his bedchamber and offer what they could offer in return for expert advice. They were so touching in their eagerness for knowledge, so unaware of their own desirability. They had the perfection of dreams. But Ian, who was after all fifty and not twenty, withstood them.

All of Scotland was hoping to see Charles Edward Stuart on the throne, and from hopes they progressed to rumors and from rumors to sightings. Then came the great victory at Falkirk. Naturally, Ian wished to do his part and naturally, being a man of influence and standing, his part must be a large one. It was the sin of ambition which gave the witches an opening.

This time the woman they sent was not young and beautiful but old and sweet. She was everyone's mother. She wore a scarf on her hair and her stockings rolled at her ankles. Blue rivers ran just beneath the skin of her legs. Out of her sleeve she drew a leather pouch.

"From the end of the world," she said. "Brought me by a black warrior riding a white elephant, carried over mountains and across oceans." She made it a lullaby. Ian was drowsy when she finished. So she took his hand and emptied the pouch into his palm, closing it for him. When he opened his hand, he held the curled shards and splinters of a unicorn's horn.

Ian had never seen a unicorn's horn before, although he knew that the king of Denmark had an entire throne made of them. A unicorn's horn is a thing of power. It purifies water, nullifies poison. The witch reached out to Ian, slit his thumb with her one long nail, so his thumb ran blood. Then she touched the wound with a piece of horn. His thumb healed before his eyes, healed as if it had never been cut, the blood running back inside, the cut sealing over like water.

In return Ian gave the witch what she asked. He had given her his godliness, too, but he didn't know this at the time. When the witch was gone, Ian took the horn and ground it into dust. He subjected it to one more test of authenticity. He mixed a few grains into a hemlock concoction and fed it to his cat, stroking it down her throat. The cat followed the hemlock with a saucer of milk, which she wiped, purring, from her whiskers.

Ian had already put down a very fine single malt whiskey, many bottles, enough for the entire McBane clan to toast the coronation of Charles Stuart. It was golden in color and 90 proof, enough to make a large man feel larger without incapacitating him. Ian added a few pinches of the horn to every bottle. The whiskey color shattered and then vanished, so the standing bottle was filled with liquid the color of rainwater, but if you shook it, it pearled like the sea. Ian bottled his brew with a unicorn label, the unicorn enraged, two hooves slicing the air.

Have you ever heard of the American ghost dancers? The Boxers of China? Same sort of thing here. Ian distributed his whiskey to the McBanes before they marched off to Culloden. Ian assured them that the drink, taken just before the battle, would make them invulnerable. Sword wounds would seal up overnight; bullets would pass through flesh as if it were air.

I don't suppose your Disney says very much about Culloden. A massacre is a hard thing to set to music. Certainly they tell no stories and sing no songs about the McBanes that day. Davie McBane was the first to go, reeling about drunkenly and falling beneath one of the McBanes' own horses. Little Angus went next, shouting and racing down the top of a small hill, but before he could strike a single blow for Scotland, a dozen arrows jutted from him at all points. His name was a joke and he made a big, fat target. His youngest brother, Robbie, a boy of only fifteen years, followed Angus in, and so delirious with whiskey that he wore no helmet and carried no weapon. His stomach was split open like a purse. An hour later, only two of the McBanes still lived. The rest had died grotesquely, humorously, without accounting for a single enemy death.

When news reached home, the McBane wives and daughters armed themselves with kitchen knives and went in search of Ian. They thought he had lied about the unicorn horn; they thought he had knowingly substituted the inferior tooth of a fish instead. Ian was already gone, and with enough time and forethought to have removed every bottle of the unicorn brew and taken it with him. This confirmed the women's suspicions, but the real explanation was different. Ian had every expectation the whiskey would work. When the McBanes returned, he didn't wish to share any more of it.

The women set fire to his home and his brewery. Ian saw it from a distance, from a boat at sea, exploding into the sky like a star. The women dumped every bottle of whiskey they found until the rivers bubbled and the fish swam upside down. But none of the whiskey bore the unicorn label. Ian was never seen or heard from again.

"Whiskey is subtle stuff. It's good for heartache; it works a treat against shame. But, even laced with unicorn horn, it cannot mend a man who has been split in two by a sword stroke. It cannot mend a man who no longer has a head. It cannot mend a man with a dozen arrows growing from his body like extra arms. It cannot give a man back his soul."

The story seemed to be over, although Prince Charles had

never appeared in it. Bobby had no feeling left in his hand. "I see," he said politely.

McBean shook him once, then released him. He fetched a pipe. When he lit a match, he held it to his mouth and his breath flamed like a dragon's. "What will I do to you if you tell anyone?" he asked Bobby. This was a rhetorical question. He continued without pausing. "Something bad. Something so bad you'd have to be an adult even to imagine it."

SO BOBBY TOLD ME none of this. I didn't see him again that day. He did not come by, and when I finally went over, his mother told me he was home, but that he was not feeling well, had gone to bed. "Don't worry," she said, in response, I suppose, to the look on my face. "Just a chill. Nothing to worry about."

He missed school the next day and the next after that. When I finally saw him, he was casual. Offhand. As if it had all happened so long ago he had forgotten. "He caught me," Bobby said. "He was very angry. That's all. We better not do it again."

It was the end of our efforts to put a Stuart on the throne. There are days, I admit, when I'm seeing the dentist and I pick up *People* in the waiting room and there they are, the current sad little lot of Windsors, and I have a twinge of guilt. I just didn't care enough to see it through. I enjoyed Charles and Diana's wedding as much as the next person. How was I to know?

Bobby and I were less and less friends after that. It didn't happen all at once, but bit by bit, over the summer mostly. Sex came between us. Bobby went off and joined Little League. He turned out to be really good at it, and he met a lot of boys who didn't live so near to us but had houses he could bike to. He dumped me, which hurt in an impersonal, inevitable way. I believed I had brought it on myself, leaving him that day, going home to a warm house and never saying a word to anyone. At that age, at that time, I did not believe this was something a boy would have done.

So Bobby and I continued to attend the same school and see each other about in our yards, and play sometimes when the game was big and involved other people as well. I grew up enough to understand what our parents thought of McBean, that he was often drunk. This was what had made his nose purple and made him rave about the Stuarts and made him slip in his snowy yard, his arms flapping like wings as he fell. "It's a miracle," my mother said, "that he never breaks a bone." But nothing much more happened between Bobby and me until the year we turned sixteen, me in February, him in May.

He was tired a lot that year and developed such alarming bruises under his eyes that his parents took him to a doctor who sent him right away to a different doctor. At dinner a few weeks later, my mother said she had something to tell me. Her eyes were shiny and her voice was coarse. "Bobby has leukemia," she said.

"He'll get better," I said quickly. Partly I was asking, but mostly I was warning her not to tell me differently. I leaned into her and she must have thought it was for comfort, but it wasn't. I did it so I wouldn't be able to see her face. She put her arm around me, and I felt her tears falling on the top of my hair.

Bobby had to go to Indianapolis for treatments. Spring came, and summer, and he missed the baseball season. Fall, and he had to drop out of school. I didn't see him much, but his mother was over for coffee sometimes, and she had grown sickly herself, sad and thin and gray. "We have to hope," I heard her telling my mother. "The doctor says he is doing as well as we could expect. We're very encouraged." Her voice trembled defiantly.

Bobby's friends came often to visit; I saw them trooping up the porch, all vibrant and healthy, stamping the slush off their boots and trailing their scarves. They went in noisy, left quiet. Sometimes I went with them. Everyone loved Bobby, though he lost his hair and swelled like a beached seal and it was hard to remember that you were looking at a gifted athlete, or even a boy.

Spring came again, but after a few weeks of it, winter returned suddenly with a strange storm. In the morning when I left for school, I saw a new bud completely encased in ice, and three dead birds whose feet had frozen to the telephone wires. This was the day Arnold Becker gave me the message that Bobby wanted to see me. "Right away," Arnie said. "This afternoon. And just you. None of your girlfriends with you."

In the old days Bobby and I used to climb in and out each other's windows, but this was for good times and for intimacy; I didn't even consider it. I went to the front door and let his mother show me to his room as if I didn't even know the way. Bobby lay in his bed, with his puffy face and a new tube sticking into his nose and down his throat. There was a strong, strange odor in the room. I was afraid it was Bobby and wished not to get close enough to see.

He had sores in his mouth, his mother had explained to me. It was difficult for him to eat or even to talk. "You do the talking," she suggested. But I couldn't think of anything to say.

And anyway, Bobby came right to the point. "Do you remember," he asked me, "that day in the McBean cellar?" Talking was an obvious effort. It made him breathe hard, as if he'd been running.

Truthfully, I didn't remember. Apparently I had worked to forget it. I remember it now, but at the time, I didn't know what he was talking about.

"Bonnie Prince Charlie," he said, with an impatient rasp so I thought he was delirious. "I need you to go back. I need you to bring me a bottle of whiskey from McBean's cellar. There's a unicorn on the label."

"Why do you want whiskey?"

"Don't ask McBean. He'll never give it to you. Just take it. You would still fit through the window."

"Why do you want whiskey?"

"The unicorn label. Very important. Maybe," said Bobby, "I just want to taste one really good whiskey before I die. You do this and I'll owe you forever. You'll save my life."

He was exhausted. I went home. I did not plan to break into McBean's cellar. It was a mad request from a delusional boy. It saddened me, but I felt no obligation. I did think I could get him some whiskey. I had some money, I would spare no expense. But I was underage. I ate my dinner and tried to think who I could get to buy me liquor, who would do it, and who would even know a fine whiskey if they saw one. And while I was working out the problem I began, bit by bit, piece by piece, bite by bite, to remember. First I remembered the snow, remembered standing by the tree watching the cellar window with snow swirling around me. Then I remembered offering to shovel the walk. I remembered the footprints leading into the cellar window. It took all of dinner, most of the time when I was falling asleep, some concentrated sessions when I woke during the night. By morning, when the sky was light again, I remembered it completely.

It had been my idea and then I had let Bobby execute it and then I had abandoned him. I left him there that day and in another story, someone else's story, he was tortured or raped or even killed and eaten, although you'd have to be an adult to believe in these possibilities. The whole time he was in the McBean house I was lying on my bed and worrying about him, thinking, Boy, he's really going to get it, but mostly worrying what I could tell my parents that would be plausible and would keep me out of it. The only way I could think of to make it right was to do as he'd asked and break into the cellar again.

I also got caught, got caught right off. There was a trap. I tripped a wire rigged to a stack of boards; they fell with an enormous clatter and McBean was there, just as he'd been for Bobby, with those awful cavernous eyes, before I could make it back out the window.

"Who sent you?" he shouted at me. "What are you looking for?"

So I told him.

"That sneaking, thieving, lying boy," said McBean. "It's a lie, what he's said. How could it be true? And anyway, I couldn't spare it." I could see, behind him, the bottles with the unicorn label. There were half a dozen of them. All I asked was for one.

"He's a wonderful boy." I found myself crying.

"Get out," said McBean. "The way you came. The window."

"He's dying," I said. "And he's my best friend." I crawled back out, while McBean stood and watched me, and walked back home with a face filled with tears. I was not giving up. There was another dinner I didn't eat and another night I didn't sleep. In the morning it was snowing, as if spring had never come. I planned to cut class and break into the cellar again. This time I would be looking for traps. But as I passed McBean's house, carrying my books and pretending to be on my way to school, I heard his front door.

"Come here," McBean called angrily from his porch. He gave me a bottle, wrapped in red tissue. "There," he said. "Take it." He went back inside, but as I left he called again from behind the door. "Bring back what he doesn't drink. What's left is mine. It's mine, remember." And at that exact moment, the snow turned to rain.

For this trip I used the old window route. Bobby was almost past swallowing. I had to tip it from a spoon into his throat and the top of his mouth was covered with sores, so it burned him badly. One spoonful was all he could bear. But I came back the next day and repeated it, and the next, and by the fourth he could take it easily, and after a week he was eating again, and after two weeks I could see that he was going to live, just by looking in his mother's face. "He almost died of the cure," she told me. "The chemo. But we've done it. We've turned the corner." I left her thanking God and went into Bobby's room, where he was sitting up and looking like a boy again. I returned half the bottle to McBean.

"Did you spill any?" he asked angrily, taking it back. "Don't tell me it took so much."

And one night that next summer, in Bryan's Park with the firecrackers going off above us, Bobby and I sat on a blanket and he told me McBean's story.

WE FINISHED SCHOOL and graduated. I went to IU, but Bobby went to college in Boston and settled there. Sex came between us again. He came home once to tell his mother and father that he was gay and then took off like the whole town burned to the touch.

Bobby was the first person that I loved and lost, although there have, of course, been others since. Twenty-five years later I tracked him down and we had a dinner together. We were awkward with each other; the evening wasn't a great success. He tried to explain to me why he had left, as an apology for dumping me again. "It was just so hard to put the two lives together. At the time I felt that the first life was just a lie. I felt that everyone who loved me had been lied to. But now—being gay seems to be all I am sometimes. Now sometimes I want someplace where I can get away from it. Someplace where I'm just Bobby again. That turned out to be real, too." He was not meeting my eyes, and then suddenly he was. "In the last five years I've lost twenty-eight of my friends."

"Are you all right?" I asked him.

"No. But if you mean, do I have AIDS, no, I don't. I should, I think, but I don't. I can't explain it."

There was a candle between us on the table. It flickered ghosts into his eyes. "You mean the whiskey," I said.

"Yeah. That's what I mean."

The whiskey had seemed easy to believe in when I was seventeen and Bobby had just had a miraculous recovery and the snow had turned to rain. I hadn't believed in it much since. I hadn't supposed Bobby had either, because if he did then I really had saved his life back then and you don't leave a person who saves your life without a word. Those unicorn horns you read about in Europe and Scandinavia. They all turned out to be from narwhals. They were brought in by the Vikings through China. I've read a bit about it. Sometimes, someone just gets a miracle. Why not you? "You haven't seen Mr. McBean lately," I said. "He's getting old. Really old. Deadly old."

"I know," said Bobby, but the conclusion he drew was not the same as mine. "Believe me, I know. That whiskey is gone. I'd have been there to get it if it wasn't. I'd have been there twenty-eight times."

Bobby leaned forward and blew the candle out. "Remember when we wanted to live forever?" he asked me. "What made us think that was such a great idea?"

I NEVER WENT inside the toy store in The Hague. I don't know what the music box played, "Edelweiss," perhaps, or "Lara's Theme," nothing to do with me. I didn't want to risk the strong sense I had that it had been put there for me—had traveled whatever travels, just to be there in that store window for me to see at that particular moment—with any evidence to the contrary. I didn't want to expose my own fragile magic to the light of day.

Certainly I didn't buy it. I didn't need to. It was already mine, only not here, not now. Not as something I bought for myself, on an afternoon *by* myself, in a foreign country with my mother dying a world away. But as something I found one Christmas morning, wrapped in red paper. I stood looking through the glass and wished that Bobby and I were still friends. That he knew me well enough to have bought me the music box as a gift.

And then I didn't wish that at all. Already I have too many friends, care too much about too many people, have exposed myself to loss on too many sides. I could never have imagined as a child how much it could hurt you to love people. It takes an adult to imagine such a thing. And that's the end of my story.

If I envy anything about McBean now, it is his solitude. But no, that's not really what I wish for either. When I was seventeen I thought McBean was a drunk because he had to have the whiskey so often. Now, when I believe in the whiskey at all, I think, like Bobby, that drinking was just the only way to live through living forever.

LILY RED

One day Lily decided to be someone else. Someone with a past. It was an affliction of hers, wanting this. The desire was seldom triggered by any actual incident or complaint but seemed instead to be related to the act or prospect of lateral movement. She felt it every time a train passed. She would have traded places instantly with any person on any train. She felt it often in the car. She drove onto the freeway that ran between her job and her house, and she thought about driving right past her exit and stopping in some small town wherever she happened to run out of gas, and the next thing she knew, that was exactly what she had done.

Except that she was stopped by the police instead. She was well beyond the city; she had been through several cities, and the sky had darkened. The landscape flattened and she fell into a drowsy rhythm in which she and the car were both passengers in a small, impellent world defined by her headlights. It was something of a shock to have to stop. She sat in her car while the police light rotated behind her, and at regular intervals she watched her hands turn red on the steering wheel. She had never been stopped by the police before. In the rearview mirror she could see the policeman talking to his radio. His door was slightly open; the light was on inside his car. He got out and came to talk to her. She turned her motor off. "Lady," he said, and she wondered if policemen on television always called women *lady* because that was what real policemen did, or if he had learned this watching television just as she had. "Lady, you were flying. I clocked you at eighty."

Eighty. Lily couldn't help but be slightly impressed. She had been twenty-five miles per hour over the limit without even realizing she was speeding. It suggested she could handle even faster speeds. "Eighty," she said contritely. "You know what I think I should do? I think I've been driving too long, and I think I should just find a place to stay tonight. I think that would be best. I mean, eighty. That's too fast. Don't you think?"

"I really do." The policeman removed a pen from the pocket inside his jacket.

"I won't do it again," Lily told him. "Please don't give me a ticket."

"I could spare you the ticket," the policeman said, "and I could read in the paper tomorrow that you smashed yourself into a retaining wall not fifteen miles from here. I don't think I could live with myself. Give me your license. Just take it out of the wallet, please. Mattie Drake runs a little bed-and-breakfast place in Two Trees. You want the next exit and bear left. First right, first right again. Street dead-ends in Mattie's driveway. There's a sign on the lawn: MATTIE'S. Should be all lit up this time of night. It's a nice place and doesn't cost too much in the off season." He handed Lily back her license and the ticket for her to sign. He took his copy. "Get a good night's sleep," he said, and in the silence she heard his boots scattering gravel from the shoulder of the road as he walked away.

She crumpled the ticket into the glove compartment and waited for him to leave. He shut off the rotating light, turned on the headlights, and outwaited her. He followed all the way to the next exit. So Lily had to take it.

She parked her car on the edge of Mattie's lawn. Moths circled the lights on the sign and on the porch. A large white owl slid through the dusky air, transformed by the lights beneath it into something angelic. A cricket landed on the sleeve of her linen suit. The sprinklers went on suddenly; the watery hiss erased the hum of insects, but the pathway to the door remained dry. Lily stood on the lighted porch and rang the bell.

The woman who answered wore blue jeans and a flannel shirt. She had the angular hips of an older woman, but her hair showed very little gray, just a small patch right at the forehead. "Come in, darling," she said. There was a faint southern softness in her voice. "You look tired. Do you want a room? Have you come to see the caves? I'm Mattie."

"Yes, of course," Lily told her. "I need a room. I met some people who were here last year. You really *have* to see these caves, they told me."

"I'll have Katherine pack you a lunch if you like," Mattie offered. "It's beautiful hiking weather. You won't get nearly so hot as in the summer. You can go tomorrow."

Lily borrowed the phone in the living room to call David. It sat on a small table between a glass ball with a single red rosebud frozen inside and a picture of the Virgin praying. The Virgin wore a blue mantilla and appeared to be suspended in a cloudless sky. The phone had a dial which Lily spun. She was so used to the tune their number made on the touch phone at work that she missed hearing it. She listened to the answering machine, heard her voice which sounded nothing like her voice, suggesting that she leave a message. "I'm in Two Trees at Mattie's bed-and-breakfast," she said. "I had this sudden impulse to see the caves. I may stay a couple of days. Will you call Harriet and tell her I won't be in tomorrow? It's real slow. There won't be a problem." She would have told David she missed him, but she ran out of time. She would have only said it out of politeness anyway. They had been married nine years. She would miss him later. She would begin to miss him when she began to miss herself. He might be missing her, too, just about then. It would be nice if all these things happened at the same time.

She took the key from Mattie, went upstairs, used the bathroom at the end of the hall, used someone else's toothbrush, rinsing it out repeatedly afterward, unlocked her door, removed all her clothes, and cried until she fell asleep.

In the morning Lily lay in bed and watched the sun stretch over the quilt and onto the skin of her arms and her hands. She looked around the room. The bed was narrow and had a headpiece made of iron. A pattern of small pink flowers papered the walls. On the bookcase next to the bed a china lady held a china umbrella with one hand and extended the other, palm up, to see if the rain had stopped. There were books. *Beauty's Secret*, one of them said on the spine. Lily opened it, but it turned out to be about horses.

A full-length mirror hung on the back of the bedroom door. Lily didn't notice until the sunlight touched its surface, doubling in brightness. She rose and stood in front of it, backlit by the sunny window, frontlit by the mirror so that she could hardly see. She leaned in closer. Last night's crying had left her eyes red and the lids swollen. She looked at herself for a long time, squinting and changing the angle. Who was she? There was absolutely no way to tell.

The smell of coffee came up the stairs and through the shut door. Lily found her clothes on the desk chair where she had left them. She put them on: stockings, a fuchsia blouse, an eggshell business suit, heels. She used the bathroom, someone else's hairbrush as well as someone else's toothbrush, and came downstairs.

"You can't go hiking dressed like that," Mattie told her, and of course Lily couldn't. "You have nothing else? What size shoe do you wear? A six and a half? Six? Tiny little thing, aren't you? Katherine might have something that will do." She raised her voice. "Katherine? Katherine!"

Katherine came through the doorway at the bottom of the stairs, drying her hands on a dish towel. She was somewhat younger than Mattie though older than Lily, middle forties, perhaps, and heavier, a dark-skinned woman with straight black hair. On request she produced jeans for Lily, a sleeveless T-shirt, a red sweatshirt, gray socks, and sneakers. Everything was too big for Lily. Everything was wearable.

Mattie took her through the screen door and out the back porch after breakfast. Beyond the edge of Mattie's sprinklers, the lawn stopped abruptly at a hill of sand and manzanita. Mattie had stowed a lunch and a canteen in a yellow day pack. She began to help Lily into it. "You go up," Mattie said. "All the way up. And then down. You can see the trail from the other side of the fence. Watch for rattlers. You hiked much?" Lily was having trouble slipping her left arm under the second strap. It caught at the elbow, her arm pinned behind her. Mattie eased the pack off and began again.

"Oh, yes," Lily assured her. "I've hiked a lot." Mattie looked unconvinced. "I'm a rock climber," said Lily. "That's the kind of hiking I'm used to. Crampons and ropes and mallets. I don't usually wear them on my back. I wear them on my belt. I take groups out. Librarians and schoolteachers and beauticians. You know."

"Well, there's just a trail here," said Mattie doubtfully. "I don't suppose you can get into trouble as long as you stay on the trail. Your shoes don't really fit well. I'm afraid you'll blister."

"I once spent three days alone in the woods without food or shelter and it snowed. I was getting a merit badge." The day pack was finally in place. "Thank you," Lily said.

"Wait here. I'm going to get some moleskin for your feet. And I'm going to send Jep along with you. Jep has a lot of common sense. And Jep knows the way. You'll be glad of the company," Mattie told her. She disappeared back into the house.

"It was in Borneo," Lily said softly, so that Mattie wouldn't hear. "You want to talk about blisters. You try walking in the snows of Borneo."

Jep turned out to be a young collie. One ear flopped over in proper collie fashion. One pointed up like a shepherd's. "I've heard some nice things about you," Lily told him. He followed

Lily out to the gate and then took the lead, his tail and hindquarters moving from side to side with every step. He set an easy pace. The trail was unambiguous. The weather was cool when they started. In an hour or so, Lily removed her sweatshirt and Jep's tongue drooped from his mouth. Everyone felt good.

The sun was not yet overhead when Lily stopped for lunch. "Eleven twenty-two," she told Jep. "Judging solely by the sun." Katherine had packed apple juice and cold chicken and an orange with a seam cut into the peel and a chocolate Hostess cupcake with a cream center for dessert. Lily had not seen a cupcake like that since she had stopped taking a lunch to school. She sat with her back against a rock overhang and shared it with Jep, giving him none of the cream filling. There was a red place on her left heel, and she covered it with moleskin. Jep lay on his side. Lily felt drowsy. "You want to rest awhile?" she asked Jep. "I don't really care if we make the caves, and you've seen them before. I could give a damn about the caves, if you want to know the truth." She yawned. Somewhere to her left a small animal scuttled in the brush. Jep hardly lifted his head. Lily made a pillow out of Katherine's red sweatshirt and went to sleep, leaning against the overhang.

When she woke, the sun was behind her. Jep was on his feet, looking at something above her head. His tail wagged slowly and he whined once. On the ground, stretching over him and extending several more feet, lay the shadow of a man, elongated legs, one arm up as though he were waving. When Lily moved away from the overhang and turned to look, he was gone.

It unsettled her. She supposed that a seasoned hiker would have known better than to sleep on the trail. She turned to go back to Mattie's and had only walked a short way, less than a city block, when she saw something she had missed coming from the other direction. A woman was painted onto the flat face of a rock which jutted up beside the trail. The perspective was somewhat flattened, and the image had been simplified, which made it extraordinarily compelling somehow. Especially for a painting on a rock. When had Lily ever seen anything painted on a rock other than KELLY LOVES ERIC or ANGELA PUTS OUT? The woman's long black hair fell straight down both sides of her face. Her dark eyes were half closed; her skin was brown. She was looking down at her hands, which she held cupped together, and she was dressed all in red. Wherever the surface of the rock was the roughest, the paint had cracked, and one whole sleeve had flaked off entirely. Lily leaned down to touch the missing arm. There was a silence as if the birds and the snakes and the insects had all suddenly run out of breath. Lily straightened and the ordinary noises began again. She followed Jep back down the trail.

"I didn't get to the caves," she admitted to Mattie. "I'll go again tomorrow. But I did see something intriguing: the painting. The woman painted on the rock. I'm used to graffiti, but not this kind. Who painted her?"

"I don't know," said Mattie. "She's been here longer than I have. We get a lot of farm labor through, seasonal labor, you know. I always thought she looked Mexican. And you see paintings like that a lot in Mexico. Rock Madonnas. I read somewhere that the artists usually use their own mother's faces for inspiration. The writer said you see these paintings by the roadside all the time and that those cultures in which men idolize their mothers are the most sexist cultures in the world. Interesting article. She's faded a lot over the years."

"You don't often see a Madonna dressed in red," Lily said.

"No, you don't," Mattie agreed. "Blue usually, isn't it?" She helped Lily out of the pack. "Did you get blisters?" she asked. "I worried about you."

"No," said Lily, although the spot on her heel had never stopped bothering her. "I was fine."

"You know who might be able to tell you about the painting? Allison Beale. Runs the county library but lives here in Two Trees. She's been here forever. You could run over tonight and ask her if you like. I'll give you the address. She likes company."

So Lily got back in her car with Allison Beale's address in her pocket and a map to Allison's house. She was supposed to go there first and then pick up some dinner at a little restaurant called the Italian Kitchen, but she turned left instead of right and then left again to a bar she'd noticed on her way into Two Trees, with a neon martini glass tipping in the window. The only other customer, a man, stood with his back to her, studying the jukebox selections but choosing nothing. Lily sat at the counter and ordered a margarita. It came without salt and the ice floated inside it uncrushed. "You're the lady staying with Mattie," the bartender informed her. "My name is Egan. Been to the caves?"

"Lily," Lily said. "I don't like caves. I can get lost in the supermarket. Wander for days without a sweater in the frozen foods. I'm afraid to think what would happen to me in a cave."

"These caves aren't deep," the bartender said, wiping the counter in front of her with the side of his hand. "Be a shame to come all the way to Two Trees and not even see the caves."

"Take a native guide," the other man suggested. He had come up behind her while she ordered.

She slid around on the bar stool.

"Henry," he told her. He wore a long black braid and a turquoise necklace. The last time Lily had seen him he had been dressed as a policeman. She'd had no sense of his hair being long like this.

"You're an Indian," Lily said.

"Can't put anything past you." He sat down on the stool next to hers. Lily guessed he was somewhere in his thirties, just about her own age. "Take off your wedding ring and I'll buy you a drink."

She slid the ring off her finger. Her hands were cold and it didn't even catch at the knuckle. She laid it on the napkin. "It's off," she said. "But that's all I'm taking off. I hope we understand each other."

The bartender brought her a second margarita. "The first one was on the house," he said. "Because you're a guest in Two Trees. The second one is on Henry. We'll worry about the third when you get to it."

Lily got to it about an hour later. She could easily have done without it. She was already quite drunk. She and Henry and the bartender were still the only people in the bar.

"It just intrigued me, you know?" she said. The bartender stood draped across the counter next to her. Henry leaned on one elbow. Lily could hear that she was slurring her words. She tried to sharpen them. "It seemed old. I thought it intrigued me enough to go talk to the librarian about it, but I was wrong about that." She laughed and started on her third drink. "It should be restored," she added. "Like the Sistine Chapel."

"I can tell you something about it," the bartender said. "I can't swear any of it's true, but I know what people say. It's a picture of a miracle." He glanced at Henry. "Happened more than a hundred years ago. It was painted by a man, a local man, I don't think anyone remembers who. And this woman appeared to him one day, by the rock. She held out her hands, cupped, just the way he drew them, like she was offering him something, but her hands were empty. And then she disappeared again."

"Well?" said Lily.

"Well, what?" Henry answered her. She turned back to him. Henry was drinking something clear from a shot glass. Egan kept it filled; Henry never asked him, but emptied the glass several times without appearing to be affected. Lily wondered if it might even be water.

"What was the miracle? What happened?"

There was a pause. Henry looked down into his drink. Egan finally spoke. "Nothing happened that I know of." He looked at Henry. Henry shrugged. "The miracle was that she appeared. The miracle was that he turned out to be the kind of person something like this happened to."

Lily shook her head in dissatisfaction.

"It's kind of a miracle the painting has lasted so long, don't you think?" Egan suggested. "Out there in the wind and the sand for all those years?"

Lily shook her head again.

"You are a hard woman," Henry told her. He leaned closer. "And a beautiful one."

It made Lily laugh at him for being so unoriginal. "Right." She stirred her drink with her finger. "How do Indians feel about their mothers?"

"I loved mine. Is that the right answer?"

"I'll tell you what I've always heard about Indians." Lily put her elbows on the counter between them, her chin in her hands.

"I bet I know this." Henry's voice dropped to a whisper. "I bet I know exactly what you've always heard."

"I've heard that sexual technique is passed on from father to son." Lily took a drink. "And you know what I've always thought? I've always thought a lot of mistakes must be perpetuated this way. A culture that passed on sexual technique from *mother* to son would impress me."

"So there's a middleman," said Henry. "Give it a chance. It still could work." The phone rang at the end of the bar. Egan went to answer it. Henry leaned forward, staring at her intently. "You have incredible eyes," he said, and she looked away from him immediately. "I can't decide what color they are."

Lily laughed again, this time at herself. She didn't want to respond to such a transparent approach, but she couldn't help it. The laugh had a hysterical edge. She got to her feet. "Take off your pants and I'll buy you a drink," she said and enjoyed the startled look on Henry's face. She held on to the counter, brushing against him by accident on her way to the back of the bar.

"End of the counter and left," the bartender told her, hanging up the phone. She gripped each stool and spun it as she went by, hand over hand, for as long as they lasted. She made it the last few steps to the bathroom on her own. The door was marked with the silhouette of a figure wearing a skirt. Lily fell through it and into the stall. On one side of her *Brian is a fox* was scratched into the wall. On the other were the words *Chastity chews.* A picture accompanied the text, another picture of a woman, presumably chewing chastity. She had many arms like Kali and a great many teeth. A balloon rose from her mouth. *Hi,* she said simply.

Lily spent some time at the mirror, fixing her hair. She blew a breath into her hand and tried to smell it, but all she could smell was the lavatory soap. She supposed this was good. "I'm going home," she announced, back in the bar. "I've enjoyed myself."

She felt around in her purse for her keys. Henry held them up and rang them together. "I can't let you drive home. You hardly made it to the bathroom."

"I can't let you take me. I don't know you well enough."

"I wasn't going to suggest that. Looks like you have to walk."

Lily reached for the keys and Henry closed his fist about them. "It's only about six blocks," he said.

"It's dark. I could be assaulted."

"Not in Two Trees."

"Anywhere. Are you kidding?" Lily smiled at him. "Give me the keys. I already have a blister."

"I could give you the keys and you could hit a tree not two blocks from here. I don't think I could live with myself. Egan will back me up on this." Henry gestured with his closed fist toward the bartender.

"Damn straight," said Egan. "There's no way you're driving home. You'll be fine walking. And, anyway, Jep's come for you." Lily could see a vague doggy shape through the screen door.

"Hello, Jep," Lily said. The doggy shape wagged from side to side. “All right.” Lily turned back to the men at the bar. “All right,” she conceded. “I’m walking. The men in this town are pitiless, but the dogs are fine. You’ve got to love the dogs.”

She swung the screen door open. Jep backed out of the way. “Tomorrow,” Egan called out behind her, “you go see those caves.”

Jep walked beside her on the curbside, between her and the street. Most of the houses were closed and dark. In the front of one a woman sat on a porch swing, holding a baby and humming to it. Some heartbreak song. By the time Lily reached Mattie’s she felt sober again.

Mattie was sitting in the living room. “Egan called,” she said. “I made you some tea. I know it’s not what you think you want, but it has some herbs in it, very effective against hangover. You won’t be sorry you drank it. It’s a long hike to the caves. You want to be rested.”

Lily sat on the couch beside her. “Thank you. You’re being very good to me, Mattie. I don’t deserve it. I’ve been behaving very badly.”

“Maybe it’s just my turn to be good,” said Mattie. “Maybe you just finished your turn. Did you ever get any dinner?”

“I think I may have had some pretzels.” Lily looked across the room to the phone, wondering if she were going to call David. She looked at the picture of the Madonna. It was not a very interesting one. Too sweet. Too much sweetness. “I should call my husband,” she told Mattie and didn’t move.

“Would you like me to leave you alone?”

“No,” said Lily. “It wouldn’t be that sort of call. David and I, we don’t have personal conversations.” She realized suddenly that she had left her wedding ring back at the bar on the cocktail napkin beside her empty glass.

"Is the marriage a happy one?" Mattie asked. "Forgive me if I'm prying. It's just—well, here you are."

"I don't know," said Lily.

Mattie put her arm around Lily and Lily leaned against her. "Loving is a lot harder for some people than for others," she said. "And being loved can be hardest of all. Not for you, though. Not for a loving woman like you."

Lily sat up and reached for her tea. It smelled of chamomile. "Mattie," she said. She didn't know how to explain. Lily felt that she often appeared to be a better person than she was. It was another affliction. In many ways Mattie's analysis was true. Lily knew that her family and friends wondered how she lived with such a cold, methodical man. But there was another truth, too. Often, Lily set up little tests for David, tests of his sensitivity, tests of his commitment. She was always pleased when he failed them, because it proved the problems between them were still his fault. Not a loving thing to do. "Don't make me out to be some saint," she said.

She slept very deeply that night, dreaming on alcohol and tea, and woke up late in the morning. It was almost ten before she and Jep hit the trail. She watched for the painting on her way up this time, stopping to eat an identical lunch in a spot where she could look at it. Jep sat beside her, panting. They passed the rock overhang where she had eaten lunch the day before, finished the climb uphill, and started down. The drop-off was sharp; the terrain was dusty and uninviting, and Lily, who was tired of walking uphill, found it even harder to descend. When the trail stopped at a small hollow in the side of a rock, she decided she would rest and then go back. Everyone else might be excessively concerned that she see the caves, but she couldn't bring herself to care. She dropped the day pack on the ground and sat beside it. Jep raised his collie ear and wagged his tail. Turning, Lily was not at all surprised to see Henry coming down the hill, his hair loose and hanging to his shoulders.

"So," he said. "You found the caves without me."

"You're kidding." Lily stood up. "This little scrape in the rock? This can't be the famous Two Trees caves. I won't believe it. Tell me there are real caves just around the next bend."

"You need something more?" Henry asked. "This isn't enough? You are a hard woman."

"Oh, come on." Lily flicked her hair out of her eyes. "Are you telling me people come from all over to see this?"

"It's not the caves." Henry was staring at her. She felt her face reddening. "It's what happens in the caves." He moved closer to her. "It's what happens when a beautiful woman comes to the caves." Lily let herself look right at his eyes. Inside his pupils, a tiny Lily looked back out.

"Stay away from me," said Lily. Was she the kind of woman who would allow a strange man in a strange place to kiss her? Apparently so. Apparently she was the kind of woman who said no to nothing now. She reached out to Henry; she put one hand on the sleeve of his shirt, one hand on his neck, moved the first hand to his back. "I gave you my car and my wedding ring," she told him. "What do you want now? What will satisfy you?" She kissed him first. They dropped to their knees on the hard floor of the cave. He kissed her back.

"We could go somewhere more comfortable," said Lily.

"No," said Henry. "It has to be here."

They removed their clothes and spread them about as padding. The shadow of the rock lengthened over them. Jep whined once or twice and then went to sleep at a safe distance. Lily couldn't relax. She let Henry work at it. She touched his face and kissed his hand. "Your father did a nice job," she told him, moving as close to his side as she could, holding herself against him. "You do that wonderfully." Henry's arm lay underneath her back. He lifted her with it, turning her so that she was on top of him, facing down. He took hold of her hair and pulled her face to his own, put his mouth on her mouth. Then he let her go, staring at her, holding the bits of hair about her face in his hands. "You are so beautiful," he said, and something broke inside her.

"Am I?" She was frightened because she suddenly needed to believe him, needed to believe that he might love her, whoever she was.

"Incredibly beautiful."

"Am I?" Don't say it if you don't mean it, she told him silently, too afraid to talk and almost crying. Don't make me want it if it's not there. Please. Be careful what you say.

"Incredibly beautiful." He began to move again inside her. "So beautiful." He watched her face. "So beautiful." He touched her breasts and then his eyes closed and his mouth rounded. She thought he might fly apart, his body shook so, and she held him together with her hands, kissed him until he stopped, and then kissed him again.

"I don't want to hurt you," Henry said.

It hurt Lily immediately, like a slap. So now she was the sort of woman men said this to. Well, she had no right to expect anything different from a man she didn't even know. She could have said it to him first if she'd thought of it. That would have been the smart thing to do. Nothing would have been stupider than needing him. What had she been thinking of? "But you will if you have to," she finished. "Right? Don't worry. I'm not making anything of this. I know what this is." She sat up and reached for Katherine's sweatshirt. She was cold and afraid to move closer to Henry. She was cold and she didn't want to be naked anymore.

"You sound angry," Henry said. "It's not that I couldn't love you. It's not that I don't already love you. Men always disappoint women. I'm not sure we can escape it."

"Don't be ridiculous," Lily told him sharply. She put her head into the red tent of the sweatshirt and pulled it through. "I should have gotten your sexual history first," she added. "I haven't done this since the rules changed."

"I haven't been with a woman in ten years," Henry said. Lily looked at his face in surprise.

"Before that it was five years," he said. "And before that three, but that was two at once. That was the sixties. Before that it was fifteen years. And twenty before that. And two. And two. And before that almost a hundred."

Lily stood up, pulling on Katherine's jeans. "I should have gotten your psychiatric history first," she said. The faster she tried to dress, the more difficulties she had. She couldn't find one of Katherine's socks. She was too angry and frightened to look among Henry's clothes. She put on Katherine's shoes without it. "Come on, Jep," she said.

"It can't mean anything," Henry told her.

"It didn't. Forget it." Lily left without the day pack. She hurried up the trail. Jep followed somewhat reluctantly. They made the crest of the hill; Lily looked behind her often to see if Henry was following. He wasn't. She went past the painting without stopping. Jep preceded her through the gate into Mattie's backyard.

Mattie and Katherine were waiting in the house. Katherine put her arms around her. "You went to the caves," Katherine said. "Didn't you? I can tell."

"Of course she did," said Mattie. She stroked Lily's hair. "Of course she did."

Lily stood stiffly inside Katherine's arms. "What the hell is going on?" she asked. She pushed away and looked at the two women. "You sent me up there, didn't you? You did! You and Egan and probably Allison Beale, too. Go to the caves, go to the caves. That's all I've heard since I got here. You dress me like some virginal sacrifice, fatten me up with Hostess cupcakes, and send me to him. But why?"

"It's a miracle," said Mattie. "You were chosen. Can't you feel it?"

"I let some man pick me up in a bar. He turns out to be a nut." Lily's voice rose higher. "Where's the miracle?"

"You slept with Henry," said Mattie. "Henry chose *you*. That's the miracle."

Lily ran up the stairs. She stripped Katherine's clothes off and put her own on. Mattie came and stood in the doorway. Lily walked around her and out of the room.

"Listen to me, Lily," Mattie said. "You don't understand. He gave you as much as he can give anyone. That's why in the painting the woman's hands are empty. But that's *his* trap. *His* curse. Not yours. When you see that, you'll forgive him. Katherine and Allison and I all forgave him. I know you will, too, a loving woman like you." Mattie reached out, grabbing Lily's sleeve. "Stay here with us. You can't go back to your old life. You won't be able to. You've been chosen."

"Look," said Lily. She took a deep breath and wiped at her eyes with her hands. "I wasn't chosen. Quite the opposite. I was picked up and discarded. By a man in his thirties and not the same man you slept with. Maybe you slept with a god. You go ahead and tell yourself that. What difference does it make? You were still picked up and discarded." She shook loose of Mattie and edged down the stairs. She expected to be stopped, but she wasn't. At the front door, she turned. Mattie stood on the landing behind her. Mattie held out her hands. Lily shook her head. "I think you're pretty pathetic, if you want to know the truth. I'm not going to tell myself a lot of lies or listen to yours. I know who I am. I'm going. I won't be back. Don't expect me."

Her car waited at the front of the house, just where she had parked it the first night. She ran from the porch. The keys were inside. Left and left again, past the bar where the martini glass tipped darkly in the window, and onto the freeway. Lily accelerated way past eighty and no one stopped her. The foothills sped by and became cities. When she felt that she was far enough away to be safe from small-town Madonnas and immortals who were cursed to endure centuries of casual sex with as many loving women as possible—which was damn few, in fact, if you believed the numbers they gave you—she slowed down. She arrived home in the early evening. As she was walking in the door, she noticed she was wearing her wedding ring.

David was sitting on the couch reading a book. "Here I am,

David," Lily said. "I'm here. I got a speeding ticket. I never looked to see how much it was for. I lost my ring playing poker, but I mortgaged the house and won it back. I lost a lot more, though. I lost my head. I'm halfhearted now. In fact, I'm not at all the woman I was. I've got to be honest with you."

"I'm glad you're home," said David. He went back to his book.

THE BLACK FAIRY'S CURSE

She was being chased. She kicked off her shoes, which were slowing her down. At the same time her heavy skirts vanished and she found herself in her usual work clothes. Relieved of the weight and constriction, she was able to run faster. She looked back. She was much faster than he was. Her heart was strong. Her strides were long and easy. He was never going to catch her now.

SHE WAS RIDING the huntsman's horse and she couldn't remember why. It was an autumn red with a tangled mane. She was riding fast. A deer leapt in the meadow ahead of her. She saw the white blink of its tail.

She'd never ridden well, never had the insane fearlessness it took, but now she was able to enjoy the easiness of the horse's motion. She encouraged it to run faster.

It was night. The countryside was softened with patches of moonlight. She could go anywhere she liked, ride to the end of the world and back again. What she would find there was a castle with a toothed tower. Around the castle was a girdle of trees, too narrow to be called a forest, and yet so thick they admitted no light at all. She knew this. Even farther away were the stars. She looked up and saw three of them fall, one right after the other. She made a wish to ride until she reached them.

She herself was in farmland. She crossed a field and jumped a low stone fence. She avoided the cottages, homey though they seemed, with smoke rising from the roofs and a glow the color of butter pats at the windows. The horse ran and did not seem to tire.

She wore a cloak which, when she wrapped it tightly around her, rode up and left her legs bare. Her feet were cold. She turned around to look. No one was coming after her.

She reached a river. Its edges were green with algae and furry with silt. Toward the middle she could see the darkness of deep water. The horse made its own decisions. It ran along the shallow edge but didn't cross. Many yards later it ducked back away from the water and into a grove of trees. She lay along its neck, and the silver-backed leaves of aspens brushed over her hair.

SHE CLIMBED INTO one of the trees. She regretted every tree she had never climbed. The only hard part was the first branch. After that it was easy, or else she was stronger than she'd ever been. Stronger than she needed to be. This excess of strength gave her a moment of joy as pure as any she could remember. The climbing seemed quite as natural as stair steps, and she went as high as she could, standing finally on a limb so thin it dipped under her weight, like a boat. She retreated downward, sat with her back against the trunk and one leg dangling. No one would ever think to look for her here.

Her hair had come loose and she let it all down. It was warm on her shoulders. "Mother," she said, softly enough to blend with the wind in the leaves. "Help me."

She meant her real mother. Her real mother was not there, had not been there since she was a little girl. It didn't mean there would be no help.

Above her were the stars. Below her, looking up, was a man. He was no one to be afraid of. Her dangling foot was bare. She did not cover it. Maybe she didn't need help. That would be the biggest help of all.

"Did you want me?" he said. She might have known him from somewhere. They might have been children together. "Or did you want me to go away?"

"Go away. Find your own tree."

THEY WENT SWIMMING together and she swam better than he did. She watched his arms, his shoulders rising darkly from the green water. He turned and saw that she was watching. "Do you know my name?" he asked her.

"Yes," she said, although she couldn't remember it. She knew she was supposed to know it, although she could also see that he didn't expect her to. But she did feel that she knew who he was—his name was such a small part of that. "Does it start with a W?" she asked.

The sun was out. The surface of the water was a rough gold.

"What will you give me if I guess it?"

"What do you want?"

She looked past him. On the bank was a group of smiling women, her grandmother, her mother, and her stepmother, too, her sisters and stepsisters, all of them smiling at her. They waved. No one said, "Put your clothes on." No one said, "Don't go in too deep now, dear." She was a good swimmer, and there was no reason to be afraid. She couldn't think of a single thing she wanted. She flipped away, breaking the skin of the water with her legs.

She surfaced in a place where the lake held still to mirror the sky. When it settled, she looked down into it. She expected to see that she was beautiful, but she was not. A mirror only answers one question and it can't lie. She had completely lost her looks. She wondered what she had gotten in return.

THERE WAS A MIRROR in the bedroom. It was dusty so her reflection was vague. But she was not beautiful. She wasn't upset about this and she noticed the fact, a little wonderingly. It didn't matter at all to her. Most people were taken in by appearances, but others weren't. She was healthy; she was strong. If she could manage to be kind and patient and witty and brave, there would be men who loved her for it. There would be men who found it exciting.

He lay among the blankets, looking up at her. "Your eyes," he said. "Your incredible eyes."

His own face was in shadow, but there was no reason to be afraid. She removed her dress. It was red. She laid it over the back of a chair. "Move over."

She had never been in bed with this man before, but she wanted to be. It was late and no one knew where she was. In fact, her mother had told her explicitly not to come here, but there was no reason to be afraid. "I'll tell you what to do," she said. "You must use your hand and your mouth. The other—it doesn't work for me. And I want to be first. You'll have to wait."

"I'll love waiting," he said. He covered her breast with his mouth, his hand moved between her legs. He knew how to touch her already. He kissed her other breast.

"Like that," she said. "Just like that." Her body began to tighten in anticipation.

He kissed her mouth. He kissed her mouth.

HE KISSED HER MOUTH. It was not a hard kiss, but it opened her eyes. This was not the right face. She had never seen this man before and the look he gave her—she wasn't sure she liked it. Why was he kissing her, when she was asleep and had never seen him before? What was he doing in her bedroom? She was so frightened, she stopped breathing for a moment. She closed her eyes and wished him away.

He was still there. And there was pain. Her finger dripped with blood and when she tried to sit up, she was weak and encumbered by a heavy dress, a heavy coil of her own hair, a corset, tight and pointed shoes.

"Oh," she said. "Oh." She was about to cry and she didn't know this man to cry before him. Her tone was accusing. She pushed him and his face showed the surprise of this. He allowed himself to be pushed. If he hadn't, she was not strong enough to force it.

He was probably a very nice man. He was giving her a concerned look. She could see that he was tired. His clothes were ripped; his own hands were scratched. He had just done something hard, maybe dangerous. So maybe that was why he hadn't stopped to think how it might frighten her to wake up with a stranger kissing her as she lay on her back. Maybe that was why he hadn't noticed how her finger was bleeding. Because he hadn't, no matter how much she came to love him, there would always be a part of her afraid of him.

"I was having the most lovely dream," she said. She was careful not to make her tone as angry as she felt.

THE VIEW FROM VENUS: A CASE STUDY

Linda knows, of course, that the gorgeous male waiting for her, holding the elevator door open with his left hand, cannot be moving into apartment 201. This is not the way life works. There are many possible explanations for the boxes stacked around his feet—he may be helping a friend move in, his girlfriend, perhaps. Someone equally blond and statuesque who will be Linda's new next-door neighbor, and Gretchen will point out that she is a sister, after all, and force everyone to be nice to her. Their few male guests will feel sorry for her, oppressed as she is by all that beauty, and there will be endless discourse on the tragic life of Marilyn Monroe.

The door slides shut. Linda reaches for the second-floor button, but so does he, and they both withdraw their hands quickly before touching. He takes a slight step backward, communicating his willingness to let her punch in the destination. She does so; the outline of the button for the second floor shines slightly. It is just below eye level. She watches it closely so as not to look at him, and she can feel him not looking at her. They share the embarrassment of closely confined strangers. The elevator does not move.

Linda is upset because she is nervous. This nervousness is in direct proportion to how attractive she finds him. She is very nervous. She tells herself sharply to stop being so juvenile.

He reaches past her and re-presses the button. “It’s always like this,” Linda tells him. “When you’re in a hurry, take the stairs.”

He turns slowly and looks at her. “I’m Dave Stone,” he says. “Just moving in.”

“Linda Connors. Apartment Two-oh-three.” So he will be living here. He and his girlfriend will move in together; they will both be neighbors, but she will still be a sister, and no one will be allowed to rip off another woman’s man.

The elevator groans and shudders. It begins to lift. “I’m transferring up from Santa Barbara,” Dave says. “Have you ever been there? I know how this is going to sound, but you really do look familiar.”

“Nope.” The elevator jerks twice before stopping. Linda is expecting it and is braced against the side. Dave stumbles forward. “Maybe you’ve confused me with some movie star,” Linda suggests. “A common mistake.” She gives the door a slight push to open it. “My roommate Lauren says I have Jack Lemmon’s chin,” she adds, and leaves him struggling to unload his boxes before the elevator closes up and moves on.

Inside the apartment Linda gets herself a glass of milk. Her mood now is good. She has stood next to a man, a strange man, and she has talked with him. She actually spoke first instead of merely answering his questions. And she tells herself, though it is hard to ever be sure of these things, that nothing about the conversation would have told him this was difficult for her.

The truth is that men frighten Linda. The more a particular man appeals to her, the more frightening he becomes. Linda knows almost nothing about men, in spite of having had a father practically her whole life. She believes that men are fundamentally different from women, that they have mysterious needs and assess women according to bizarre standards on which she herself never measures very high. Some years back she read in "The Question Man," a daily column in the *San Francisco Chronicle*, that men mentally undress women when they pass them on the street. Linda has never recovered from the shock of this.

One of Linda's roommates, a red-haired woman named Julie, is curled up with a book. It is a paperback entitled *The Arrangement.* Julie likes books with explicit sex. Julie already knows she is destined to be some married man's lover and has told Linda so. Linda reads Jane Austen. For fun.

"Have you seen what's moving in next door?" Julie asks.

"I met him. Big, blond . . . his name is Dave."

"Chiseled features," says Julie. "That's what you call those. And he's not the only one. There's a little dark one, too, and a couple of brothers who haven't arrived yet."

Four of them. And four women inside Linda's own apartment. There seems to Linda to be a certain inescapable logic at work here. She pictures a quadruple wedding (where she is the only one technically entitled to wear white, but no one need know this) and then life in a cozy suburban quadruplex. It is only with some effort that Linda remembers that Dave did not really seem to be her type, being unquestionably more attractive than she is. "Not my type" is the designation Linda applies to men who pay no attention to her. It is an infinite set. Those few men who are Linda's type she invariably dislikes. She drinks her milk and makes the realistic decision to forget Dave forever. They'll always have their elevator ride. . . .

WELCOME TO Comparative Romance I. You have just experienced the Initial Encounter. The point of view is female: We shall be sticking to this perspective through most of this term. And we shall access only one mind at a time. This gives a more accurate sense of what it would be like to be an actual participant. It is not uncommon for those inexperienced in the process of absorption to have an uncomfortable reaction. Is anyone feeling at all queasy? Claustrophobic? No? Good.

Then let me make a few quick points about the Encounter and we will return. You must remember, owing to the time required by Transmission and Processing, that these events are not current. We are involved here in a historical romance. The location is the city of Berkeley, before its secession. The year, according to local calculation, is 1969, a time thought by some to have been critical in the evolution of male/female relationships. Can anyone here provide a context?

Very good. In addition to the war, the assassinations, and the riots, we have a women's movement which is just becoming militant again. We have many women who are still a little uncomfortable about this. "I believe in equal rights for women, but I'm not a feminist," is the proper feminine dogma at this time. To call oneself a feminist is to admit to being ugly. Most women are reluctant to do this. Particularly on the West Coast.

Are there any questions? If not, let's locate ourselves and Linda at Encounter Number Two. Are we all ready?

Well?

I'm taking that as an affirmative.

LINDA MEETS DAVE again the next morning on the stairs. He is returning from campus and invites her in for a cup of coffee in exchange for her advice in choosing classes. She is on her way to the library but decides it would be more educational to see the inside of apartment 201. She has an anthropological curiosity about men living together. What do they eat? Who does the dishes? Who cleans the toilets? Her hands are cold so she sticks them into the opposite cuffs of her sweater sleeves as she follows Dave back up the stairs.

Her first impression is that the male sex is much neater than the sex to which she belongs herself. Everything has already been unpacked. There are pictures on the walls, tasteful pictures, a small print of Rembrandt's thoughtful knight, the gold in the helmet echoing the tones of the shag carpet, a bird's-eye view of the Crucifixion, a bus poster which reads WHY DO YOU THINK THEY CALL IT DOPE? The dishes all match; the avocado Formica has been sponged so recently it is still wet.

Linda is so busy collecting data she forgets to tell Dave she doesn't really want coffee. He hands her a steaming cup and she notices with dismay that he has not even left her room to soften the taste with milk. She uses the cup to warm her hands, smells it tentatively. "Did you know," she asks him, "that in Sweden they have a variation on our bag ladies they call 'coffee bitches'? These are supposed to be women who've gone mad from drinking too much coffee. It gives you a whole new perspective on Mrs. Olsen, doesn't it?"

She hears a key turning in the door. "Kenneth," says Dave, and Kenneth joins them in the kitchen, his face a little flushed from the cold air, his eyes dark and intense. Kenneth gives Linda the impression of being somehow concentrated, as if too much energy has been packed into too small a package.

"This is Linda," Dave tells Kenneth.

"Hello, Linda," Kenneth says. He starts moving the clean dishes out of the drainer and onto the shelves. "I love this place." He gestures expansively with a plastic tumbler. "We were right to come here. I told you so." He is sorting the silverware. "I've been over at Sproul, what—half an hour? And in that time I got hit with a Frisbee, someone tried to sign me into the Sexual Freedom League, I listened to this whole debate on the merits of burning New York City to the ground, and a girl came up out of nowhere and kissed me. This is a great place."

"What was the pro side of burning New York?" asked Dave. "I've got relatives there."

"No more blackouts." Kenneth puts a coffee cup away, then takes it out again immediately. Linda sees her chance.

"Take mine," she urges. "I haven't touched it. Really." She gives Dave an apologetic smile. "Sorry. I meant to tell you before you poured. I hate coffee."

"It's okay," he says evenly. "I'll never ask you over for coffee again." He turns to Kenneth. "Tell Linda what happened last night."

"Oh, God." Kenneth takes Linda's coffee and sips at it. He settles into the chair next to her, leaning back on two legs. Linda decides she is attracted to him as well. She looks away from him. "Last night," he begins, "this guy came to our door looking for a friend of his named Jim Harper. I said we were new to the building, but I didn't think there was a Jim Harper here."

"I don't know a Jim Harper," Linda says. "In fact, you're practically the only men. Except for— "

"So he says Jim Harper might be living under an alias and have we seen any little brown guys around. I say, 'Is he a Negro?' and he says, 'No, he's just a little brown guy.' "

"So," Dave finishes, "Ken tells him we'll set out some snares tonight and let him know in the morning if we've caught anything. Who are the other men in the building? Are they little and brown?"

"There's only one. Dudley Petersen. And no. He's middle-aged, middle-sized, medium coloring. We think he's a CIA agent, because he's so cunningly nondescript and he won't tell us what he does."

"You could live your whole life in Santa Barbara without anyone coming to your door looking for small, brown men," Kenneth tells Linda. "I love this place."

Linda does not respond. She is thinking about Dudley. Last summer he'd gone to Hawaii for two weeks—on vacation, he said, but she wasn't born yesterday. She knows a Pacific Rim assignment when she sees one. He'd asked her to water his ferns. Apparently she'd been overzealous. She wouldn't have thought it possible to overwater a fern. There'd been bad feelings on his return. But while she had access to his apartment she'd found a shelf of pornographic books. Quite by accident. She'd brought them downstairs and shared them with her roommates. Really funny stuff—they'd taken turns reading it aloud: "He had the largest hands Cybelle had ever seen." . . . "'No,' she moaned. 'No.' Or was she saying 'More. More?'" . . . "Her silken breasts swelled as he stroked them. She drew his head down until his mouth brushed the nipples."

It all reminded her of an article the *Chronicle* had once run in the women's section. An expert in female psychology (an obscure branch of the larger field) had argued that small-breasted women were using their bodies to repress and reject their femininity because they would rather be men. Under hypnosis, with the help of a trained professional, these women could come to accept themselves as women and their breasts would grow. This happy result had been documented in at least three cases.

What had struck Linda most about the article was its very accusing tone. Men liked women to have large breasts; it was highly suspect, if not downright bitchy, the way some women refused to provide them. Linda feels Kenneth looking at her. Mentally undressing her? Why, even as they speak, Dave and Kenneth are probably asking themselves why her breasts are so small. Because she is cold and nervous, Linda has been sitting with her arms crossed over her chest. Now she deliberately uncrosses them.

"When do the rest of you arrive?" she asks distantly.

Dave looks himself over. "I'm all here," he says. "This is it."

"No. Your other roommates. The brothers."

There is a moment's silence while Dave and Kenneth drink their coffee. Then they both speak at once. "We couldn't afford the apartment just the two of us," Kenneth says, while Dave is saying, "The Flying Zukini Brothers? You mean you haven't met them yet? You are in for a treat."

"They're here already," Kenneth adds. "God, are they here.

They have presence, if you know what I mean. Even when they're not here, they're here."

"Go home while you can," advises Dave. "Go home to your small brown men." His eyes are just visible over the tilted rim of his coffee cup.

Footsteps stamp at the doorway. There is a sound of keys. "Too late," says Dave ominously as the door swings open. Two clean-cut men in T-shirts which show their muscled arms try to come through the door together. They catch, in charmingly masculine fashion, at the shoulders. They are nice-looking, but somehow Linda knows the quadruple wedding is off. No one would take the last name of Zukini anyway, not even if they hyphenated it.

"I got a car!" says the first of the brothers through the door. "I mean, I put the money down and it's sitting in the basement. I drove it home!" He accelerates into a discussion of RPMs, variations in mileage, painless monthly payments. Man talk. Linda is bored.

"Linda, this is Fred," says Dave. "The other one is Frank."

"You want to go see the car?"

"I got a class."

"Good thinking."

Linda shifts from one foot to the other, feeling awkward and grateful for Fred's noise, which makes it less obvious. She wants to say something intelligent before she pushes her way through the clot of men blocking the door, and the longer she puts it off the more awkward it becomes. She gives up on the intelligent part. "Thanks for the coffee," she says to Dave. She narrowly misses Fred's fist, which has swung good-naturedly past her ear and settled into Kenneth's shoulder.

Kenneth covers the spot with his right hand. "Don't do that

again, Fred," he says, his tone deceptively light. And then Linda is out in the hall and the door closes behind her.

WE HAVE REACHED the end of the Second Encounter. Let's take a moment to reorient ourselves, and then perhaps you have questions I can answer. Yes? You. In the back.

The *Chronicle*? No, I believe it is a major newspaper with some particularly well-known columnists. Did you have another question?

Well, yes. I know it wasn't painted by Rembrandt and you know it wasn't painted by Rembrandt and in fifty years everyone will know it wasn't painted by Rembrandt, but in 1969 it was a Rembrandt. There was another question, wasn't there? Yes. You. Speak loudly, please.

Well, I'm not sure I want to answer this. We are experiencing these events as Linda does; to give you an objective assessment of Linda's physical appearance would taint this perspective.

Let's imagine a reality for a moment, an objective, factual you. How do others perceive you? How do you perceive others' perceptions of this you? We are now at two removes from the objective reality; we have passed it through two potentially distorting filters—others' perception of you and your perceptions of others—and yet for the purposes of relationships this is absolutely the closest to reality anyone can come. So this is where we will stay. Linda is small and thin; you experience this with Linda. She perceives herself as ordinary so you will share this perception. But I will point out that, although Linda imagines her appearance to be a liability, still she dresses in ways that support it. She cultivates the invisibility she feels so hampered by.

The point you raise is an interesting one with its own peculiarly female aspects. The entire issue, women's perceptions of their own bodies, is strange and complex and one of you might consider it as a possible term paper topic. Let's collect a little more data and then discuss it further. We'll pick up the Third Encounter a bit early to give you a chance to see the women together first. And let me just give you this bit of insight to ground your thinking on this subject. There are four women involved in this next Encounter, four relatively intelligent women, and yet all four share the same basic belief that anyone who looks at them closely will not love them. They feel that their energies in a relationship must go primarily to the task of preventing the male from ever seeing them clearly.

Are we ready? All right.

DINNER IS OVER, and the women of apartment 203 are still sitting around the table. They are holding a special financial meeting. Item one: Someone has made two phone calls to Redwood City and is refusing to acknowledge them. This is of interest only to Linda; the phone is in Linda's name. Item two: Was the Sara Lee cake which Julie consumed unassisted a cake bought with apartment funds or a personal cake?

Julie's position is completely untenable. She argues first that it was her own private cake and second that she most certainly did not eat it alone. It is the most flagrant case Linda can imagine of someone trying to have her cake and eat it, too, and

Linda says so. Julie is a closet eater and has developed a number of techniques for consuming more than anyone realizes. She will open the ice cream container from the bottom and shovel away unnoticed until someone else tries to serve herself and the ice cream collapses under the spoon.

Julie can seldom decide if she is dieting or not. This ambivalence forces her to rely on an ancient method of weight control. If, after polishing off a chocolate cake, it turns out she is on a diet after all, she throws it up. Of course this step, once taken, is irrevocable. Julie thinks that she is fat, although the whole time Linda has known her she never has been.

"Self-induced vomiting is hard on the stomach lining," says Gretchen. Gretchen is as short as Linda, but more muscular and athletic. She is a feminist and says so. "This is what finally destroyed Roman culture."

"Lead in the pipes," contends Linda.

"What?"

"They used lead in their water pipes. Eventually they were all brain-damaged."

"The process was accelerated by self-induced vomiting."

Julie is not listening. She is holding her red hair in her fingers, isolating single strands and splitting the ends. Julie does this routinely, although she spends extra money on special shampoos for damaged hair. Gretchen bites her fingernails. Lauren, who is black and so beautiful that strange men approach her on the street and say, "Hey, foxy lady," to her, pulls out her eyelashes when she is nervous and has done such a thorough job she now wears false eyelashes even to class. Linda bites her lips. She was told once as a child that her eyes were her best feature; she ceased to have any interest in the rest of her face. And then later she read in Chekhov that an unattractive woman is always being told she has beautiful eyes or beautiful hair. Linda's most recent compliment is that she has nice teeth. It is hard to get excited about this.

Someone knocks on the door. The women's hands all drop to their laps. "Come in," says Lauren.

It is Dave. Linda's breath quickens slightly. He has brought a penciled sign which he claims to have found Scotch-taped to the doorknob of 201. *Attention!! it says. Emergency!!! Clothes drier in basement refusing to fonction! Suzette.*

"What do you make of this?" Dave asks. He is wearing a dark blue T-shirt which reads KAHOALUAH SUMMER CAMP—TURN YOUR LIFE AROUND. It looks good on him.

"Suzette lives directly above us," Linda tells him. "Apartment Three-oh-three. Just a guess, but I'd say she's got a load of wet laundry and she'd like you to fix the dryer. She's a foreign exchange student from France," she adds. "Which explains the exclamation marks."

Gretchen shakes her head, moves her dark and heavy bangs off her forehead with the back of one wrist. She has to shampoo daily, and even so her hair is oily by evening. "It's because you're male, of course. She thinks mechanical abilities are linked to the Y chromosome."

"It's shaped like a little wrench," Julie points out.

"Or maybe she read your aura." Lauren's smile is particularly innocent. She examines her fingernails. "I wonder what color an electrician's aura would be?"

"Bright?" suggests Linda. Dave is looking at her. He is waiting for an explanation. "Suzette's a little strange," she tells him. "She communicates with Venusians. She writes herself notes from them; they guide her hand. It's called automatic writing. I think. And she reads the magnetic field around people's heads." Linda swallows uncomfortably. "She's very pretty."

"If you like pretty," says Gretchen. It is a trick question.

Dave dodges it. "I don't know how to fix a dryer."

"I'll tell you what." Lauren folds her hands and smiles up at him. "You go up there and explain that in person. I imagine she'll forgive you. Apartment Three-oh-three. Just above this one. You can't miss it."

Dave takes his note and edges back out the door. Linda feels her aura dimming around her ears.

"I bet they thought living in an apartment building with nothing but women in it would be out of sight," says Gretchen. Her tone suggests malicious satisfaction. "Serves them right if it's just one broken dryer after another."

"Is the dryer broken?" Julie asks. "I used it this afternoon, fading my jeans. It was working fine then." She looks at Lauren and they both start to laugh. "Poor, poor Dave. He'll never leave Suzette's apartment alive. He'll walk through that door and one thing will lead to another."

One thing is always leading to another in Julie's own romances. The phrase mystifies Linda, who feels that, logically, a gaping chasm must separate polite "Hello, I got your note" sorts of conversation from passionate sex. "What does that mean, Julie?" she asks, perhaps more vehemently than she might have wished. "'One thing leads to another.' That never ever happens to me. Can you describe that?"

Julie looks embarrassed, but more on Linda's behalf than her own. "Oh, come on, Linda," she says. "You know."

Linda turns to Lauren. "Tell me about the first time one thing led to another when you were out with Bill."

"Don't be a voyeur," says Lauren.

Julie laughs and Linda looks at her questioningly. "Sorry," she offers. "It just struck me as funny that you should be accused of voyeurism. You're the last of the prudes."

"How the hell can you tell?" Linda demands. "Have I passed up a number of opportunities to be licentious? Alert me when the next one comes along."

"She's not a prude," Gretchen objected. "Just naive. And very smart. It's an unexpected combination, so nobody knows what to make of it. And, of course, men don't care about smart anyway."

Linda rises from the table with dignity. "I'm going to my room now," she says, "because my presence seems to be having such a dampening effect on your desire to discuss me." She starts down the hall, and it occurs to her that the route is absolutely identical to the one between the kitchen and the bedrooms in apartment 201. Or 303. She dredges up a parting shot. "There's no way I'm going to pay for two phone calls to Redwood City I didn't even make. I'll take out the phone first. Try me." She goes into her (and Gretchen's) bedroom and closes the door. She lies across the bed she has very sensibly decided never to make. It would just have to be done again tomorrow. Every tomorrow. The blankets form comfortable little hills and valleys beneath her. And above her? Directly over her head, one thing is leading to another. She tries to imagine it.

DAVE: I got your note. I came as soon as I could.

SUZETTE: I've been waiting. (Their eyes lock.)

DAVE: (gazing at her) I don't know how to fix a dryer, Suzette. I wish I could.

SUZETTE: It doesn't matter. Nothing matters now that you're here.

(Dave steps through the door. Suzette closes it slowly, sensuously, behind him. She presses against it with her back. They are both breathing audibly.)

SUZETTE: I was just about to slip into something more comfortable. (She removes her sweater.) Would you like to watch?

DAVE: (grabbing her) Suzette! (Her silken breasts begin to swell.)

Linda makes them swell larger and larger until they pop like balloons. It is a fleeting satisfaction. She consigns the phrase "One thing leads to another" to the large set of things she doesn't understand and nobody is ever going to explain to her, a set which includes the mysterious ailment known as hemorrhoids.

Gretchen comes into the room, ostensibly to find her English Lit assignment, but the quarter has not even started yet. Linda is not fooled. Gretchen just wants to see if she is angry. "Julie made the calls," Gretchen says. "Of course."

"Has she admitted it yet?"

"Any moment now." Gretchen fusses with the things on her desk. "Hey, Linda?"

Linda rolls onto her side and looks at Gretchen. "Yeah?"

"We all love you just the way you are."

"I know that," says Linda.

. . .

ALL RIGHT. That was Encounter Number Three. Let's just take a moment to stretch and shake off the effects of the absorption. Or sit quietly. Return to yourselves. When you feel ready, we'll discuss what we've absorbed.

Yes? Is everyone back now? Good. Questions?

Very good. You are very quick; I wondered if anyone would pick this up. We do have an agent on the scene, although our control of her is limited to suggestion only. The note, for example, was our idea, but the spelling was all her own. We communicate with her in the manner Linda described and we have identified ourselves as Venusians, a wildly implausible cover which she accepted without hesitation. We hope with her help to have some input into the pacing of the romance. At present it is not unusually slow but cannot be said to be developing quickly either. And we have so much ground to cover this term.

I did say we'd come back to this topic and I take your point. Lauren would be an interesting focus for us later; certainly the additional variable of being black in a predominantly white culture adds yet another complication to the issue of women and their bodies. The other three women represent differentiated approaches to the topic: Julie dislikes her body and abuses it; Gretchen dislikes her body but believes politically in the injustice of current standards of physical beauty and is attempting to substitute standards of health and strength instead; Linda is interesting because, in fact, she likes her body quite well, she just doesn't expect anyone else to. Linda perceives her major shortcoming to be the size of her breasts, although she is mystified as to the reasons men desire more here. As long as Linda is our focus, we will share this mystification. Later in the term, when we switch to the male point of view, these things may become clearer. Let me just emphasize that it is hard to exaggerate the importance of these physical aspects, perceptions, and self-perceptions to the question of romance. Yes?

I must tell you that I find your remarks both alarming and repelling. It is one thing to agree, as we all must for the sake of the study, on the principle of physical relativity. We can accept that they find each other attractive even if we do not find them so. We can do our best to dispose of our own physical standards and prejudices in those areas where they seem likely to cloud the study. We can even remind ourselves that they might find us just as repellent as we find them. But it is quite another thing to speculate as you have just done on their physical intimacies with such specificity of detail. You are in danger of losing your academic detachment and, frankly, I will not be able to allow your continued participation if I see any more evidence of such imaginative and sympathetic absorption. Is that clear?

Yes? No, this is a good question. Of course you have not heard of Redwood City. No one important has ever lived in Redwood City and no one important ever will. The mystery is not that anyone would deny having placed phone calls to such an area; the mystery is that anyone could find someone there to call in the first place.

We are going to skip the fourth and fifth Encounters. They are brief and concern themselves only with a discussion of possible professors and classes. You will remember them, once absorbed. And I'm going to time our approach so that we pick up another critical memory of the period that has lapsed. Are you ready? Stay with me now.

THE BOYS IN apartment 201 had decided to give a party. Kenneth had come in the evening to extend the invitation. It was to be a small affair, limited to people who lived in the building and a few who could be persuaded to spend the night, since the city of Berkeley was under curfew.

"We'll just sit out on the terrace and yell 'Fascist pigs' at the passing police cars," Kenneth said. "It'll give us a chance to meet our neighbors in a relaxed social setting."

Two days later he invited the entire Cal ROTC on an impulse. Linda hears him arguing with Dave about it as she rises slowly toward the second floor in the sticky elevator. "It's going to be fine, Dave," Kenneth is saying. "You worry too much. Getting arrested for violating curfew will radicalize them." Linda gets out of the elevator and Kenneth catches the door with his hand, batting it back so that he can get in. "Later," he says cheerfully as the door closes, making him disappear from the left to the right.

Dave looks at Linda sourly. "Did you hear?" he asks. "Can you imagine what our apartment is going to look like after a bunch of cadets have partied there? What if they just don't go home? What if they pass out all over the place? They're all going to be physical as hell." They hear Kenneth's feet below them, pounding the sidewalk. He has an eleven o'clock class. Linda can see, reading Dave's watch sideways, that it is 11:02. Dave moves his arm suddenly to brush his hair back with his hand. The watch face flashes by Linda. She likes Dave's hands, which are large and rather prominently veined. She tries to find something not to like about Dave. "Come on in," Dave offers. "I'll make you a cup of hot chocolate."

"I hate chocolate," says Linda.

"Of course you do. I knew that. Come in anyway. I've got a problem, and I'm surrounded by Zukinis. Did Kenneth tell you that Frank registered Peace and Freedom last Monday? Yesterday he switched to Republican. I don't even pretend to understand the intricate workings of his mind."

Linda follows Dave into apartment 201. Her palms are sticky with sweat, which strikes her as adolescent. The whole world is wondering when she is going to grow up, and she is certainly no exception. Linda has hardly seen Dave since the night he went up to Suzette's. She wishes she could think of an artful way to find out how that evening ended. Or when it ended.

Dave puts a yellow teapot on the stove. Not a stray dish, not a fork left out anywhere. The avocado Formica gleams. Before, Linda believed they were neat. Now she is beginning to feel there may be something unhealthy about it. The neatness seems excessive.

Fred Zukini is sitting at the kitchen table. The wastebasket is beside his chair; every few moments he crumples a piece of paper and drops it in. There is a stack of library books by his left elbow. His arm is bent to support his head. "Please don't make a lot of noise," he requests.

Dave lowers his voice. "You want to know his class load? This is the absolute truth. He's got music for teachers, math for teachers, and volleyball."

"Is he going to be a teacher?" Linda asks.

"God help us. We spent all yesterday listening to him learn to sing 'Twinkle, Twinkle, Little Star' by numbers. I don't know if it was music or math. Today, at breakfast, he demonstrates the theory of the conservation of milk."

"The what?"

"How you can pour one large glass of milk into two small ones with no resulting loss of volume. Then he asks me to correct a paper he's working on. The assignment is for two pages; he's done ten. I can't say I was enthusiastic, but I wouldn't want it said that I discourage initiative. So I look at it. He's hovering by my elbow, all nervous, because it's his first college paper and I'm a seasoned junior. Eight pages are a direct quote. Out of one book. I tell him, 'You can't do that,' but he says it's exactly what he wants to say."

"How are your own classes?" Linda asks. "Did you get into MacPherson's?"

"I did, but I had to lie about my major. And you didn't tell me he threw chalk."

"Only when he's provoked. It's no fun if you're not surprised. Did he throw it at *you*?"

"No, but I jumped about a foot out of my chair anyway." Dr. MacPherson teaches Economic History and is one of Linda's favorite professors. He can tell you about the Black Plague so that you feel you're actually there. If you are momentarily overcome, however, and he thinks your attention is wandering, he sends a piece of chalk singing past your ear.

The teapot whistles asthmatically. Dave gets out the instant coffee, makes himself a cup in a green enamel mug, and puts the coffee jar away. They tiptoe past Fred, who groans for their benefit and crumples another piece of paper. They sit on the living room couch at a respectable distance apart. No one's leg touches anyone else's. "You said you had a problem," Linda hints. Please, please don't let it be Suzette.

"Yeah," says Dave. He blows on his steaming cup. "I do. It's Mrs. Kirk up in the penthouse. She hates me. She started hating me Tuesday morning and she refuses to stop. It's because of the sign I had in our window. Maybe you saw it?" Linda shakes her head. "Well, I'd spent a bad night because a number of our neighborhood cats were out looking for each other. And I made this small and tasteful sign for our window. It said THE ONLY GOOD CAT IS A DEAD CAT."

Dave blows on his coffee again and takes a quick sip. Linda remembers how silly she always thought it was, as a child, the habit grown-ups had of making drinks so hot they couldn't drink them and then having to wait until they cooled. Sometimes they waited too long and had to heat the drink all over again. A bad system.

"How can you drink that?" she asks. "Thirty seconds ago it was boiling."

"You blow right next to the side," Dave says, "and then you only drink the part you've blown on. I could teach you, but when would you use it? Tea? Do you drink tea?" Linda shakes her head. "No, you hate tea. Am I right?"

Linda smiles and watches Dave blow and take another sip. It's a larger sip. She thinks he's showing off.

"It was a small and tasteful sign," Dave repeats. "A very restrained response considering the night I'd just been through. You probably heard them, too?"

Linda shakes her head again.

"Well, I can't explain that," Dave says. "You must be a very sound sleeper. So Mrs. Kirk thinks my sign was aimed at her particular cats who are, apparently, too well-bred to yowl all night. She's called the manager and she's threatening to call the SPCA. The manager asked me to go and smooth it over with her, since she's an old and valued tenant, in contrast to myself. And I did try. I'm not proud. She won't even open the door to me. She thinks I'm only pretending to be sorry in order to gain access to her apartment and bludgeon her cats. She told me she just wished we lived in England where they know how to deal with people like me, whatever the hell that means."

"So what do you want from me?"

Dave smiles ingenuously. "You're very popular, Linda. Did you know that? I can't find a single person who doesn't like you. I bet even Mrs. Kirk likes you. Couldn't you go up and tell her you and I were having this casual conversation about cats and I just happened to mention what models of catdom her cats are? Invite her to the party. Invite her cats."

Linda doesn't respond. She is too surprised by the assertion that she is popular. She is liked by other women; she always has been. In high school she had seen clearly that girls who were popular were almost always those not liked by other girls; this was, in fact, the most reliable indication of popularity, the dislike others of your own sex had for you. It was believed to be the price a woman paid for being beautiful, although Linda knew beautiful women who were not popular and Linda knew also of women who were not so beautiful, but insisted other women hated them in an attempt to fool men into thinking they were. Men were instantly sympathetic to this. Sometimes Linda had even seen this work. Surely being popular has nothing to do with Mrs. Kirk's opinion.

"Please," says Dave. "It's a small favor."

"No, it's not," Linda informs him. Mrs. Kirk is the ex-wife of a state senator. He has been married twice since and although he is now free as a bird again, his interest in sending her alimony checks on schedule has dwindled. Six months ago, shortly after the dissolution of his last marriage, he was picked up for drunk driving. A small newspaper article reported the event. Page 29. Mrs. Kirk cut it out and posted it in the elevator in case anyone had missed it. She added her own caption: *Would you vote for this man?* But Mrs. Kirk is a bit of a drinker herself. Any visit to the penthouse is an occasion for Bloody Marys and long discussions on the inadvisability of giving your heart and the best years of your life to swine. It is not the conversation Linda wishes to avoid, however. It is the drinks. Linda can hardly face tomato juice alone; add liquor and it becomes a nightmare. And there is no way to refuse a drink from Mrs. Kirk. Linda looks at Dave's hands. "But I'll do it anyway," she says.

Fred slams a book closed. "Could you be a little quieter?" he calls from the kitchen. "I really have to concentrate."

"Don't respond," Dave warns her. "Don't say anything. He's fishing for help. He's dying to tell you what his assignment is."

They sit quietly for a moment. The sun has moved down the wall to Linda's face; on the opposite wall the painted sun illuminates the knight's helmet in the Rembrandt and never moves. Dave shifts closer to Linda on the couch but still does not touch her.

Linda focuses on the painting. She feels very warm, but she

tells herself it is the sun. "We'll make a deal," says Dave. He has lowered his voice, but his tone is nothing more than friendly. "You go talk to Mrs. Kirk for me and I'll get Dudley's fingerprints for you at the party. Then we'll be even. Are your roommates coming?"

"Yes," says Linda. But she is lying. They have no intention of attending and they all told her so last night.

She goes home and tries to persuade them again. "I don't think I can lose fifteen pounds by Friday," says Julie. "I can't have fun at a party if I'm fat."

"Sorry. Bill and I are going to a movie," says Lauren. "If we can agree on something. *Dutchman* is on campus, but he wants to see the new Joey Heatherton epic in the city."

"It's about Vietnam," says Julie. "Give the man a break. I'm sure his interests are political."

"Listen to this," says Gretchen. She is holding the *Chronicle*, folded open to the women's section, in two white fists. The strain in her voice tells Linda she is about to read from Count Marco's column.

"I don't want to hear it," says Linda. "Why read it? Why torture yourself?"

There is no stopping Gretchen. "He's complaining about the unattractiveness of women you see in hospital emergency rooms," she says. "'Set aside a flattering outfit, loose, no buttons, of course, and a pair of fetching slippers. Think ahead a little.' He's concerned that, in the case of an emergency, we may become eyesores. God! I'm going to write the *Chronicle* another letter."

"Any attention to a columnist, they consider good attention.

The more letters he provokes, the more secure his job. He's ridiculous. Just don't read him."

"It's not trivial," says Gretchen. "You think it is, but it's not. They pay this flaming misogynist to write antifemale poison, and then they put it in the women's section. Can't they just move his column? Is it too much to ask? Put it in the goddamn sports section." Her voice has risen steadily in volume and pitch until she hits its limits.

Linda reaches out and brushes Gretchen's bangs back with one hand. They won't stay; they fall back into Gretchen's outraged eyes.

"It's important," Gretchen says.

"About this party—"

"I don't want to go." The newspaper crackles in Gretchen's hands. "I told you that."

"Why not?"

"I just don't like them. They look like fraternity escapees. Jock city. Fifties time warp. Have you ever tried to have a conversation with Fred Zukini? He thinks Bernadette Devlin is a French saint. He told me he saw the movie about her."

"Dave and Kenneth are nice."

"Shall I tell you about this party?" Gretchen asks. She takes a deep breath; she is talking more slowly and has regained control of her voice. "I know about this party. We're talking party games. We're talking people passing oranges around using only their chins and everyone maneuvering to be the lucky guy who gets his orange from the woman in the low-cut blouse with the Mae West body. We're talking beer cans that people have crushed with their hands, collecting like flies on the windowsills."

"They've ordered a keg," says Linda.

"Excuse the pun, but I rest my case."

Lauren is standing behind Linda. She clears her throat in a way that makes Linda turn to look at her. She is combing her hair higher and wider. "Julie says you've got a thing for Dave. But Gretchen says you don't." Her voice is quiet. "Who's right?"

Linda tries to think what answer she wants to give. She takes too long.

"If we thought you liked him we would never have sent him up to Suzette's. You've got to know that," Lauren says.

"Even if he is all wrong for you," adds Gretchen.

"It's all right," Linda tells them. "He was going to meet Suzette sooner or later." But come to the party. You're supposed to be my friends. She doesn't say it out loud so nobody does it.

ARE WE ALL BACK? Does anyone have any questions or comments to make?

Actually, the curfew was more of an annoyance factor. If you could demonstrate persuasively to the police that your reasons for being out were nonpolitical, you were likely to get off with a warning and the instructions to go right home. Unless you were a male with long hair. Later the National Guard brought tanks into Berkeley and stationed them at critical intersections, but even this was primarily for show. Though you must remember that there was real fighting and some serious injury.

Well, cats are one of those topics on which you find only partisans. You love cats or you hate cats; no one is indifferent. I can't explain this. Perhaps these questions are taking us a little far afield. The course is Romance. The point of view is female. Does anyone have a question that is a little more penetrating?

No, no, we will be looking at the romances of older (and younger) women later. Mrs. Kirk will not be a focus, although we will be meeting her. Her partiality for alcohol would make her a difficult subject. Absorption is tricky enough without the added complication of chemical abuse. Let me tell you, though, that on the two occasions when Mrs. Kirk's husband has remarried, his wives have both been thirty-three years of age. He himself was fifty-two and then fifty-eight. Mrs. Kirk herself is now fifty-eight, and in 1969 if she had become enamored of a man of thirty-three, even in Berkeley, this would have been considered humorous or pathetic. Yet Mrs. Kirk at fifty-eight, judging by appearance alone, has aged less than Mr. Kirk at fifty-eight. There may be variables in this situation, the significance of which we have not yet grasped. Keep the issue in mind, though for the purpose of our current case study all the participants are contemporaries. In the back there?

He was not really a Count. Yes?

Those changes are sexual. The course is Romance. We will not be discussing them this term, although you will find them even more pronounced when the subjects are younger and male.

I must mention to you the possibility of sensory overload in this next Encounter. We are going with Linda to the party. The room is smoky and hot; the music is loud and primitive. This will be an exercise in academic detachment. Ready?

GRETCHEN HAD OFFERED Linda grass before she left, but Linda had refused. She wanted to keep her wits about her, but now, standing in the open doorway to 201, she realizes suddenly that in a couple of hours she will be surrounded by drunken strangers. And she will still be sober. There is nothing to drink but beer, and she finds the taste of beer extremely vile.

The Doors are on the stereo: "Twentieth Century Fox." Linda is glad Gretchen is not there. Just yesterday Gretchen had called Leopold's to ask them to remove records with sexist lyrics from the bins. She had a list of the most outrageous offenders.

"Sure," the salesman on the phone had said. "Anything for you chicks. Why don't you come down and we'll talk about it. Are you a fox?"

"No, I'm a dog," said Gretchen, slamming down the phone and repeating the conversation to Linda. "Male chauvinist pig!"

Linda passes Dave on her way in. He is in the kitchen washing some glasses. Suzette is with him, perched on the countertop. She has dressed for the evening as Nancy Sinatra, short skirt, white boots, mane of sensuous hair. She is leaning into Dave's face, saying something in a low, intimate whisper. Linda cannot hear what she says, doesn't even want to know. Anything Suzette says is rendered interesting and charming by that damned accent she has. Linda doesn't say hello to either of them.

She finds Kenneth and he hands her a beer, which she accepts tactfully. "I was just thinking of you," Kenneth says. "I'm glad you're here. I've got someone I think you'll like." He uses his elbows to force a path through the ROTC. Linda has to follow very closely; it closes up behind them like water. At the end of the path is the living room couch. On the couch is a thin, pale woman with eyeliner all around her eyes. She's done her lashes like Twiggy, tops and bottoms. No lipstick, but she's wearing a skirt and nylons. This surprises Linda, who glances around quickly and sees that a lot of people in the room have legs. She is wearing jeans herself, not Levi's, since Levi's doesn't make a jean small enough to fit her, not even boys' jeans, which are too large at the waist and too small through the hips, but as close to Levi's as she is capable of coming. They should have been appropriate to the occasion, but Gretchen was right. Linda finds herself in the fifties, where it is still possible to underdress. Where did Kenneth find these people?

Next to the woman on the couch is a man, and this is who Kenneth introduces her to. "Ben Bryant," he says. "A writer. Ben, this is Linda Connors." He looks pleased. "A reader," he adds. "She reads everything. She even reads nonfiction." He starts to introduce the woman, his hand is opened in her direction, but he never finishes. "And this is—" he says. "Margaret! You made it! Far out!" and he is gone, a little heat remaining where he had been standing. Linda moves into it.

A man behind her is talking above the music in a loud voice. "But *Sergeant Pepper* is the best album ever made. The Beatles have ennobled rock and roll."

Another man, higher voice, responds. "Ennobled! They've sanitized it. It used to be black! It used to be dangerous!"

Linda smiles at Ben even though she is nervous and he is wearing a thin sweater vest with leather buttons, which she doesn't think looks promising. "I don't really read that much," she says. "Kenneth is easily impressed."

"Melanie and I," says Ben, "were just discussing the difference between male and female writers. I was comparing Jane Austen to Joseph Conrad."

"I like Austen," says Linda warningly.

"So do I. What she does, she does well. But you must admit the scope of her work is rather limited."

"Must I?" Linda's uncomfortableness is disappearing.

"The difference between the two, as I was just telling Melanie, is the difference between insight and gossip."

Linda looks at Melanie. Her face is impassive. "I'm not so sure a clear distinction can be made between the two. Who knows more about people than the gossip?"

"You're playing devil's advocate," says Ben comfortably.

"I'm expressing my true opinion."

Ben settles back in the couch, crossing his arms. "I don't want you to think that I think the differences are biologically determined. No. This is a sociological limitation. Women's writing is restricted because women's lives have been restricted. They're still capable of writing well-crafted little books."

Linda opens her mouth and Gretchen's voice comes out. "You've lived a pretty full life?" she asks.

"I've traveled. Extensively."

"So have I. I was in Indonesia when Sukarno fell. Grown men circumcised themselves in the hope of passing as Muslims." Linda sees Ben shift slightly in his seat. "Circumcised *themselves*. Someday I may want to write about the things I've seen." She has won the argument, but she has cheated to do it. Linda has never even been to Santa Barbara. Dr. MacPherson was in Indonesia when Sukarno fell and has described it so vividly Linda knows she can carry it off if she is challenged. She isn't. Ben is looking at his lap. Linda's mood is black. She has been at the party maybe fifteen minutes and already she has betrayed her sex. Worse, she has betrayed Jane Austen. She isn't fit to live. Linda punishes herself by taking a large sip of beer. And another. She holds her breath and swallows and decides she has paid enough. She abandons her glass by the couch and pointedly directs her words to Melanie. "Excuse me," she says. "There's someone I have to talk to."

Linda shoves her way over to the stereo and Kenneth. "Don't introduce me to any more writers," she says.

"Didn't you like Ben?" Kenneth asks. "Fred, let Linda pick out a record." Fred Zukini is just about to put the Association on. It is a lucky thing Linda came along. She asks for *Big Pink*. She wants to hear "The Weight."

Kenneth turns the music up. He has one arm draped around Margaret; he kisses her on the neck. He smiles at Linda, but it is definitely a get-lost kind of smile. Linda responds, spotting an empty chair in a corner and retreating to it.

She sees Dave again, sitting under the Rembrandt, talking with Dudley Petersen. She cannot quite hear their words, though the young man with the high voice who disliked the Beatles is still clearly audible. "No, no, no," he is saying. "We're talking about the complete failure of the dialectic."

Suzette has found Dave again, too, and in the sudden silence between "Tears of Rage" and "To Kingdom Come," Linda hears Suzette ask Dave if she can sit on his lap. Well! Linda can't help feeling this is somehow lacking in subtlety. Her father told her, advice she has never needed, not once, that boys do not like to be chased and he was a boy himself and should know, but there Suzette is, settling herself in, laughing like Simone Signoret, and this appears to be just one more area in which Linda has been sadly misled. The situation is hopeless. Linda looks at her shoes and wonders how early she can go home. In fact, Linda likes Suzette for being so brazenly weird. Gretchen likes her, Julie likes her, Lauren likes her—add them together and it should have been enough to prevent such popularity.

Linda leans back and closes her eyes, listening to the conversations close to her. To her right, two women are laughing. "So he doesn't have a condom," one says. "'I figured you'd be on the pill,' he tells me and I say, 'Listen, bucko, we have a saying among my people—the person who plans the party should bring the beer.' 'Your people?' he asks and I say, 'Yeah, my people. You know. Women.'" The second woman's voice is soft and throaty. "Probably just never heard women called people before," she offers.

Farther from her, Linda hears someone suggesting a party game. Everyone is to lie down with their heads on someone else's stomach and then all laugh simultaneously. Score another one for Gretchen.

She hears Frank Zukini asking some woman what her major is. Penetrating question, Linda thinks. "Drama," the woman answers. "I'm a thespian." There is a long pause, and Frank's voice when he responds betrays shock. "Whatever's right," he says, at last.

And then Suzette's voice, close to Linda's ear, indicates that Dave's lap is unoccupied again. "I have a message for you," Suzette tells her.

Linda sits up and opens her eyes. "For me?"

"Yes. From the Venusians. They're very interested in you, Linda. They ask about you a lot."

"How flattering," says Linda. "Extraterrestrial attention. What's the message?"

Suzette's hair is the color of the knight's helmet and surrounds her face like an aura. "They said not to do anything they wouldn't do."

"Suzette," says Linda, smiling at her, "tell them to relax. I never do anything."

Dudley Petersen passes. Linda knows he sees her, but he goes in another direction. Still brooding about his ferns. But Mrs. Kirk joins her, carrying her beer in a pewter mug with a hinged lid and a glass bottom. "Marvelous party," says Mrs. Kirk. "No hippies. Just a lot of nice young people enjoying themselves."

"I'm not enjoying myself," Linda tells her. "I'm having a terrible time."

"It's because you're not drinking. Kenny! Kenny!" Mrs. Kirk waves a plump hand and her bracelets ring out commandingly. "Linda needs a beer!"

Kenneth supplies one, giving her an empty glass wrapped in a paper towel at the same time. "The glass is a gift from Dave," he informs her. "And Dave says not to handle it too much. Would you like to tell me what's going on?"

Linda takes the glass and her spirits lift ridiculously. But briefly. "It's evidence," she says. She watches Kenneth weave his way back to Dave. Kenneth wants to invite the police department, any off-duty officers and anyone they are willing to let out of jail. He argues with Dave about it. Dave is holding the phone clamped tightly together and refusing to release it.

"Hey, Linda." It's Fred Zukini. "You still haven't seen my car. You want to? I got a tape deck, now, and I put a lock on the gas cap and I put sheepskin on the seats."

Linda takes a long drink of her beer and then sets it and the empty glass back under the seat where they'll be safe until she can retrieve them. She follows Fred to the elevator, passing through a nasty, acrid smell by the couch where Ben Bryant is smoking a pipe. With tobacco in it.

Fred doesn't seem the sort to seduce her in the basement. Too much risk to the car, for one thing, and Linda doesn't like him so she is relaxed and calm, picking her way through the couples who have opted for romantic subterranean lighting. Fred stops at a polished red VW bug and runs his hand over the curves of the trunk. "I got extra locks on the doors, too," he says. "Because of the tape deck. I'm going to get leather for the steering wheel."

Linda leans over, peering into the car's interior. Above the soft and snowy sheepskin, next to the steering column, a set of keys dangles. "You've left your keys in it," Linda tells Fred. "Anyone could take it."

Fred pushes her roughly aside, pressing his forehead against the window. "It's locked." His voice breaks. "It's all locked up. The keys are locked inside."

"Oh," says Linda. She thinks for a moment. "Maybe you could get in with a coat hanger. I've seen that done."

"Linda, the windows are closed. And it's got special locks."

"Oh." Linda thinks again. "I guess you'll have to break a window."

Fred runs a hand through his hair, but it is too short to be disarranged. His face is anguished. "Could you let me think this through?" he requests. "God, Linda, could you be quiet and leave me alone for a bit?"

Linda makes her way back to the elevator, the heels of her shoes snapping on the cement floor. A white-faced cadet stumbles across her path. He moans once, a pathetic, suffocated sound. "Oh, no," he says. He falls against the first of the washing machines, claws it open, and throws up into it. He looks at Linda and throws up again.

There is a message here, Linda decides. A message from the Venusians. The message is to go home. Go home to her roommates who were so right when she was so wrong, and Linda feels that all she will ever ask for the whole rest of her life is not to forget and wash her clothes in the first machine or spend another second with anyone named Fred or Frank or Kenneth or—

The elevator opens slowly, suspensefully, and Dave is inside. "I thought you might need rescuing," he says. "Mrs. Kirk gave me the keys to the penthouse. She says you can see all of San Francisco from there. Want to come?"

"Why not?" Linda answers coldly. "As long as I'm in the elevator anyway." She joins him. They face front. No one's shoulder touches anyone else's. The elevator does not move. Linda jabs the topmost button. And again. The elevator gives a startled lurch upward. About the third floor, Linda asks where Suzette is. Maximum aplomb. A casual, uninterested question. She is merely making conversation.

"Sitting on Frank's lap. Apparently he's a very old soul. A teacher. A guru, would you believe it? He has a yellow aura. Suzette just about died when she saw it."

"Too bad for you," says Linda. The elevator has stopped, but its door is sticking. Linda has to wedge her foot in to force it open.

"I'm not interested in Suzette." Dave sounds surprised. "Linda, the woman communicates with Venusians." He fits Mrs.

Kirk's key into the lock. "You're not drunk, are you? I mean not even a little. You hate beer?"

"Yes."

"Just a lucky guess."

"But I'm working on it," Linda tells him. "I'm growing. I'm changing."

"Oh, no. Don't do that," says Dave. They enter the penthouse and are attacked by a mob of affectionate cats, escaping to the terrace with their lives and a quantity of cat hair. The evening couldn't be more beautiful, absolutely clear, and the lights on the hills extend all the way to the water, where Linda can actually see the small shapes of the waves, forming and repeating themselves endlessly over the bay. The air is cold, and somewhere below she hears the sound of breaking glass.

"Did that come from the basement?" Linda asks with some interest.

Dave shakes his head tiredly. "The apartment. That's what I get for leaving Kenneth in charge." He moves closer to Linda, putting his hands around her shoulders, making her shake. She can't think clearly and she can't hold still. The entire attention of her body is focused suddenly on those places where his hands are touching her. "My apartment is full of drunks and it's after curfew," Dave says. "I'm going to kiss you now unless you stop me."

And what Linda feels is just a little like fear, but no, not like that at all, only it is so intense that she is not quite able to participate in the first kiss. She does better on the second, and by the third Dave has moved from her mouth to her neck and is telling her that he fell in love with her the first time he saw her, that first day in the elevator, when he saw she had Jack Lemmon's chin.

WELL. THERE WE ARE. This seems to me to be a natural breakpoint, and although I can't deny that we could learn a great deal more by going on here and, time permitting, we may return and do this later in the term, for now I want to bring this experience to some sort of close. The course is, after all, Romance and the focus is courtship, not mating, and let me add that the process of absorption is rather—well, untested in situations involving actual chemical changes in the subject's physical system. We don't want to find ourselves as subjects in someone else's lab test, now, do we? Of course we don't. Let's let the lab work this out first.

We did go far enough with Linda to make some final observations concerning women and the physical aspects of romance. These are the sort of concerns which will continue to occupy our attention, as we determine whether or not they are universal, specifically female, or merely manifestations of a particular personality type.

I'm speaking, more specifically, of the body/mind split which occurred at the moment Dave touched her. I thought it was very pronounced. Did anyone not feel this? Yes, very pronounced. Linda's body began to take on, in her own mind, a sort of otherness. Partly this was inherent in her conscious decision to feel whatever her body was feeling. A decision to be physically swept away is a contradiction in terms even when carried out successfully, and I feel Linda was relatively successful. But this is only the most straightforward, simplest aspect of the split.

Linda's arousal was dependent upon Dave's. Not upon Dave himself. Upon Dave's arousal. Did you notice? In the earlier encounters we didn't find this. Linda responded to his hands, to his face, to his voice, to various secondary male characteristics. She found him attractive. Mentally and physically. But toward the end she was much more aroused by the fact that he found her attractive. I don't want to get into a discussion of evolution or of psychology. I merely point this out; I ask you to consider the implications. We have a sort of loop between the male and the female, and the conduit is the female's body. It has been said—and we will be trying to determine, as we move on to other subjects, different ages, different sexes, whether it has been oversaid—that any romantic entanglement between a male and a female is, in fact, a triangle, and the third party is the female's body. It is the hostage between them, the bridge or the barrier. At least in this case. Let's be cautious here. At least for Linda. I'm ready for questions.

I would imagine that being told you had a nice chin was about as exciting as being told you had nice teeth. But this is just a guess. Linda was hardly listening at this point.

They went to *Dutchman*, a movie in which a white female seduces and destroys a black male. It made for an uncomfortable evening. Yes?

Well, the Joey Heatherton choice would have been problematical, too. No, I understand your interest. We'll look at Lauren more later. I promise.

Nobody has a clue as to what the lyrics to "The Weight" mean. I doubt that the man who wrote it could answer this question. He was probably just making it rhyme.

Are there any more questions?

Anything at all?

Then I'm ready to dismiss you. Be thinking about what you've absorbed. Next time we'll begin to look for common themes and for differences. It should be enlightening. The course is Comparative Romance. The point of view is female. We'll start next time with questions. When you've thought about it some more, I'm sure you'll have questions.

GAME NIGHT AT THE FOX AND GOOSE

The reader will discover that my reputation,
wherever I have lived, is endorsed
as that of a true and pure woman.

—*Laura D. Fair*

Alison called all over the city trying to find a restaurant that served blowfish, but there wasn't one. She settled for Chinese. She would court an MSG attack. And if none came, then she'd been craving red bean sauce anyway. On the way to the restaurant, Alison chose not to wear her seat belt.

Alison had been abandoned by her lover, who was so quick about it she hadn't even known she was pregnant yet. She couldn't ever tell him now. She sat pitifully alone, near the kitchen, at a table for four.

YOU'VE REALLY SCREWED UP THIS TIME, her fortune cookie told her. GIVE UP. And, in small print: CHIN'S ORIENTAL PALACE.

The door from the kitchen swung open, so the air around her was hot for a moment, then cold when the door closed. Alison drank her tea and looked at the tea leaves in the bottom of her cup. They were easy to read. He doesn't love you, they said. She tipped them out onto the napkin and tried to rearrange them, YOU FOOL. She covered the message with the one remaining wonton, left the cookie for the kitchen god, and decided to walk all by herself in the dark, three blocks up Hillside Drive, past two alleyways, to have a drink at the Fox and Goose. No one stopped her.

Alison had forgotten it was Monday night. Sometimes there was music in the Fox and Goose. Sometimes you could sit in a corner by yourself listening to someone with an acoustic guitar singing "Killing Me Softly." On Monday nights the television was on and the bar was rather crowded. Mostly men. Alison swung one leg over the only empty bar stool and slid forward. The bar was made of wood, very upscale.

"What can I get the pretty lady?" the bartender asked, without taking his eyes off the television screen. He wore glasses, low on his nose. Alison was not a pretty lady and didn't feel like pretending she was. "I've been used and discarded," she told the bartender. "And I'm pregnant. I'd like a glass of wine."

"You really shouldn't drink if you're pregnant," the man sitting to Alison's left said. "Two more downs and they're already in field goal range again."

The bartender set the wine in front of Alison. He was shaking his head. "Pregnant women aren't supposed to drink much," he warned her.

"How?" the man on her left asked.

"How do you think?" said Alison.

"Face mask," said the bartender.

"Turn it up."

Alison heard the amplified *thwock* of football helmets hitting together. "Good coverage," the bartender said. "No protection," said the man on Alison's right.

Alison turned to look at him. He was dressed in a blue sweater with the sleeves pushed up. He had dark eyes and was drinking a dark beer. "I asked him to wear a condom," she said quietly. "I even brought one. He couldn't."

"He couldn't?"

"I really don't want to discuss it." Alison sipped her wine. It had the flat, bitter taste of house white. She realized the bartender hadn't asked her what she wanted. But then, if he had, house white was what she would have requested. "It just doesn't seem fair." She spoke over her glass, unsure that anyone was listening, not really caring if they weren't. "All I did was fall in love. All I did was believe someone who said he loved me. He was the liar. But nothing happens to him."

"Unfair is the way things are," the man on her right told her. Three months ago Alison would have been trying to decide if she were attracted to him. Not that she would necessarily have wanted to do anything about it. It was just a question she'd always asked herself, dealing with men, interested in the answer, interested in those times when the answer changed abruptly, one way or another. But it was no longer an issue. Alison was a dead woman these days. Alison was attracted to no one.

Two men at the end of the bar began to clap suddenly. "He hasn't missed from thirty-six yards yet this season," the bartender said.

Alison watched the kickoff and the return. Nothing. No room at all. "Men handle this stuff so much better than women. You don't know what heartbreak is," she said confrontationally. No one responded. She backed off anyway. "Well, that's how it looks." She drank and watched an advertisement for trucks. A man bought his wife the truck she'd always wanted. Alison was afraid she might cry. "What would you do," she asked the man on her right, "if you were me?"

"Drink, I guess. Unless I was pregnant."

"Watch the game," said the man on her left.

"Focus on your work," said the bartender.

"Join the Foreign Legion." The voice came from behind Alison. She swiveled around to locate it. At a table near a shuttered window a very tall woman sat by herself. Her face was shadowed by an Indiana Jones–type hat, but the candle on the table lit up the area below her neck. She was wearing a black T-shirt with a picture on it that Alison couldn't make out. She spoke again. "Make new friends. See distant places." She gestured for Alison to join her. "Save two galaxies from the destruction of the alien armada."

Alison stood up on the little ledge that ran beneath the bar, reached over the counter, and took an olive, sucking the pimiento out first, then eating the rest. She picked up her drink, stepped down, and walked over to the woman's table. Elvis. That was Elvis's face on the T-shirt right between the woman's breasts. ARE YOU LONESOME TONIGHT? the T-shirt asked.

"That sounds good." Alison sat down across from the woman. She could see her face better now; her skin was pale and a bit rough. Her hair was long, straight, and brown. "I'd rather time travel, though. Back just two months. Maybe three months. Practically walking distance."

"You could get rid of the baby."

"Yes," said Alison. "I could."

The woman's glass sat on the table in front of her. She had finished whatever she had been drinking; the maraschino cherry was all that remained. The woman picked it up and ate it, dropping the stem onto the napkin under her glass. "Maybe he'll come back to you. You trusted him. You must have seen something decent in him."

Alison's throat closed so that she couldn't talk. She picked up her drink, but she couldn't swallow either. She set it down again, shaking her head. Some of the wine splashed over the lip and onto her hand.

"He's already married," the woman said.

Alison nodded, wiping her hand on her pant leg. "God."

She searched in her pockets for a Kleenex. The woman handed her the napkin from beneath the empty glass. Alison wiped her nose with it and the cherry stem fell out. She did not dare look up. She kept her eyes focused on the napkin in her hand, which she folded into four small squares.

"When I was growing up," she said, "I lived on a block with lots of boys. Sometimes I'd come home and my knees were all scraped up because I'd fallen or I'd taken a ball in the face or I'd gotten kicked or punched, and I'd be crying and my mother would always say the same thing. 'You play with the big boys and you're going to get hurt,' she'd say. Exasperated." Alison unfolded the napkin, folded it diagonally instead. Her voice shrank. "I've been so stupid."

"The universe is shaped by the struggle between two great forces," the woman told her. It was not really responsive. It was not particularly supportive. Alison felt just a little bit angry at this woman who now knew so much about her.

"Good and evil?" Alison asked, slightly nastily. She wouldn't meet the woman's eyes. "The Elvis and the anti-Elvis?"

"Male and female. Minute by minute, the balance tips one way or the other. Not just here. In every universe. There are places"—the woman leaned forward—"where men are not allowed to gather and drink. Places where football is absolutely illegal."

"England?" Alison suggested and then didn't want to hear the woman's answer. "I like football," she added quickly. "I like games with rules. You can be stupid playing football and it can cost you the game, but there are penalties for fouls, too. I like games with rules."

"You're playing one now, aren't you?" the woman said. "You haven't hurt this man, even though you could. Even though he's hurt you. He's not playing by the rules. So why are you?"

"It doesn't have anything to do with rules," Alison said. "It only has to do with me, with the kind of person I think I am. Which is not the kind of person he is." She thought for a moment. "It doesn't mean I wouldn't like to see him get hurt," she added. "Something karmic. Justice."

"'We must storm and hold Cape Turk before we talk of social justice.'" The woman folded her arms under her breasts and leaned back in her chair. "Did Sylvia Townsend Warner say that?"

"Not to me."

Alison heard more clapping at the bar behind her. She looked over her shoulder. The man in the blue sweater slapped his hand on the wooden bar. "Good call. Excellent call. They won't get another play in before the half."

"Where I come from she did." Alison turned back as the

woman spoke. "And she was talking about women. No one gets justice just by deserving it. No one ever has."

Alison finished off her wine. "No." She wondered if she should go home now. She knew when she got there that the apartment would be unbearably lonely and that the phone wouldn't ring and that she would need immediately to be somewhere else. No activity in the world could be more awful than listening to a phone not ring. But she didn't really want to stay here and have a conversation that was at worst too strange and at best too late. Women usually supported you more when they talked to you. They didn't usually make you defensive or act as if they had something to teach you, the way this woman did. And anyhow, justice was a little peripheral now, wasn't it? What good would it really do her? What would it change?

She might have gone back and joined the men at the bar during the half. They were talking quietly among themselves. They were ordering fresh drinks and eating beer nuts. But she didn't want to risk seeing cheerleaders. She didn't want to risk the ads with the party dog and all his women, even though she'd read in a magazine that the dog was a bitch. Anywhere she went, there she'd be. Just like she was. Heartbroken.

The woman was watching her closely. Alison could feel this, though the woman's face remained shadowed and she couldn't quite bring herself to look back at her directly. She looked at Elvis instead and the way his eyes wavered through her lens of candlelight and tears. Lonesome tonight? "You really have it bad, don't you?" the woman said. Her tone was sympathetic. Alison softened again. She decided to tell this perceptive woman everything. How much she'd loved him. How she'd never loved anyone else. How she felt it every time she took a breath, and had for weeks now.

"I don't think I'll ever feel better," she said. "No matter what I do."

"I hear it takes a year to recover from a serious loss. Unless you find someone else."

A year. Alison could be a mother by then. How would she find someone else, pregnant like she was or with a small child? Could she spend a year hurting like this? Would she have a choice?

"Have you ever heard of Laura D. Fair?" the woman asked.

Alison shook her head. She picked up the empty wineglass and tipped it to see if any drops remained. None did. She set it back down and picked up the napkin, wiping her eyes. She wasn't crying. She just wasn't exactly not crying.

"Mrs. Fair killed her lover," the woman told her. Alison looked at her own fingernails. One of them had a ragged end. She bit it off shorter while she listened. "He was a lawyer. A. P. Crittenden. She shot him on the ferry to Oakland in November of 1870 in front of his whole family because she saw him kiss his wife. He'd promised to leave her and marry Mrs. Fair instead, and then he didn't, of course. She pleaded a transient insanity known at that time as emotional insanity. She said she was incapable of killing Mr. Crittenden, who had been the only friend she'd had in the world." Alison examined her nail. She had only succeeded in making it more ragged. She bit it again, too close to the skin this time. It hurt and she put it back in her mouth. "Mrs. Fair said she had no memory of the murder, which many people, not all of them related to the deceased, witnessed. She was the first woman sentenced to hang in California."

Loud clapping and catcalls at the bar. The third quarter had started with a return all the way to the fifty-yard line. Alison heard it. She did not turn around, but she took her finger out of her mouth and picked up the napkin. She folded it again. Four small squares. "Rules are rules," Alison said.

"But then she didn't hang. Certain objections were made on behalf of the defense and sustained, and a new trial was held. This time she was acquitted. By now she was the most famous and the most hated woman in the country."

Alison unfolded the napkin and tried to smooth out the creases with the side of her palm. "I never heard of her."

"Laura D. Fair was not some little innocent." The woman's hat brim dipped decisively. "Mrs. Fair had been married four times, and each had been a profitable venture. One of her husbands killed himself. She was not pretty, but she was passionate. She was not smart, but she was clever. And she saw, in her celebrity, a new way to make money. She announced a new career as a public speaker. She traveled the country with her lectures. And what was her message? She told women to murder the men who seduced and betrayed them."

"I never heard of her," said Alison.

"Mrs. Fair was a compelling speaker. She'd had some acting and elocution experience. Her performance in court showed training. On the stage she was even better. 'The act will strike a terror to the hearts of sensualists and libertines.'" The woman stabbed dramatically at her own breast with her fist, hitting Elvis right in the eye. Behind her hand, Elvis winked at Alison in the candlelight. "Mrs. Fair said that women throughout the world would glory in the revenge exacted by American womanhood. Overdue. Long overdue. Thousands of women heard her. Men, too, and not all of them entirely unsympathetic. Fanny Hyde and

Kate Stoddart were released in Brooklyn. Stoddart never even stood trial. But then there was a backlash. The martyred Marys were hanged in Philadelphia. And then . . ."

The woman's voice dropped suddenly in volume and gained in intensity. Alison looked up at her quickly. The woman was staring back. Alison looked away.

"And then a group of women hunted down and dispatched Charles S. Smith in an alley near his home. Mr. Smith was a married man and his victim, Edith Wilson, was pregnant, an invalid, and eleven years old. But this time the women wore sheets and could not be identified. Edith Wilson was perhaps the only female in Otsego County, New York, who could not have taken part." Alison folded her napkin along the diagonal.

"So no one could be tried. It was an inspiring and purging operation. It was copied in many little towns across the country. God knows, the women had access to sheets."

Alison laughed, but the woman was not expecting it, had not paused to allow for laughter. "And then Annie Oakley shot Frank Butler in a challenge match in Cincinnati."

"Excuse me," said Alison. "I didn't quite hear you." But she really had and the woman continued anyway, without pausing or repeating.

"She said it was an accident, but she was too good a shot. They hanged her for it. And then Grover Cleveland was killed by twelve sheeted women on the White House lawn. At teatime," the woman said.

"Wait a minute." Alison stopped her. "Grover Cleveland served out two terms. Nonconsecutively. I'm sure."

The woman leaned into the candlelight, resting her chin on a bridge she made of her hands. "You're right, of course," she said. "That's what happened here. But in another universe where the feminine force was just a little stronger in 1872, Grover Cleveland died in office. With a scone in his mouth and a child in New York."

"All right," said Alison accommodatingly. Accommodation was one of Alison's strengths. "But what difference does that make to us?"

"I could take you there." The woman pushed her hat back so that Alison could have seen her eyes if she wanted to. "The universe right next door. Practically walking distance."

The candle flame was casting shadows which reached and withdrew and reached at Alison over the table. In the unsteady light, the woman's face flickered like a silent-film star's. Then she pulled back in her chair and sank into the darkness beyond the candle. The ball was on the ten-yard line and the bar was quiet. "I knew you were going to say that," Alison said finally. "How did I know you were going to say that? Who would say that?"

"Some lunatic?" the woman suggested.

"Yes."

"Don't you want to hear about it anyway? About my universe?" The woman smiled at her. An unperturbed smile. Nice even teeth. And a kind of confidence that was rare among the women Alison knew. Alison had noticed it immediately without realizing she was noticing. The way the woman sat back in her chair and didn't pick at herself. Didn't play with her hair. Didn't look at her hands. The way she lectured Alison.

"All right," Alison said. She put the napkin down and fit her hands together, forcing herself to sit as still. "But first tell me about Laura Fair. My Laura Fair."

"Up until 1872 the two histories are identical," the woman said. "Mrs. Fair married four times and shot her lover and was convicted and the conviction was overturned. She just never lectured. She planned to. She was scheduled to speak at Platt's Hotel in San Francisco on November 11, 1872, but a mob of some two thousand men gathered outside the hotel and another two thousand surrounded the apartment building she lived in. She asked for police protection, but it was refused and she was too frightened to leave her home. Even staying where she was proved dangerous. A few men tried to force their way inside. She spent a terrifying night and never attempted to lecture again. She died in poverty and obscurity.

"Fanny Hyde and Kate Stoddart were released anyway. I can't find out what happened to the Marys. Edith Wilson was condemned by respectable people everywhere and cast out of her family."

"The eleven-year-old child?" Alison said.

"In your universe," the woman reminded her. "Not in mine. You don't know much of your own history, do you? Name a great American woman."

The men at the bar were in an uproar. Alison turned to look. "Interception," the man in the blue sweater shouted to her exultantly. "Did you see it?"

"Name a great American woman," Alison called back to him.

"Goddamn interception with goal to go," he said. "Eleanor Roosevelt?"

"Marilyn Monroe," said a man at the end of the bar.

"The senator from California?" the woman asked. "Now that's a good choice."

Alison laughed again. "Funny," she said, turning back to the woman. "Very good."

"We have football, too," the woman told her. "Invented in 1873. Outlawed in 1950. No one ever got paid to play it."

"And you have Elvis."

"No, we don't. Not like yours. Of course not. I got this here."

"Interception," the man in the blue sweater said. He was standing beside Alison, shaking his head with the wonder of it. "Let me buy you ladies a drink." Alison opened her mouth and he waved his hand. "Something nonalcoholic for you," he said. "Please. I really want to."

"Ginger ale, then," she agreed. "No ice."

"Nothing for me," said the woman. They watched the man walk back to the bar, and then, when he was far enough away not to hear, she leaned forward toward Alison. "You like men, don't you?"

"Yes," said Alison. "I always have. Are they different where you come from? Have they learned to be honest and careful with women, since you kill them when they're not?" Alison's voice was sharper than she intended, so she softened the effect with a sadder question. "Is it better there?"

"Better for whom?" The woman did not take her eyes off Alison. "Where I come from the men and women hardly speak to each other. First of all, they don't speak the same language. They don't here, either, but you don't recognize that as clearly. Where I come from there's men's English and there's women's English."

"Say something in men's English."

"'I love you.' Shall I translate?"

"No," said Alison. "I know the translation for that one." The heaviness closed over her heart again. Not that it had ever gone away. Nothing made Alison feel better, but many things made her feel worse. The bartender brought her ginger ale. With ice. Alison was angry, suddenly, that she couldn't even get a drink with no ice. She looked for the man in the blue sweater, raised the glass at him, and rattled it. Of course he was too far away to hear even if he was listening, and there was no reason to believe he was.

"Two-minute warning," he called back. "I'll be with you in two minutes."

Men were always promising to be with you soon. Men could never be with you now. Alison had only cared about this once, and she never would again. "Football has the longest two minutes in the world," she told the woman. "So don't hold your breath. What else is different where you come from?" She sipped at her ginger ale. She'd been grinding her teeth recently—stress, the dentist said—and so the cold liquid made her mouth hurt.

"Everything is different. Didn't you ask for no ice? Don't drink that," the woman said. She called to the bartender. "She didn't want ice. You gave her ice."

"Sorry." The bartender brought another bottle and another glass. "Nobody told me no ice."

"Thank you," Alison said. He took the other glass away. Alison thought he was annoyed. The woman didn't seem to notice.

"Imagine your world without a hundred years of adulterers," she said. "The level of technology is considerably depressed. Lots of books never written because the authors didn't live. Lots of men who didn't get to be president. Lots of passing. Although it's illegal. Men dressing as women. Women dressing as men. And the dress is more sexually differentiated. Codpieces are fashionable again. But you don't have to believe me," the woman said. "Come and see for yourself. I can take you there in a minute. What would it cost you to just come and see? What do you have here that you'd be losing?"

The woman gave her time to think. Alison sat and drank her ginger ale and repeated to herself the things her lover had said the last time she had seen him. She remembered them all, some of them surprisingly careless, some of them surprisingly cruel, all of them surprising. She repeated them again, one by one, like a rosary. The man who had left was not the man she had loved. The man she had loved would never have said such things to her. The man she had loved did not exist. She had made him up. Or he had. "Why would you want me to go?" Alison asked.

"The universe is shaped by the struggle between two great forces. Sometimes a small thing can tip the balance. One more woman. Who knows?" The woman tilted her hat back with her hand. "Save a galaxy. Make new friends. Or stay here where your heart is. Broken."

"Can I come back if I don't like it?"

"Yes. Do you like it here?"

She drank her ginger ale and then set the glass down, still half full. She glanced at the man in the blue sweater, then past him to the bartender. She let herself feel just for a moment what it might be like to know that she could finish this drink and then go home to the one person in the world who loved her.

Never in this world. "I'm going out for a minute. Two minutes," she called to the bartender. One minute to get back. "Don't take my drink."

She stood and the other woman stood, too, even taller than Alison had thought. "I'll follow you. Which way?" Alison asked.

"It's not hard," the woman said. "In fact, I'll follow you. Go to the back. Find the door that says WOMEN and go on through it. I'm just going to pay for my drink and then I'll be right along."

VIXENS was what the door actually said, across the way from the one marked GANDERS. Alison paused and then pushed through. She felt more than a little silly, standing in the small bathroom that apparently fronted two universes. One toilet, one sink, one mirror. Two universes. She went into the stall and closed the door. Before she had finished she heard the outer door open and shut again. "I'll be right out," she said. The toilet paper was small and unusually rough. The toilet wouldn't flush. It embarrassed her. She tried three times before giving up.

The bathroom was larger than it had been, less clean, and a row of urinals lined one wall. The woman stood at the sink, looking into the mirror, which was smaller. "Are you ready?" she asked and removed her breasts from behind Elvis, tossing them into a wire wastebasket. She turned. "Ready or not."

"No," said Alison, seeing the face under the hat clearly for the first time. "Please, no." She began to cry again, looking up at his face, looking down at his chest, ARE YOU LONESOME TONIGHT?

"You lied to me," she said dully.

"I never lied," he answered. "Think back. You just translated wrong. Because you're that kind of woman. We don't have women like you here now. And anyway, what does it matter whose side you play on? All that matters is that no one wins. Aren't I right? Aren't I?" He tipped his hat to her.